Eos

The Long, Dark Road Of Horse & Human

Blythe Ayne

Eos

The Long, Dark Road
Of Horse & Human

Blythe Ayne

EOS

Blythe Ayne

Emerson & Tilman, Publishers
129 Pendleton Way #55
Washougal, WA 98671

www.BlytheAyne.com
https://shop.BlytheAyne.com
Blythe@BlytheAyne.com

EOS

ebook ISBN: 978-1-957272-36-8
Paperback ISBN: 978-1-957272-37-5
Hardbound ISBN: 978-1-957272-38-2
Large Print ISBN: 978-1-957272-39-9
Audio ISBN: 978-1-957272-40-5

[**FICTION** / Fantasy / Paranormal
FICTION / Fantasy / Contemporary
FICTION / Magical Realism]
BIC: FM

DEDICATION:

To Horse Lovers
Wherever You May Be

Table of Contents:

Chapter I

Lori Awakening

*L*ori woke with the strange sensation of floating. She reached out to touch the mattress, trying to fully wake up, taking in the peculiar translucent-ivory moonlight. It stirred about the bedroom, restless, haunted and haunting, prying into every niche and nook.

A pulsing thrum came through the bed—this motion, this muffled sound had awakened her.

But ... *what was it?*

Nathan, sleeping soundly on the remote side of the king-sized bed, jumped up with a start. "*Cayuse,*" he whispered. Slipping out of bed, he grabbed his jeans off the chair and pulled them on.

Lori watched the moonlight pour onto him as if discovering what it had been searching for, his beautiful muscles standing out in bas relief, chiseled alabaster in the living light as he pulled on his shirt.

"What ... what is it?" Lori whispered. "What's that sound? What are you doing?"

Nathan turned and looked at her as if surprised to see her there. "You're awake ...."

"Have been. The ... the sound, and the ... I feel something ... through the earth ... *what is it?*"

"Cayuse," Nathan said simply, moving across the bedroom.

"Cayuse," Lori repeated. "What's ...."

Nathan didn't bother to button his shirt. "Go back to sleep."

"What's cayuse?" Lori asked as he bolted from the bedroom.

"Mustangs," he said from the stairwell.

Lori leapt up from the bed, grabbed the comforter off the hope chest at the foot of the bed, and, flinging it around her shoulders, hurried to the stairs.

"Wild horses?" She scurried down the back stairs. "*Wild horses, Nathan?*"

He already stood on the back porch, pulling on a pair of cowboy boots—the kind of cowboy boots cowboys worked in.

He looked over his shoulder at her, distracted. Then stepped back into the kitchen and strode down the hall to bang on a door. "Taffy, cayuse, come on."

"I'm up, Boss. Be right out."

At that moment, Beau, Nathan's son, came into the kitchen and flipped on the glaring, fluorescent lights, tugging on his shirt.

Mrs. Hinds, the housekeeper, came down the opposite hall, turning on lights in her wake, while Taffy stepped out of his room. As if choreographed, the two of them came into the kitchen at the same moment.

"Cayuse," Mrs. Hinds nodded. "Solstice. Didn't even realize it." She glanced at the calendar. "Yep. Tomorrow. Full moon."

Lori took in the activity flowing about her, mystified and clueless. "*Wild horses, Mrs. Hinds?*" she asked in a small, confused voice.

"Sure, Missus, wild horses."

"They're coming close, Boss," Taffy said. "*Listen!* Coming right in. Kinda weird."

Nathan, who had stepped back out onto the porch, nodded, then glanced at Beau. "What are you gawking at?" he growled.

Lori turned to see Beau giving her an unabashed look of lust. She pulled the comforter close around her.

"Get your boots on, pervert." Nathan picked up a pair of boots and flung them into the kitchen. "And keep your damn eyes in your sockets. Lori, go back to bed! Come, Taffy, Beau." He stepped outside.

Mrs. Hinds bustled about, making coffee. "Coffee and breakfast ready when you get back."

Suddenly, only Mrs. Hinds stood with Lori in the luminous, vast kitchen.

Mrs. Hinds busied herself, not even glancing at Lori.

"Breakfast?" Lori asked. "It's two a.m."

Mrs. Hinds glanced at Lori as if recalling she was there. "They'll likely be out for a couple hours," she answered, her sturdy farm-stock frame orchestrating pots and pans and oven and stovetop with the grace of a conductor.

"But, Mrs. Hinds, *what* are they doing?"

"What are who doing? The mustangs?"

"No. Nathan and Taffy. And, well, Beau."

"Nathan and Taffy are trying to capture a few of the cayuse. Beau is, without a doubt, getting underfoot." She muttered something else Lori couldn't make out.

"What?"

"That Beau. For a seventeen-year-old kid, he's trouble like a baby."

"Yes. Well...." Lori pulled the comforter yet closer around her. "Babies don't ...."

Mrs. Hinds halted her activity, hands full of kitchen utensils, and looked at Lori. "Right. Babies don't look at their father's wife like she's Thanksgiving dinner and he's got a fork in his hand."

Lori couldn't help giggling, though it came out jittery and nervous. "Yes, Mrs. Hinds, that's an apt picture. He makes me ...."

The thundering of the herd of mustangs crested the near hill, and even the spoon on the counter rattled.

"*Oh!*" Lori whispered.

"I hear you, Missus. He needs to be socialized. Fat little brat. Coming in close, that herd. Never knew them to come this close."

"But ... what ... why did you mention the solstice? What does that have to do with ...." Lori heard the three quarter horses tear out from the horse barn.

"There they go," Mrs. Hinds observed, busying herself again with preparations. "The cayuse come around on summer solstice. You can pretty much set your watch to it. But they've never come this close."

"But ... I don't understand. Horses can't ... don't ... they don't have calendars or watches!"

Mrs. Hinds guffawed a big belly laugh. "True, true. Horses don't have calendars or watches. Very funny."

"I'm not being funn ... *hmmm*." Lori stopped in utter confusion, thinking what a strange world she lived in! Things she said, meant to amuse never got a small crack of a smile, and something she said, wanting really, truly to understand, got a full-fledged guffaw.

"To tell the truth, Missus, I don't know why the wild herd comes around as if they *do* have calendars. I really don't know. I just know ... *they do!* Anyway, you'd better do as the Boss ordered, and go back to bed."

"I will," Lori retorted, raising her chin, "do precisely as I please, and not be treated as if I'm a peer to Beau. *Goodness, Mrs. Hinds!*"

Mrs. Hinds didn't turn around, she just nodded. "Think I'll make some cornbread," she said.

"That sounds lovely." Lori knew she'd irritated Mrs. Hinds with her comment, but she couldn't grasp why. Why must she always do as Nathan said? She had her own mind!

"Guess I'd better get dressed if I'm staying up all night." She turned and stole back up to the bedroom. Stepping out onto the balcony, she looked toward the scream and thunder of the wild horses. She saw them suddenly crest the ridge, surprisingly close to the ranch.

The moon moved over them like a restless tide, their hides glowed in the fretful light, their racing hooves churned, appearing suspended above the surface of the ridge. Lori caught her breath at the other-worldly sight.

The horses bolted along the ridge, then came down toward the ranch, apparent victims of lunacy.

Why would they come toward the ranch?

The two rows of giant oaks lining the wide driveway blocked much of her view, but she briefly saw the herd of little horses, with Nathan and Taffy close behind on their larger quarter horses, the dogs baying, closing in.

Shivering, Lori stepped back inside. It was a troubling drama, entirely beyond her understanding. The chill of the night crept into her, her bare feet now numb with cold, while the wide bed, with its pile of inviting blankets in the shifting-silver moonlight, lured her.

"I'll just lie down for a moment," she murmured, curling up under the blankets. She could hear, at a near distance, Nathan and Taffy shouting over the thud of hooves.

As she closed her eyes, the image of a perfect, golden-silver little horse came into her mind, clear as the disturbing moonlight. Trying to stay awake, wondering about the vision of the shining little horse, sleep beguiled her.

She slipped like a pebble beneath its lilting waves.

*   *

Lori woke hours later, sun streaming through the windows, bright and buoyant, the events of the night before seeming remote and unreal. Despite the cheerful sunlight, she felt oddly disoriented and a little bit sad. She didn't know why.

Looking across the expanse of bed, she couldn't tell if Nathan had even returned to bed. She heard voices in the kitchen and wondered if everyone—*but herself!*—had been up all night. She showered, then pulled on a pair of jeans and a chartreuse silk shirt.

It was quiet as she padded downstairs to the kitchen. She hoped the men had gone out, but they were still lolling about the kitchen, the silence but a momentary preoccupation with eating. Mrs. Hinds was nowhere in sight, and Lori surmised she was engaged in her endless cleaning, washing, sorting, repairing, and organizing chores.

Lori poured herself a bowl of granola smothered in almond milk, and ate, standing by the kitchen window, contemplating the oaks.

Beau, too animated to sit, stood on the far side of the table inhaling a waffle, which disappeared under a mountain of peanut butter. *"Wow, it was great!"* he blurted, flinging his arm out. A blob of peanut butter went flying from his waffle, and landed, *splat!*, in Lori's granola.

Nathan and Beau burst into guffaws, and even Taffy chuckled. But he got up and came around the table, took Lori's bowl, dumped the contents into the cat's bowl, rinsed her bowl out, and poured in fresh granola and almond milk.

Lori watched him quietly. "Thanks, Taffy," she said, taking the offered bowl.

"Did you see that?" Beau howled. *"Ker-plop, he-he!* Like I planned it!" He burst into noisy guffaws, his belly sticking out from his tee shirt, jiggling. *"Sooooo funny!* Shoulda seen your face, Lori."

"Yeah, funny, Beau. For an adolescent." Lori gave Nathan a pointed look.

"Okay, Beau, enough," Nathan said. "Tell Lori what we did last night, with less theatrics."

"Huh?"

"Don't wave your arms about."

"Oh. Yeah. Okay. Well, it was like that herd of mustangs was...."

"Were," Nathan corrected.

"Uhhh ... *were* trying to get to our horses. Don't you think, Dad?"

Nathan shrugged. "So it seemed."

"Yeah—and so they're, like, two-hundred of 'em running like crazy...."

"Beau...."

"What?"

"Don't exaggerate."

"They *were* running like crazy, Dad."

"Yes. But there weren't two-hundred."

"No? *Really?* That's what it looked like to me. But the moon was so bright, it like, made the horses have shadows. I got confused."

"You sure did," Taffy nodded. "Got completely turned around, and started heading back over the ridge."

"Yeah. That was strange. I was like ... like ... I like, heard someone or somethin'. It seemed like someone called to me. But I guess it was just the horses screaming. Those cayuse were screaming, like, you know, like ... they sorta sounded like people ... didn't they, Dad?"

"I didn't notice that, no. Anyway, there were probably about fifty, which is plenty enough."

"No kidding? Only fifty?" Beau looked puzzled. "Huh. Well, anyway, they were running and the moon full, no clouds, everything bright, but grey, and we ... we come up to 'em. And to my eyes, they all looked the same. Just a big bunch of screaming wild horses. *Except that one.*"

"Yes. That palomino," Nathan interjected.

"Yeah," Beau agreed, then whispered, "*That palomino.*"

"Arabian body," Taffy said. "High stepping, too."

"Yeah," Beau agreed. "So we roped some of 'em, and Dad got that palomino. She was wild and screaming! Made me ...." Beau shuddered his whole body. "*Creepy!* Dad got her and another, and Taffy got three. Couldn't get my eyes to focus on any of 'em. Just all blurred and screaming. Got me all turned around in my head."

That would finally be going the right direction, Lori thought. But she restrained herself from saying it aloud.

"I don't see like them two in the night," Beau went on. "Everything looks grey and runs together. But the horses screamed and screamed, and we got those five. The rest run off, back over the ridge, but they were screamin' too, lookin' back."

Lori shook her head in dismay at the image of the traumatized creatures. Why make them so unhappy, she could not imagine. Nathan had plenty of horses, what could he possibly want with more? Especially these little, scruffy, wild ones. "So—what are you going to do with them?" she asked Nathan.

He exchanged a look with Taffy. "Oh, we'll figure out something, Hon," he answered evasively.

"You're not *going* to figure out something—you *have* figured something out. You wouldn't get up in the middle of the night and gallop around the countryside to capture wild horses just because you didn't happen to be doing anything else."

"Well, maybe we would. We've been known to do even stranger things." Nathan stood. "All right, enough piddling around. We've got work to do. Come on, guys." He went out the back door with Taffy close behind. Beau grabbed Nathan's plate and wolfed down the remains of the waffle on it while edging toward the back door.

"Beau...." Lori stepped in front of him.

"*Um?*"

"What does your father have in mind with those horses?"

Beau's jaw worked at the bulging mass in his already chubby cheeks. "Fog food," he said around the waffle.

"What? Swallow, Beau. You're seventeen, where are your manners?"

"In my armpit. Dog food."

Lori's expression went from puzzlement to exasperation. "Why can't we even speak the same language?"

"I answered both your questions. My manners are in my armpit. The horses are dog food."

Lori gasped.

"Aw, jeez, Lori. When'r ya goin' to get used to ranch life? Everything was born to die."

"What an awful outlook." She stepped back from him as if slapped by his comment.

"You better not whine to my dad after you nagged me to tell you, or I'll stop telling you stuff." Beau let his eyes wander up and down Lori's body, then turned and slammed the back door on his way out.

Lori had repeatedly tried to pretend he didn't look at her like that—after all, he was just a kid. But with only a six-year difference in their age, while Nathan was fifteen years her senior, Beau appeared to think this gave him "ogling rights."

Shaking herself to purge the contamination of Beau's visual assault, Lori went onto the back porch and slipped on her boots, curious to look at the hapless wild horses.

As she stepped outside, a small dust devil swirled up, catching early-falling oak leaves. It swirled around her, sighing and swishing. She stood, mesmerized in the midst of the swirling, dancing leaves.

She saw Taffy step out the back of the horse barn, saddle in hand, and, glancing toward the motion that caught his eye, a look of mystification and surprise grew on his face, first seeing the weird wind, and then realizing Lori stood in the midst of it.

Lori looked at him through the whirling, flying leaves and shrugged, raising her palms up in her own gesture of bewilderment. No dust or dirt swirled in the spiraling wind, just the happy oak leaves, batting about her, billowing her long, red-blond, hair around in a vortex.

Taffy stepped toward her, and, instantly, the vortex dropped, all the leaves falling and drifting to the ground about her.

"*Weird!*" Lori called to Taffy.

"I've never seen such a thing in my life!" Taffy called back. "I guess the leaves like your green shirt!" He laughed.

"I guess you're right!"

Taffy returned to his chores, and Lori headed to the back side of the horse barn, to the far corral, away from the barn and the other horses, where she found the ragged band of little wild horses.

The five cayuse, bunched up in the far corner of the corral, whinnied as she approached. She could see the whites of their eyes, the poor creatures crazed with fear. Why didn't they try to escape?

Then she realized that their short legs were no match for the height of the corral. Stuck out here far from everything, she figured that Nathan didn't want his horses to see the cayuse. They were probably worked up enough hearing and smelling them.

"Hey, hey, beauties," she said softly, stepping up on the bottom rail of the corral. "Hey."

They looked at her with flared nostrils, but as she waited patiently, they calmed, the whites of their eyes returned to big, luminous orbs, their nostrils stopped flaring.

The four scruffy little stallions, one paint, the other three, varying shades of brown, gathered around the palomino, protecting the little mare, although she was the tallest among them, on long, graceful, blonde, legs.

The palomino moved toward Lori, while the others remained clustered near her, her slow gait a dance of beauty, her sliver-golden coat catching the sun and reflecting it back. She made eye contact with Lori. Some unfathomable thing in Lori shifted as she felt herself flow into the little horse's glowing light.

"That palomino's a pretty little filly," Taffy said, coming up from behind.

Shocked out of the peculiar altered reality, Lori nearly fell off the fence. "*Oh!* You startled me!"

"Sorry." Taffy stepped up on the rail beside her, barely able to peek over the top rail. "Didn't mean to scare you."

"Yes. She's ... she's beautiful. And, there's something ... about her ... don't know how to express it ...."

"Yeah. I know what you mean. She just looks right at ya."

Lori nodded. "Here they are, terrified to death, and she walked right up to me. I was trying to think of how to convince Nathan not to ...."

"He's not. He intends to keep her, break her. She's small, but she looks like good breeding. We figure she's a runaway and was lucky enough to happen on a wild herd, and to be female so the stallion took her in. It's possible, though, that she's a half-breed, and just came out with the best of fine bones and beauty.

"I could bet her mother had a dalliance with a pure-bred out in a pasture. Anyway, the Boss is planning on giving that one a chance to prove herself."

"Good," Lori said, sighing deeply. There was nothing fun about the thought of going head-to-head with Nathan. But she was preparing to.

"Yeah," Taffy went on. "He's thinking she'll make a good mount for you, if she can be broken. She looks pretty young. I think there's hope." Taffy jumped down from the fence. "I'd better get back to work."

Lori watched him move around the barn with a warmhearted smile. After she'd married Nathan—just a year ago next month—on a whirlwind romance, he'd brought her here to live on his horse ranch, located between the villages of "No," and "Where" she liked to say. To herself of course, not out loud. She soon became grateful for Taffy, as an unspoken bond formed between them. He had an uncanny sense of her bouts of feeling like she didn't belong, and would chat with her, just when she needed it most. He'd become Lori's one-and-only real-true friend.

Despite their physical differences, there was something similar—very similar—Lori thought, under the surface of physical trappings.

The ex-jockey was a little king's squire sort of man, barrel-chested and bandy-legged—an altogether homely, charmingly elfin sort of person, diffident, intelligent, soft-hearted, with deep-set, sparkling brown eyes over gaunt cheekbones, a pointy nose, a thin-lipped, wide grin, and wild, wiry, brown hair, bushy at the sides and thinning at the top. His out-in-the-elements weather-beaten skin was etched with permanent lines of kindliness around his eyes and mouth.

But on horseback! On horseback he transformed into a godly centaur, as if his funny little body had been built to be on a horse.

Lori had not seen a horse that could throw him.

She returned her attention to the little wild palomino, who continued to study her calmly. There appeared to be communication passing between her and the four little stallions. Lori wondered what they had to say to one another, what they were experiencing, what they understood about their current dire situation.

An inevitable plan hatched in Lori's mind. No way would she allow these beautiful creatures to be *literally* fed to the dogs! She'd steal out in the night and let them loose. She hated to let the beautiful little palomino go, but it was probably all or nothing. Would the palomino stay when her brothers left? Would her brothers leave, if Lori attempted to keep the palomino? Not, Lori knew, not in a month of blue moons.

How would she explain it to Nathan? If they were *all* gone, well, they'd figured a way to get out. But if the one most able to get out, with her long, golden legs, was the only one that remained, all eyes would be on Lori.

She reached her hand toward the little filly, still several paces away, who approached Lori and let her pat her muzzle, sniffing her hand, sniffing at the silk shirt. She made a soft nickering sound.

"Don't worry, Miss Lovely, I'll take care of you." She stepped down from the corral and walked back to the house, then wandered to the wide, sweeping front yard, needing to move away from the little horse that had so immediately grabbed her heart. She must not form an attachment, she silently admonished herself.

Too late! Her heart replied.

In the front yard, the giant, gnarled, oaks cast fat shadows over the grass and immaculately trimmed landscape. Lori frequently offered up a prayer of gratitude that Nathan had not downed the ancient oaks when he'd had the formal mansion built for his first wife, Claire, that replaced the modest farmhouse he'd grown up in. Lori had already learned that it was Nathan's way to completely change things once he owned them.

Or he tried to, when he believed he owned something. Hence, their love-and-frustration-wrought relationship.

Claire must have been such a milquetoast, Lori mused, sitting down under one of the oaks, leaning back against the comforting strength of its trunk. However, from the few bits she'd learned about Claire, mostly from Taffy, but occasionally from Mrs. Hinds, too, it seemed she'd been willful and challenging. Not milquetoast in the least.

Everyone appeared intent on keeping Claire's memory dusted and folded, in a bell jar of silent remembrance. *And Beau!* Who *ever* Claire may have been, she must have done quite a psychological number on him, given how he still went into ballistic bouts of tears, the very few times she *had* been mentioned.

Yes, it was sad and too bad that he'd lost his mother, Lori thought, remembering her own childhood, when her mother suddenly disappeared. Her father had so checked out after that, that she emancipated herself, and lived on her own from the age of fifteen.

But Beau, in this environment of plenty, was left to develop any which way, like a feral animal. *Why* did Nathan, who ruled his roost with a "velvet-gloved iron hand," turn a blind eye and deaf ear to Beau's dysfunctions?

"What's this blue study, Miss Lori?" Taffy asked as he trotted up on Vladimir. He jumped off the horse and squatted down on the grass by her.

She smiled at him, twirling the stem of an oak leaf between her fingers. "Just thinking about ... about marrying in haste and now repenting at leisure."

"Aw, you don't mean that!" Taffy cocked his head attentively.

"No. You're right. I love Nathan, of course. A bit less 'madly' than I used to, though."

"Well, sure!" Taffy nodded. "That's the nature of so-called romantic love. If it weathers the first few rounds, it shifts to something steady, patient. Mature."

"*Ugh,* Taffy, not *mature!* I don't want to think of myself as 'mature' just yet. It sounds so matronly."

Taffy chuckled. "Nothing wrong with being mature, dear girl—sensible, reliable, levelheaded."

"Well, Taffy," Lori exclaimed, "you've just described yourself."

"Guess I'm mature, then."

"I guess."

A companionable silence fell between them. Just then a clamorous flock of nuthatches flew into the oak branches above, followed by nearly as many chickadees. Lori and Taffy spontaneously laughed at their chittering, chattering, flitting among the branches.

"It's like the trees just sprung forth these little birds!" Lori giggled.

"Indeed!"

Looking up among the animated branches, Lori felt herself relax. "But ... despite the problems, there's so much to love here."

"There is," Taffy agreed simply. "So much to love. And so much to do. I can dally no more, I've got work to get done." Taffy stood and mounted Vladimir, then ambled down the driveway, waving as he went.

Lori watched the tiny man on the massive horse until they disappeared over the crest of the hill. The thought that the little horseman, along with the grandmotherly oaks surrounding her, would see to it that no harm came to her, gave her comfort.

*   *

That night, Lori woke suddenly in the middle of the night, dreaming about the wild horses. Did she hear them screaming? She listened. No. All was still. The shocking moonlight roiled about the bedroom, as if an alchemy had blended silver and alabaster into a single, animate, breathing, element, flooding the room from floor to ceiling, weighing down the bedding with its alabaster weight.

She kicked the bedding from her and moved toward the balcony without even glancing at Nathan, deep in the land of his dreams.

As she passed the three-way mirror, her reflection so stunned her, she couldn't move. Her bare arms white as the silk of her peignoir, her face white as stone, her red-blonde hair glowing a brilliant silver, her entire body radiating a silvery-white light that undulated in waves around her head and flowed out her fingertips. The iridescence swirling about her held her, mesmerized.

As she stared, transfixed, at her reflection, she became overwhelmed with drowsiness, even her fascination with the angelic light couldn't keep her awake. She crawled back into bed—again, she heard a scream, but like that of a girl, not the wild horses.

And yet, the tranquilizing sleep overtook her.

Chapter II

Dawn:
Transmogrification

In the middle of the night, the moonlight stirred restlessly among the oaks and poured into the place where my brother, my three near-brothers, and I were imprisoned. I felt the changes begin. I begged the moonlight to let me escape, and to help me let my brothers escape, to let us all fly on the moonlight back to the herd.

But it was not to be.

I tore around the corral, crazed with pain, alone with the mystery of what I felt in my blood, in my body—

everything changing, changing, moment by moment. *My bones!* My beautiful bones—shifting.

My brothers could only stand by and watch my frenzied agony, while, in our shared mind, they also had to feel my pain, unable to do anything.

I charged into the midst of the knot of my brothers, bucking and crying, as I felt my deep memory, my connection with them, fading, even as I endured the changes—the changes every Eos must pass through, at least once.

The immensity of my grief of separation from them was greater than the physical pain—I would soon be irrevocably parted from my brothers.

Suddenly thrown violently to the ground, my shoulders pulled flat across my back, my view of the world moved crazily as my eyes shifted to the front of my head, my muzzle receded to a small hard cartilage between my eyes, my ears shrank to the sides of my head, and I felt my skull, and even the shape of my brain shifting, changing. *Changed.* All that I knew, had ever known, shifted away. Left me.

I watched in horror as my lovely, silken fetlocks disappeared and my perfect, bell-shaped hooves lengthened into soft, flat, peculiar extensions. My forelegs shortened, my hind legs rounded, and my long, beautiful back shrank, as my hind legs shot out at an entirely different angle from my body. My silver-golden mane fell in waves to these strange legs, while my precious, warm golden coat of fur fell to the ground.

I couldn't stop writhing as I screamed, I couldn't stop fighting the changes. Finally, I became exhausted and I just gave in to it. I lay there, exhausted, weak, cold, confused.

Then ... *then!* Suddenly a power rushed through me. I leapt up from the ground to rear up on my hind legs, only to discover that my forelegs were no longer useful for standing or running or jumping.

I took a few steps away from my brothers on these odd, soft, furless, hoof-less, flat feet. I looked back at the black earth where I had changed—there, the shape of my former self—my golden coat, shed upon the dirt.

I watched as the night wind caught it, swirled it up and around, sparkling and glittering in the light of the fat, round, moon. Shocked as I stared at the tufts of my fetlocks tossing about, my heart breaking while the golden outline of my previous form blew away, erased from the black earth. *Erased.*

I began to call out, but instead of my beautiful, full voice, I heard, from my own vocal cords, a shrill, pale voice. I cried, and brought the strange, soft objects my forefeet had become up to my face.

"*Ah, ahhh, Ahhhh-h-h-h ....*" I sobbed, as my brothers stood helpless in the moonlight. I cried to the night —to all the ages since the dawn of time.

My brother and my three near-brothers stood close together, quiet, inconsolably sad. They'd known that I, their little sister, must transform. Since the beginning of time, we shared through deep memory, the transmogrification of each Eos on the first solstice they reached maturity.

In this odd moment when I was no longer horse, but not quite yet human, the silence of the loss of deep memory echoed through me, an unfathomable void. I couldn't hear what my brothers thought to one another. I could sense they were sad. I knew they were frightened—the fright that ran through all of us since we'd been captured the night before.

I made soft sounds with my strange, weak voice, and they gathered close to me. I patted them with my awkward new limbs, trying to comfort them. Then I realized, as ugly as I felt myself to be, these thin growths at the ends of what had been my forelegs may be useful.

I recalled what the men had done when they put us in this cage. I moved, cautiously on the two legs, to the gate. I studied it, then fumbled with it with the small— but flexible!—pale, bare *things* that grew in the place of where my hooves had been. The gate opened—*easily!*

I felt a tiny ray of hope. There *was* power in this body! I pushed open the gate and called to my brothers. They came to me, and each in turn, first my three near-brothers, and last, my precious, twin-brother, forehead to forehead, as we each sealed a memory of love and devotion that sank into my new, unfamiliar, mind.

They then ran from the horse prison, their beautiful tails and manes streaming in the moonlight, their calls of love and their good-byes floating back to me over the drumlins.

I ran after them, but I, who had always outrun them, could not now even catch up. I stood on the top of a hillock, watching my brothers, my beautiful brothers, with my peculiar new eyes through which everything, *everything!* had a different color, a different depth. A different *look*.

I stared at them until I could no longer see the slightest flicker of their manes, until I could not hear the faintest sound of their voices.

Then I turned, and, looking down the hill at the huge house and the oaks and the long horse house, I shuddered from cold and from fear. How could I keep warm with this awful, furless, skin?

I went back down to the horse house and into the beautiful little palomino's stall. I tried to communicate with her, but my sounds came out perplexing and meaningless. Even so, she appeared to understand me and nuzzled me affectionately. I gathered up some of the blankets the horses wore and wrapped myself in them, curling up in a pile of straw in the corner of the lovely warm stall.

Although I felt so sad and frightened, exhaustion overcame me from the transformations, which I could feel continuing, though with less intensity. Every inch of my peculiar new body ached. I felt like I'd fallen off a cliff. And I had no idea what to do—I didn't have a teacher like every other Eos. But, I reasoned, if I slept for a while I would know what to do when I woke up.

Chapter III

Lori:
A Homeless Girl

"**L**ori—Lori! *Wake up!*" Nathan shook her roughly.

"Wha ...?" Lori rolled over and tried to focus on Nathan. "What?"

"Is something wrong with you?"

"I don't know ... I ...." Lori tried to remember her experience in the night. "That is, I had the strangest ...."

Nathan sat down on the edge of the bed and ran his fingers across Lori's brow. "Had the strangest what?"

"I don't know. I guess it was a dream. I thought I heard the horses, the little wild horses, scream. But I woke up, and saw myself, like ...." she pointed to the ornate, floor to ceiling mirror, "like in a light. No. Like I *was* light. So real, but it must have been a dream ... I came back to bed and fell asleep ... or ... I don't know."

"Just a dream," Nathan affirmed.

"A very strange dream ...."

"But right now, Lori, we have a very real *not* dream." He stood looking down at her with an expression Lori could not read. Not desire. Not disappointment. But both, somehow, at once. "Taffy and I need your help—I'll be in the kitchen." He strode from the room like a man on a mission.

Lori sat up on the edge of the bed, still feeling groggy and disoriented, trying to clear her head. She finally stood, somewhat shaky. Mystified by why, she pulled on a pair of jeans and a sweatshirt. She stepped into the bathroom wondering at Nathan saying he and Taffy "needed" her. They'd never "needed" her for anything. What could it be?

She pulled a brush through her hair, and as she looked in the mirror, the memory of the stone white illumination, light-filtering image of herself in the night overtook her mind.

"Are you coming?" Nathan called up the back stairs.

"Yes. Yes, *I'm coming*." She tore her gaze from the mirror and scurried down the back stairs.

In the kitchen, Mrs. Hinds acted overly busy at the stove, while Beau stood by the back door as if on a leash he would surely break.

Nathan and Taffy hovered by the stairs, a study in tall and small, waiting for her.

"Put on your boots, Lori," Nathan urged. "Sit down, Beau, you're not leaving the house. Don't let him out, Mrs. Hinds."

"Don't worry. If he makes a move, I'll box his ears."

"Aw, you can't even reach 'em, so how ya goin' to box 'em?"

Mrs. Hinds wielded a bread knife through the air. "Don't talk back to me, boy, or I'll cut them off and put them in a box before you know it."

Beau returned his attention to his father. "Come on, Dad, let me see her, too!"

Nathan gave Beau a thunderous look. "*Stay put!*" he ordered, holding the back door open for Lori, as she quickly pulled on her boots.

"This morning," he said, taking long strides to the horse barn, "when Taffy came out to feed and water the horses, he found ...." they entered Twinkle's stall, ".... *her.*"

Taffy sat on a bale of straw beside a pile of horse blankets. As Lori's eyes adjusted to the darkened interior of the stall, she saw something wrapped up in the blankets. Or ... *someone.*

Nathan stood off to the side of the Dutch door while Lori cautiously approached the pile of blankets.

"We tried to get her to come inside," Taffy said. "But she refuses to move. And she won't say anything. Also, she seems not to be wearing any clothes."

"Hi there. Are you all right?" At the sound of Lori's soft voice, the girl moved the blanket to look at her. "Don't be afraid. I won't hurt you." The blanket fell from her head and her brilliant blonde hair shone in the dark stall like a light. Lori gasped when she saw the girl's eyes—she'd seen these eyes before, and recently.

"What's your name?" Lori knelt on the floor in front of the girl. "I'm Lori. And this is Taffy, and that's Nathan," she gestured, then patted the girl's shoulder. "Everything is all right, don't be afraid."

"You're doing great," Taffy whispered. "She wouldn't let me get near her at all without screaming. When Nathan first came in, she went ballistic."

"She needs a woman right now, don't you, poor girl? Who needs all these growly, hard-skinned men?"

"Thanks, Lori, that's an insight," Nathan grumbled.

The girl jumped and gave a frightened look toward him.

"My goodness, Nathan," Lori continued in the same soft voice, "I'm trying to attend to her needs right now, not yours. Have a little understanding." She continued to softly pat the girl's shoulder.

"I think it would be best if you two made yourselves scarce," Lori continued. "And get Beau out of the house. I'll try to get her up to my room and put some clothes on her."

"*Your* room? *Our* room."

"What *is* your problem, Nathan?" Though shocked and frustrated with Nathan, Lori kept the tone of her voice calm. "Do you not see before you a defenseless, frightened, speechless, naked girl? I've never seen you behave so ridiculously."

It was the first time Lori had flat-out stood up to Nathan.

A dumbfounded look crossed his features.

"She's right," Taffy stage-whispered, standing slowly. "Let's get Beau and check the fence in the north sector."

"Who's the Boss here?" Nathan demanded, though in a slightly muted voice.

The girl began to whine.

"At the moment, Nathan, this girl," Lori moved closer to her and put an arm around her shoulders. "Now, please go!"

Taffy opened the stall door and held it open for Nathan.

"What if she bolts?" Nathan asked.

"Oh, my goodness, she's not going to bolt!" Lori continued in her soft, placating voice, wanting to yell.

Nathan and Taffy finally left.

"There now, they're gone. We'll give them a few minutes to get Beau out of the house, and get saddled up and leave. They won't need Twinkle right now."

At the mention of her name, Twinkle came to them and nuzzled them both. "Twinkle loves us, pretty girl, doesn't she?"

The girl nodded, but said nothing, and Lori wasn't sure if she really had nodded.

"Let's go in the house and see what I've got that you can wear. *Oh!* And you're hungry, too, for sure! We'll have to see if we can find out who your people are, but first things first. Right now, I just want you to know that I'm not going to let anything hurt you."

Lori continued to talk softly to the girl until she heard the men mount and gallop toward the north. "Good! Let's go inside, the only obstacle we have now is Mrs. Hinds. If we're lucky, she'll leave us alone." Lori stood. "Come on." She gestured for the girl to follow her, but she just watched as if waiting for Lori to make a move she didn't trust.

"It's all right." Lori bent over her and grabbed her shoulders firmly, pulling her to a standing position. The girl stood only about three inches shorter than Lori. "My goodness, you're tall, aren't you?" Lori put her arm around her and directed her to the stall door. "Sometimes those men just don't know how to do a thing, isn't that right?" Lori noticed that her soft babbling seemed to lead the girl like a rein. Every time Lori paused, the girl faltered.

Finally, they made it to the back door. Mrs. Hinds stood there, holding the door open for them.

"I didn't really believe the men when they told me," she whispered. "A naked girl way out here where no one ever comes."

"Mrs. Hinds, you've lived around here for a long time ...."

"Sixty-one years."

"Does she resemble any of the families in the area?"

Mrs. Hinds shook her head. "The only person she looks the least bit like is yourself, Missus."

"Really? You think so?" Lori studied the girl's face for a moment. "I'll take her upstairs and see if she'd like to have a nice hot bath and get some clothes on. I'll bet she's hungry too. Maybe you could bring up something simple, like a salad and sandwich and a glass of juice?"

"Sure," Mrs. Hinds nodded. "Poor creature. I can feel she's gone through some incredible experience."

Lori nodded, stunned at Mrs. Hinds' surprising sensitivity.

But when Lori and the girl got to the foot of the stairs, the girl balked, backing away from the stairs, looking around frantically.

"You're afraid of the stairs? But it's easy ... see?" Lori put one foot on the first step, then the other on the same step. "We'll just take them one at a time, see?"

She stepped back down and put her arm around the girl and coaxed her quietly until, finally, she took the first step. She looked surprised, then ran up the whole flight, with strange little sounds of curiosity and delight. She looked back down at Lori.

"You *are* a strange one." Lori followed and led the girl into her room and her closet. "Do you see anything you like? You're close enough to my size to fit anything."

The girl appeared attracted to the rainbow of colors of the clothes. Holding the horse blanket close, she reached out to lightly touch the fabrics.

"I'll start running the bath while you decide what you like. Don't go anywhere."

Lori went into the bathroom and started running the water, pouring in aromatic bath salts and bubble bath. When she returned to the closet, the girl sat on the floor in the middle of a jumble of Lori's shoes. She had a different pump in each hand, rhythmically tapping the heels against the floor.

Lori laughed. "It sounds like you're galloping!" She kneeled down on the floor beside her, grabbed up two pumps and joined in.

A moment later, Mrs. Hinds stood at the closet door, holding a tray. "Are the children hungry?"

Lori looked up, slightly sheepish. "This kid is. Oh, gosh, I forgot about the bath." She ran and turned off the bath water, then returned with a terry bathrobe.

"I know you don't seem to care about any of my clothes, but it's too hard to eat in a horse blanket. Here, put your arm in here."

While Mrs. Hinds set up their brunch in the bay window, Lori got the girl in the bathrobe and brought her and the horse blankets out of the closet. "Besides, dear, the horse blankets are pretty stinky." She dropped them outside the bedroom door. "I love the smell of horses, but it's not appropriate for the boudoir. Now, let's wash our hands." She led the girl to the sink in the bathroom and helped her wash her hands, then they returned back to the bay window where Mrs. Hinds had spread a charming feast.

"Why, this is lovely, Mrs. Hinds, thank you."

She made the girl sit, then handed her a glass of mango-peach juice.

The girl just stared at it.

"Like this," Lori sipped at her own glass of juice. "Mmmm! So good!"

The girl imitated Lori, then swallowed the entire contents of the glass without a breath.

"*She's thirsty!*" Lori handed the girl her own glass, and she finished it off as well. Then Lori started on her salad and the girl picked up her spoon, attempting to imitate her.

"Not quite." Lori handed her a fork.

The girl looked at it in curiosity, put it down, then wolfed down the salad with her fingers, followed by devouring the entire plate of sandwiches as Lori and Mrs. Hinds watched in amazement.

"She eats like a horse," Mrs. Hinds observed.

"She *does* have an appetite," Lori agreed. "At least there doesn't seem to be anything wrong with her physically. But ... she hasn't said a word." Lori patted the girl's hand. "How about that bath?" She came around the table and led the girl into the bathroom.

"Do you need me?" Mrs. Hinds called from the bedroom as she cleared up the brunch.

"I think we'll manage all right. But I'm guessing she'd love some of that apple pie you made yesterday if there's any left. I have the feeling she only quit eating because there was no more food."

"Apple pie, on its way."

Lori checked the temperature of the bath water, and when she turned to face the girl, she saw her mesmerized by the mirror. The fingers of one hand were entangled in her hair, while her other hand splayed across the mirror, her eyes full of amazement.

"Have you never seen yourself?" Lori gently removed the bathrobe and tried to get the girl to step into the bathtub, but she recoiled.

"*N-i-i-i!*" She cried, eyes wide with fright.

"No?" Lori asked. "You mean no? You don't want to get into the water?"

"*No!*" the girl said.

"Okay ... okay. At least you spoke a word. I'll tell you what. I'll give you a sponge bath, how's that?" Lori got a washcloth and soaped it up. The girl seemed to love the warmth of the cloth against her skin.

While Lori toweled her dry, Mrs. Hinds knocked at the door. "The police are here, missus."

"Who called the police?"

"The Boss, before he and Taffy went out to work."

"I see. Jeez, can't we even get clean and dressed and relaxed before we get interrogated? Could you bring me my sea green silk lounge outfit, Mrs. Hinds?"

Mrs. Hinds brought the outfit and Lori managed, finally, to get the girl in it. "Something tells me she won't wear anything confining."

"Yep. We'd better get back downstairs, or the police will think we're behaving suspiciously."

Lori laughed. "Too many police procedural shows, Mrs. Hinds."

The girl laughed in a perfect mimic of Lori. "*No!*" she said, and laughed again. She rubbed her hands over the silk covering her body.

"No?" Mrs. Hinds said.

"It's her only word. I think she likes the silk."

Mrs. Hinds nodded. "I can understand that."

The three of them went down the wide, sweeping, front stairs, where, in the foyer stood a policeman and a policewoman.

Lori went to them with her hand extended. "Good morning. I'm Mrs. Tanner. Can we get you some tea or coffee?"

"No thanks, ma'am," the policeman replied. I'm Officer Mandrake and this is Officer Womak. We're here in response to a report of a runaway."

"Please, be seated," Lori gestured. "Mrs. Hinds, perhaps you'd be kind enough to bring us some tea. I'm dying for some, and our guests may change their minds."

"Yes, Missus." Mrs. Hinds turned to leave.

"Oh! And the apple pie for the girl."

"Yes, Missus. I have it ready, in the kitchen. Shall I bring it in?"

"I think so, yes. I'm sure the police have seen people with ... approximate manners before."

Mrs. Hinds nodded and left.

"Is this the girl?" the policeman asked after everyone was seated.

"Yes." Lori put a protective arm around her. She sat close to Lori on the sofa and eyed the policeman with caution. She held her head up and sniffed the air.

"She seems apprehensive of us," he said, making a note.

"Well, ahm, I believe it's just you. She appears to have a strong fear of men, which is why I had the men leave the house until she and I became a little better acquainted. I ... I hesitate to tell you what to do, but I think she'd be much calmer if the woman officer did as much of the talking as possible."

They exchanged a glance. "All right, Officer Womak, it's all yours."

Officer Womak cleared her throat. "I'm in training, but I'll do my best."

Mrs. Hinds brought the tea tray in. She handed the girl a plate with the apple pie and a fork. They all quietly watched in fascination as the girl, eschewing the fork, ate the pie with her fingers in four bites.

"Is there any more pie, Mrs. Hinds?" Lori asked.

"Yes, there's another one."

"Would you care for some?" Lori asked the officers. "It's obviously very good."

They chuckled, but declined.

"Perhaps another piece for our young friend, then, Mrs. Hinds."

Mrs. Hinds nodded and left.

Lori poured cups of tea while officer Womak asked about the details of the girl's appearance and behavior, the girl devoured the second piece of pie, then fell asleep, hard and fast, against Lori's shoulder.

After a few more questions, which Lori answered to the best of her ability although she knew nothing about the girl, the police stood.

"Thank you, Mrs. Tanner," Officer Mandrake said to Lori. "And thank you for the tea. We'll take the girl now. I assume the expensive silk outfit she's wearing is yours. Would you rather put her in something less— designer? And perhaps you'd have some shoes and a jacket ...."

"Take her? Why would you take her? She's perfectly all right here until you find her people. As you can see, she feels safe with me."

"Your husband instructed us to take her."

"Phooey to what he said. Sometimes he doesn't think things through. The poor girl has obviously been through a traumatic experience, why add to it?"

"Missus," Mrs. Hinds interrupted, "if I might point out, the Boss was pretty clear on that point."

"Well, then, 'the Boss' can just take it up with me."

"And she does apparently eat ...."

"Like a horse?" Lori finished. "So what? Nine out of ten of the creatures living on this property eat like horses."

"That's because they're ... horses," Mrs. Hinds observed.

"I think we should take her," Officer Mandrake said. "We have a decent facility for runaways. You don't have to worry about her."

His voice startled the girl awake. She looked around in alarm.

"Please don't take her," Lori begged. "Really! Mrs. Hinds, shame on you!"

"I'm just trying to keep the peace. I have concern for the girl, but the Boss will blame me if his orders aren't carried out. He'll dock my pay for her expenses."

"He will *not* do that, Mrs. Hinds, on threat of divorce. If he tries, I'll fire *him*. He's probably the wealthiest man for miles around, he can't share a bit of it?"

The girl had started to breathe heavy and fast, making a small, nervous sound with each breath.

"Let's just do it quickly," Officer Mandrake stood, "for the sake of the least anxiety."

He came over to the girl and grabbed her by the shoulders, pulling her to her feet. She went wild, throwing her head and kicking. Her hair flew into the officer's eyes, blinding him. "Assistance, please, Officer Womak."

"Yes, sir." She came and stood by his side. "What should I do, sir?"

"Restraints."

"Handcuffs?" Officer Womak and Lori exclaimed together.

"No," Lori pleaded. "Please, please, oh my God, what's going on here? She's not a criminal, and I am telling you officers, to please respect my request—*do not do that to her!*"

Right then the girl went limp in a dead faint. Lori lifted her feet onto the sofa, while Office Mandrake checked her breathing.

"Please, let her be for now," Lori whispered. "I assure you, I can handle my husband, if anyone can. I'll call my doctor and have her come out to take a look at the girl this afternoon."

The two officers exchanged a look, then officer Womak nodded. "All right, Mrs. Tanner. But please have the girl available in case we find a relative."

"Of course!" Lori accompanied them to the door. "And thank you for being so—humanitarian."

"We're not ogres, Mrs. Tanner," Officer Mandrake said. "We simply have a job to do, which is to protect people. Especially underage people."

"*Absolutely!*" Lori agreed, holding the front door open. "Please stop by any time. On or off duty. Really, you must try Mrs. Hinds' apple pie sometime."

"Thanks," Officer Womak nodded.

Lori closed the door with a great sigh of disgust-laced relief, and hurried back to the girl. "Thank goodness," she muttered. "Honestly, what is *with* people?"

Mrs. Hinds had a cold compress on the girl's forehead, patting her hand. But she gave Lori a look that said, "You've done it now."

"You greatly underestimate my power, Mrs. Hinds. And if Nathan tries to cut your pay, or make *any sort* of negative comment to you, you'd better let me know. I'll make up the difference myself. Why, the silk lounge suit the girl has on is probably almost one of your paychecks."

"Closer to two, Missus."

"*No!* Really? Pay cut, nonsense, you need a raise. Now, if you would, please call my doctor, give her a thumbnail sketch of what's going on, and see if she can come out this afternoon."

While Mrs. Hinds was on the telephone, the girl regained consciousness. She looked anxiously around her, but when she saw only Lori, she relaxed.

"That's right—nothing to worry about now. How are you feeling? Can you get up? Maybe you need more food. Let's go to the kitchen."

The girl followed along docilely, rubbing her hands up and down the silk of her outfit.

Mrs. Hinds got off the telephone. "The doc'll be out about three this afternoon."

"That's fine." Lori opened the refrigerator. "See anything you'd like?"

The girl stuck her head in the refrigerator and sniffed. She pulled out a head of lettuce and tore into it as she roved about the kitchen.

"Oddest manners *I* ever saw," Mrs. Hinds observed under her breath.

The girl spied the remains of the apple pie on the counter and dug into it with all fingers.

"Sorry, Mrs. Hinds, I know that pie was for dinner."

Mrs. Hinds shrugged. "If the pie was the only thing I had to be concerned about, I'd be real pleased."

The girl grabbed her stomach and groaned.

"Hmm, I guess she's finally reached—or exceeded—capacity. I'll take her back up to my room."

In the bedroom, the girl went into the closet and curled up in the corner on the floor.

"We don't sleep on the floor, dear. Come on." Lori took her by the hand to her side of the bed and pulled back the blankets. "Sleep here. Come, lie down. See?

Isn't that comfortable? I'll just pull the drapes and it'll be nice and cozy and dark."

The girl fell immediately asleep. Lori stretched out on top of the blankets on the other side of the bed intending to watch over the girl, but she, too, soon fell fast asleep.

Chapter IV

Lori:
Missing Cayuse

"What's going on?" Nathan barked, waking Lori and the girl. "Is that all you ever do anymore, Lori, sleep?"

Lori jumped up from the bed. "Hush, Nathan. There's no need to yell. I don't know what's come over you."

"Some child takes over my house and my bedroom, my express orders to have her removed are ignored, my housekeeper and my wife have declared mutiny, horses have been stolen from me, and *you don't know what's come over me?*"

The girl came around the bed and stood behind Lori, but, Lori noticed, she didn't seem as frightened as she had been.

"Horses stolen? When? Which horses?"

"The cayuse. Apparently last night. With all the muddle around this girl, I didn't even check on them until just now when we rode back in. The gate open, the corral empty. Did you hear anything?"

"Last night, yes, I woke up when I thought I heard … something. It was very strange, last night. I—well, never mind that. But, yes, I guess maybe I did hear something."

Nathan strode over to the balcony, threw the curtains open and stepped out. He stood with his back to Lori, musing. "Must be gypsies or something. Horses stolen, and I'm left with this mute girl."

Lori joined him on the balcony, the girl close behind. "But why, Nathan, would anyone steal those little wild horses? I mean—wouldn't they steal horses that are worth money?"

Nathan gave Lori a studied look. "That is a very logical thought."

"I'm extremely capable of logical thought."

"Of course you are. But, you just out-thought me."

"Brace yourself! There's more where that came from."

Nathan almost chuckled.

"As far as the girl being mute—she said "no," this morning. So she's not exactly mute. I think she's got some kind of amnesia, but the doctor—*oh!* What time is it?"

Nathan glanced at his watch. "Just about two-thirty."

"My doctor is coming at three to check the girl over. But let me get her situated in one of the guest rooms. And you can have your kingdom back."

"Yes," Nathan agreed, "if you insist on the girl staying here, I do prefer her in a guest room."

Lori took the girl's hand. "Come on dear, let's decide which room is yours." In the bedroom doorway Lori turned to Nathan. "And don't you *dare* give Mrs. Hinds a hard time. We have to talk about giving her a raise."

"*A raise!* I just gave her a raise two years ago!"

* *

"I'm sure I don't know why Nathan had so many bedrooms made in this house," Lori said as the two of them walked down the hall. "He never has any company. Let's see if you like this room." Lori opened the door to a room three doors down, that also faced the great oaks lining the driveway. The sweet, dappled light and shadow of the oaks played about the room. Oak leaves danced across the walls in bright shades of orange and gold and green.

"*Oh! Oh!*" the girl exclaimed, rushing up to the wall, reaching out to pluck at a leaf.

Lori laughed, while the girl turned to her with a puzzled expression. "It's not real, dear. I painted the leaves on the walls."

The girl's puzzled expression remained. She turned to the wall again to stroke the leaf, and then she moved on to others, touching them, trying to find their edges.

"I will have to show you how I did that. But I'm very happy to learn that they look that real. Everyone else in this household seems to have no clue why I painted oak leaves on the walls of this little room. I was beginning to wonder, too. But I see now, it was for this very moment."

Lori sat on the edge of the little white chenille-covered bed, watching the girl work her way around the room, touching all the leaves as she went, until she came to the mirror of the dresser, where, once again, she became completely taken by her reflection.

Lori got up and stood by her. "You see that beautiful girl?"

The girl started when Lori came by her. She looked over at Lori and then back to the mirror. She touched Lori's face and then her own, and Lori could see that she was having a new insight that the girl in the mirror was, in fact, herself.

"*Nii, nii,*" she murmured.

At that moment, Mrs. Hinds came to the door of the bedroom. "The doctor is here, Missus."

"Oh, goodness, we're not even settled. Thank you, Mrs. Hinds. Would you mind terribly bringing her here?"

"Not in the least."

Lori took the girl's hand. "My doctor is here. She's nice, and I want to make sure you're all right, because I don't know what happened to you that you came to be in the barn. So, don't worry, all right?"

"Hi, Lori," the doctor greeted, entering the room. "Thank you, kindly, Mrs. Hinds," she called, as Mrs. Hinds made an unceremonious retreat down the hall.

"She doesn't want any part of this I fear, Edna," Lori said.

"Just as well," the doctor replied, shutting the door quietly and coming into the room.

"Hi there," she said to the girl, who looked at her with curiosity. "Shall we sit over here?" She gestured to the bed. Lori took the girl's hand and sat by her on the bed.

"Have you noticed anything that concerns you other than the not talking?" The doctor pulled up a chair and sat in front of them.

"No. Like what?"

"Well ... just, anything."

"No. She seems ... perfect. But she does appear to be suffering from amnesia. She tried to pluck the leaves off the wall, and doesn't seem to realize that they aren't real. Then, just before you came, she became fascinated with her reflection in the mirror. She did that before. She didn't seem to realize it was herself. I walked up to her, and she looked shocked that the real me and the mirror me were the same. She was just putting that together when you came."

"Ummm ...." the doctor nodded, taking the girl's hand. "That's good. No resistance to my touch."

"Yes. Very good," Lori agreed. "Would you like me to leave?"

"*No!*" the girl exclaimed.

Both Lori and the doctor jumped, then giggled.

"Well, then, I guess you'll stay! She's not mute. And she understands us. I'll just check her vitals and ...." The doctor dropped off, engaged in a perfunctory check of the girl's eyes and pulse and limbs. The girl calmly let the doctor check her over, while continuing to hold Lori's hand.

Lori watched a strange expression growing on the doctor's face as she ran her hand over the girl's scapulae, an expression that grew as she checked out the girl's thigh bones.

When she was through, she patted the girl's hand. "You're very fortunate to have Lori take care of you, my girl." The doctor gathered her paraphernalia and put it back in its case. "By-bye, for now, pretty girl." She stepped from the room, and Lori followed, pulling the door to, but not shutting it completely.

"Is there something to be concerned about?" Lori asked.

"I ... I don't think so, but just to be sure, I think it'd be a good idea to get a few x-rays."

"There *is* something wrong with her. I could tell by your expression."

The doctor shook her head. "Don't become alarmed, Lori. I wouldn't say there's anything wrong with her, there's just a bit of an anomaly, and I'd like to have a couple x-rays. Do you mind taking her?"

"Of course not, Edna."

"I'd like to set it up for tomorrow, if I can get it arranged."

"Really? There must be something very worrying ...."

"Not to worry, Lori." The doctor headed down the hall to the front stairway. "You know how I'm inclined to err on the side of caution."

"True," Lori agreed. "But yes, set up the appointment for x-rays, and give me the details."

A few minutes later Lori returned to the girl in the "Oak Leaf Room."

The girl stood in the doorway, watching for her.

"You were *sooooo* good for the doctor! I'm very proud of you."

"X-rays?" the girl asked.

"Oh! My, you are quite the smarty, aren't you? Don't worry. They just take pictures of your bones. Doesn't hurt one bit. Between the two of us, I think the doctor is being a fussbudget, but, we'll humor her, won't we?" Lori grinned at the girl, but her frown did not go away.

Lori took the girl's hand and led her to the dresser. "Sit here and let me brush your beautiful hair." The girl obediently sat, and Lori began to brush the thick, long, pale blond hair. "Such beautiful hair. You could make a fortune as a hair model, and your face and body are perfect too. Not that I'd recommend modeling. It's a crazy, manic life style that I'm very happy to have left. Plus, you seem to be a private sort of person."

Lori made long thin braids at the girl's temple, pulled them back, and clipped them with a pale blue hair clip. "What do you think of that? Pretty?" She held up a mirror so the girl could see the braids clipped with the blue jewelry. The girl studied the braids and the hair clip, slowly reaching up and touching them gently. She turned and grinned up at Lori.

"I'm so glad you like it!" Lori pulled up the little boudoir chair and sat next to the girl. "All right now, I have to name you. I can't go on calling you 'you,' or 'the girl.' Even if it's not your real name, just something that feels right. How about—Julie?"

The girl looked at Lori as if she didn't understand a word. "No, that's not right. Maybe—I know! *Dawn!* We found you at dawn and your gorgeous hair is golden like dawn."

The girl took Lori's hand and rubbed her cheek against Lori's fingers. "That *is* your name, isn't it?" Lori whispered.

The room shifted and faded. Lori found herself on a wide open prairie, the wind blowing across her face and the smooth flow of four thin strong legs beneath her, as she ran along a crest. She looked out and saw the ocean at a distance. Then she heard the rhythm of hooves—she looked behind her and saw one, two, three hundred small, perfect, radiant horses, cresting the hill behind her.

Their beauty and their familiarity overwhelmed her. *They were her tribe.* They ... were ... hers. They tossed their heads and nickered in adoration as they gathered around her.

She looked out to the sea, awash in the perfect moment.

"So, what was the doctor's verdict?" Nathan asked, appearing in the doorway.

"Oh!" Lori exclaimed, shocked nearly into a faint. "*Oh!*" She gathered herself rapidly. "You startled me! Goodness, Nathan, don't sneak up on a person!"

"The door was open. I'll not be accused of 'sneaking' in my own house!"

Dawn stood and moved to the corner at Nathan's raised voice. Lori jumped up to stand by her. "It's all right. He's not yelling at you! He's yelling at me."

Nathan softened his voice, but the tone of disapproval remained. "I'm not yelling at all, Lori. But I do have the right to know about the condition of someone staying under my roof. Especially when I'm paying for a doctor's private visit."

"Yes," Lori agreed, calmly. "You do. Let's go down and talk about this calmly over a cup of tea. We needn't have this conversation in front of the girl."

"Does it matter? Mute and probably deaf."

"She's neither, Nathan. Please ...."

"All right," he begrudgingly agreed as his footsteps receded down the hall.

"I'll be right down." Lori turned to Dawn. "Let's see, what might you find interesting?" Her eye took in the little bookshelf, where she'd put a few books of photographs and paintings. "Here, maybe you'd enjoy looking at these books?" She pulled one from the shelf and sat by Dawn again.

She opened the book, and the first picture was of a giant oak, so much like the ones out the window, so much like the leaves painted on the walls.

Dawn gasped, then pointed at the wall.

"Yes, clever girl! I used these pictures to inspire my painting of the leaves on the walls." She put the book in Dawn's lap. "You can look through here." She pointed at the little bookshelf. "And you can look at all those books, too. I have to go downstairs and talk with grouchy Nathan. You'll be all right here on your own, won't you?"

Dawn, utterly engrossed in the book, turned the page. "Yes," she said softly.

"Oh, see, your memory is coming back!" She kissed the top of Dawn's head. "All right, then. I'll come back up and look at the pictures with you in a little while."

* *

Lori went down to join Nathan in the kitchen. He stood chatting with Mrs. Hinds in a subdued voice, but the conversation stopped dead the moment she stepped into the room.

"What are the two of you plotting?" she asked, a bit teasing, but mostly serious.

"Nothing," Nathan answered dismissively. Mrs. Hinds headed down the hall, making herself scarce.

Lori glanced at the table and saw it had already been set for tea. She poured a big mug of tea and handed it to Nathan.

"No, thanks, Lori."

"Hmmm, as you please." She sat and stirred some honey into the mug of steaming tea.

"I want to know what the doctor said."

"Yes. I know. Is there any reason why you can't politely sit with me? Really, is there any reason you can't?"

"No, Lori." Nathan sat across from her. "There's no reason I can't sit with you."

Lori knew she needn't speak her thoughts, they would not help anything. But she did, anyway. "I don't understand why you're being … the way you're being. I just … I mean … I've never seen you this lacking in compassion. I can't sort it out, this behavior of yours."

"I'm not used to having people I don't know in my house."

"Oh, Nathan. Please disabuse me of thinking you're that remarkably petty. She's a *girl*, Nathan. A child.

Maybe thirteen years old. What, in all the names of the heavens, is threatening about her?"

"Threatening? Nothing is 'threatening' about her."

"Then *stop* acting like it!" She struggled to keep from blurting the next thought that came to mind and managed to keep it unspoken. But the thought hurt deeply just the same. The unspoken words—next month is our first anniversary, and I'm feeling there will be nothing to celebrate.

No, she did not speak those words. But she felt them.

"Now, Lori, is there something about the girl you don't want to tell me? What did the doctor discover?"

"The girl is fine. Edna did, though, seem to think there was some anomaly with her thigh bones. She wants me to take her for x-rays."

"And there we have it," Nathan nodded, like all his suspicions had been confirmed. "Who's paying for these x-rays?"

"You will, Nathan," Lori answered, sipping at her tea, seemingly calm, but daring him to cross her.

"I think not. I think it's time to have the police come and take care of her, whatever she needs. And I'll file a report for my stolen horses while I'm at it."

Shocked, Lori retorted, "You will not call the police, Nathan. And you'll get over a few wild horses outsmarting your fence and getting away. Horrible, horrible, your plan to make dog food of those beautiful creatures."

"Who told you that?"

"Beau."

Nathan moved uncomfortably in his chair but remained silent while the little kitchen clock chatted *tick-tock, tick-tock,* on the wall. Finally, he sighed deeply. "Don't you really believe she ought to be in the care of the police?"

"I most certainly do not. *How can you even ask?*"

He poured himself a mug of tea. "She will be fine with them, Lori."

"It doesn't matter. *She's fine here.* I agreed to take her to have x-rays tomorrow, and that's what I intend to do." Lori poured another mug of tea, stirred some honey into it, then stood and headed for the stairs. She didn't even turn around as she said, "Do not hit below the belt, Nathan. I can go back to Seattle in a heartbeat."

Nor did she wait for his reply as she returned upstairs to the Oak Leaf room and Dawn.

The girl hadn't moved an inch, so engrossed in the book. Lori sat beside her, still agitated from the impossible conversation with Nathan. "How dare he," she muttered under her breath.

Dawn looked up from the book. "No sad," she said.

Lori chuckled. "All right, sweetie. No sad. I won't be sad."

"No x-rays," Dawn said.

"Oh, dear. Don't worry, Dawn. Nathan doesn't want you to have x-rays, you don't want to have x-rays, and *I* don't think you need them. But what about the doctor? She'll insist. Let's just do it and be done."

Lori watched Dawn turn the pages of the oversized picture book, amazed at the grace of her movements—she'd changed so much in even a few short hours.

"No x-rays," Dawn said, sighing deeply as she turned the page.

Chapter V

Dawn: Neighborhood Friends

eep in the night, when the house and the yard were still and peaceful, the inhaling and exhaling of all the sleeping creatures a cocoon of tranquility, I crept from my warm, sweet, little bed, quietly pulling on all the clothes available to me. Then I tiptoed past Lori and Nathan's room and down the back stairs.

As quietly as possible, I found a big black bag and stuffed as much food from the counter, the refrigerator, and the little room Mrs. Hinds called "the pantry," into the bag as it could hold. I stepped onto the back porch, slipped on Lori's warmest jacket and a pair of her boots.

Then I snuck out the back door to the horse house—well, they call it the horse barn—and swooped up a couple of horse blankets. I patted Twinkle and leaned into her, willing myself to know deep memory through her, but only sensing the faintest thoughts, as I could tell she wondered what I was up to.

I turned away from her and ran out of the horse house and through the paddock. Carrying my bag of food and blankets, I ran up into the hills, stopping only when I knew I was far enough away not to be seen.

I looked up at the thinning moon—it had to be close to quarter before my skeleton would completely finish its transformation into human form and I *must not* be x-rayed until my transformation was complete. There was a lot I didn't know, but I did know that.

Looking down the hill toward the house, which I could barely see behind the oak trees, I now understood that it wasn't only the smell of horses that made me come too close to the ranch two nights before, endangering myself and my brothers—*I'd been drawn to Lori.*

Somehow, I didn't understand yet exactly how, but *somehow*, Lori and I were linked. She'd known my name, my real name.

Turning away from the ranch, I continued up the steep hillside. I remembered seeing the mouth of a little cave the herd and I had passed as we sped across the hills in the full moon. It'd be perfect for me to hide out in while my transformation continued.

I came to the mouth of the little cave and beat back the brush growing over its opening, reminding me of all that was awful about this body. I could hardly smell the grass as it scratched my bare, fragile skin. I could not run fast, and I deeply feared the ability of people to easily catch me.

The worst and most confusing of it all was the loss of deep memory. I felt small and frail and unprotected. I remembered things, in a shadowy way, that had been in my deep memory, like when the first Eos, long before the rise of human history, had metamorphosed into human form, but it didn't seem like a part of my own memory. It felt like someone had told me about it.

If I died now, all my memories would die with me. What could be more sad or more lonely or more pointless for having lived, than that? Oh, I would do anything to have not changed, even though I knew each female Eos would transmogrify, just as Eos always has. I must stay in this form at least until solstice, when I could change back or stay human, as I chose.

At that moment, I couldn't imagine choosing to stay in this body. But I have some small wisdom, and I knew intellectually, if not emotionally, the stories of Eos. Most stayed human for some time, if only to do the work of helping to prevent humans—who, sadly, have no deep memory, no shared mind—from self-destructing.

I knew I could not decide in that moment what I would do six months in the future. It took all of my thinking, intuition, and wisdom just to decide what I ought to do in the present moment.

I spread the blankets on the floor of the shallow cave near the back wall, grateful for the over-growth of golden grasses at its mouth, which the wind played through, creating an enchanting, reedy melody.

The comforting smell of Twinkle in the blankets relaxed my tired mind, letting me create images of standing asleep with my herd. That thought alone let me relax, and the more I relaxed, the more I'd sleep, and the more I slept, the less I'd have to eat. Soon, my metamorphosis would be complete and I could return to Lori.

But I hoped that her man, that "Nathan," would not continue in his big voice about my being there, he frightened me so. What if Lori decided, because of him, to try to find another place for me to stay? What would I do then?

But my even more immediate concern was that I may not have enough food to satisfy the raging hunger. I'd never known such an appetite, and I knew I must take good care of myself during the transformation, getting enough sleep, and eating enough to feed the hot engine of the metamorphosis.

Comforted by the warm fragrance of the golden grasses and Twinkle's blankets, as if I rested in a primordial nest, exhaustion rolled over me, and a deep, dreamless sleep took me into its comforting arms, while the wind blew a lullaby through the grasses.

I woke after a few hours. The edgy light of the waning full moon had turned the golden grasses to silver. I felt a radiating hunger like an angry fire. I knew I must make the food I had last, but I couldn't stop eating once I began.

I studied the small pile of bread, vegetables, and a few apples and oranges that were left. And this large purple thing, I wasn't sure what it was, but it didn't attract me to bite into it. I didn't have enough food to get me through another day at this rate.

Stepping cautiously out of the cave, I peered at the rolling hills, inhaling the night air. No creature stirred. I smelled a wood fire on the air from a nearby home.

Standing in the cool moonlight, all my mixed-up emotions swirled around. Mostly I simply felt—*lonely*. I imagined sitting by Lori looking at one of her beautiful books.

I'd never, ever, been this completely, this utterly, alone. The herd always stuck together. But I *had* experienced grief. Wild, raging, inconsolable grief. The recollection came to me now, unbidden, of the night my mother was shot by drunken, crazed men, chasing the herd from vile meanness, flying across the hills in a vehicle that nothing stopped, their rancid odor, stale and foul.

A gentle breeze brought me back to this moment. My face felt suddenly cold, and I raised my hands to touch my cheeks. I saw my fingers sparkling in the moonlight with wetness. I realized these were the tears deep memory told about.

Human tears.

Crying for my mother, my beautiful, exquisite mother, who, palomino like myself, looked like horizontal lightning, galloping across the ridge on a full-moon night such as tonight.

I sat on the giant rock by the cave opening, holding my hands, palms up, in my lap, thinking about my astounding mother. I let my human emotions pour through me in this new sense of mourning, and with this strange feeling of love, I watched the drops of grief fall into my palms. I watched in my mind—this new and different mind—my mother's dance across the little hills, her delicate, elegant hooves beating a rhythm into the earth-bound grasses.

I thought of those times when she looked back at me, picked me out of the herd with her glance, the times she thought to me, "you, my daughter, are Eos. I will teach you all you must know before your first transition."

But she didn't have the opportunity to teach me everything she knew. And now, for reasons I didn't understand, I'd been brought to Lori. And with Lori I would stay. *Whatever it took!*

The fading fringe of deep memory sank into a pool in my mind that I could not hold on to—it slipped away unbidden. I closed my fists on my tears and stood. I had an as yet unknown calling. I would honor Eos, I would honor my mother, whatever may come.

But first, I must come fully *into* this body, I must stop fighting it, stop disliking it.

In short, I must become human, in my mind. As I wrapped my thoughts around these insights, the night took on a different, yet so-amazing beauty. *The way these eyes saw!* Dimensions danced about in completely different intricacies. Different aspects of *everything* appeared important.

Feeling the hot hunger again, I had the sudden realization that, as a human, I could go near where humans lived and perhaps find more food.

I stole through the tall grasses and looked over the ridge of the hill that dropped sharply away to a small house far below. No lights came through its windows, but from the chimney glided the incense of wood smoke, like a lazy gray mane stretching across the milky moonlit sky.

I slipped down the hill, noticing both my grace and awkwardness on the steep slope. I became rapidly more acquainted with my footing, more familiar with the way my changed senses processed information.

I had less visual depth, but I saw *color*—even in the night! Wonderful, and to my new eyes, *blazing* color. The horse house below appeared to glow an intense, friendly, red.

The grasses brushed against my bare hands, immediate and intimately delightful, while I still feared my immense vulnerability. I became aware of my feet—even my toes, in the boots—feeling the bumps and valleys in the terrain of the earth as I could never have imagined.

The scent of the wood smoke grew strong as I reached level ground and crept up to the little farmhouse, where I now also smelled a variety of vegetation. I came to the white rail fence surrounding the yard of the house, then moved around to the back of the horse house and sat on the ground on the short, domestic grass to decide what to do next.

A big black and silver dog came around the barn, uttering a throaty growl. He approached me, then paused. I sensed his confusion at the sight of me, a person, sitting quietly on the grass, in the night. He stretched out his body, long and low, growling, slinking toward me. When he got a few feet away, he stopped, teeth bared. Friend or foe? I felt him ask. What sort of creature are you?

Ah! So clever, this dog, knowing I was not as I seemed, neither fully horse nor fully human.

I felt my own alarm. The herd occasionally had to deal with packs of wild dogs, chasing us, nipping at our fetlocks, while we kicked back at them. But I understood this domesticated animal, he'd been trained to protect his home. I hoped he'd not attack a human sitting defenselessly on the ground.

"*Nii,*" I nickered softly to him. With this ridiculous nose, I could not resonate a decent horse sound, but I could at least speak horse language.

The dog raised his snout to the air, remaining crouched on the grass, sniffing at me. I didn't move a muscle, while, still crouching, he began to make a slow circuit about me. When he came back to face me, I extended my hand. He decided to cautiously accept me. He stood and barked in a friendly manner his tail half-wagging.

"*Shhh!*" I feared the worst, waking up people if he began even friendly barking. At that moment I heard the velvety *pad-pad* footsteps of a horse, coming around the side of the barn, ears forward in curiosity.

I looked up at a beautiful roan quarter horse, the luminosity of his huge, friendly eyes fixed on me, his magnificent hide glowing in the stark light. I told the horse of my hunger, and, although I confused him by being able to communicate with him, he let me know that human food grew in the patch of earth between where we were and his person's house. He gave me a mental picture of the man coming out to collect vegetables and berries and taking them inside. Sometimes the man even kneeled down and nibbled right there among the vegetation.

I stood and patted the horse, scratching under his forelock. He tried to nuzzle me in return, inhaling my scent. I backed away, in sad longing. Then I bent over and shadowed the dog, who led me to a low wire fence around many vegetables. The fence probably kept out the chickens and ducks I saw sleeping in a little wooden house nearby.

I stepped over the fence into the garden. *What a feast!* All kinds of food grew in plentiful, tidy rows, along with low bushes filled with sweet berries, and standing tall along the back edge of the garden, delicious sweet corn.

I took off Lori's jacket and filled it with food. One day I would repay this farmer. I didn't know how, but I'd not forget the kindness of the dog and the horse, and the generosity of the farmer, unaware though he may be of my theft.

As I crept from the garden, a light came on in the little house. I froze on the spot, and the dog stopped too, poised beside me, as we both watched the little light. A minute later it turned off, and I made my way back up the hill. The dog kept me company, but when I got to the crest of the hill, I patted him and sent him home.

I watched him trot back down the hill, his tail a graceful black plume, skipping along in opposition to the smooth swing of his feet. As he came to the bottom of the hill another dog began barking. My new friend answered with a couple of sharp barks, looking across the open terrain, then disappeared in the shadows of the little house.

The near dog barked again, joined by another. I smelled horse on the night air. I heard them now, too, not far away.

My heart pounded in fear as I dashed to my little cave, crawled in, and pulled the grasses over the entryway.

The barking of the dogs and the nickering of horses, along with the thud and rumble of hooves through the earth, came closer.

The sound of human voices broke over the hill.

I curled up, pulling the horse blankets tightly around me, trembling.

Chapter VI

Lori: Missing!

In the middle of the night, unable to sleep, Lori wandered down the hall to look in on Dawn. She cracked open the Oak Leaf room door—the moonlight spilled across the walls, lighting up the bright orange-yellow-green leaves she'd painted, glowing with an animated energy.

But, much to Lori's shock, Dawn was not in her little bed. Hoping against hope that Dawn had become hungry in the night, Lori rushed downstairs into the kitchen, but the lights were out, and no one was there.

Seeing the empty fruit bowl on the table, Lori opened the refrigerator to see it nearly bare, and the bread box on the counter, empty.

She stepped onto the back porch to go to the barn and discovered her work boots and one of her jackets missing.

Opening the screen door, she peered into the strange, moving, eldritch moonlight. So odd how everything seemed to be moving and still at the same time. The bright moonlight had always unnerved her, ever since she'd moved out here to the wide open spaces of the country.

But now, looking for the homeless girl, it seemed that every leaf and blade of grass knew something she did not.

Across the yard, Vladimir, up against the fence of the paddock, watched her with intensity. What was he doing out of his stall? She slipped into another pair of her boots, from among the neat row of boots, and hurried out to the paddock.

She reached up and patted Vladimir as he leaned his head over the fence to her.

"Where did that girl go, my friend?" she mused aloud.

Almost, it seemed, almost as if he understood her, he made a gravelly-grumbly sound. Lori looked up the hillside, then turned and hurried back inside.

*   *

Eos ~ 72

"But Nathan, she's missing, she's disappeared. How can you be so ... so callous about a girl, alone, out here in the country, at night?"

After coming inside, Lori roused Nathan to get him to look for Dawn. But if he would not go, she was prepared to go out on her own.

"I assure you, Lori, she's all right. She'll either be back, or she's decided to return to her family. Please stop trying to make someone else's problems ours. And stop making a pet of her, she's a person with a mind of her own."

Lori's argumentative frustration quieted to a silent fury. She dug out a scarf and gloves and crossed the bedroom, giving Nathan a disgust-filled glance. "I don't know what's your problem with that poor, innocent girl. But whatever it is, it's very unattractive. I wonder if you'll even bother to come looking for *me* if I don't come back."

She stormed out of the bedroom, ran downstairs, and pounded on Taffy's door.

"Yes?" Taffy called, sounding sleepy, but stirring about.

"Saddle Vladimir for me, Taffy, please," Lori called through the door.

"What?" She heard rapid shuffling while she wrapped up in the scarf and pulled on her gloves. Taffy stumbled out, hair askew, sleepiness in his eyes.

"I'm terribly sorry to disturb you in the middle of the night, Taffy, but I need a mount. Dawn has disappeared. I must look for her and Nathan refuses to even budge from the bed. I don't understand him, and frankly, I'm bored nearly to tears trying to figure him out. If he can let a girl wander around in the countryside in the middle of the night, where no one knows what might befall her, he's made of ... well, I don't even know *what* he's made of."

Without waiting for a response, Lori turned, hurried back down the hall and out the back door. If Taffy wouldn't help her either, she'd go alone. She heard the back door slap behind her as Taffy ran up to her, pulling on a jacket.

"Wait, Lori, wait. I'll saddle Twinkle for you, but Vladimir is too much, especially in this kind of night light. He spooks easily. I'll go with you, of course, you know that."

He grabbed her elbow with a gentle yet profound strength. "Relax. Don't be angry. If you intend to ride across these hills in this moonlight, you must have your wits about you. It's worse than darkness, false shadows everywhere, something looks like a hole that's not, and then the hole you can't even see is where your horse breaks her leg."

"Okay," Lori pulled loose from his grip. "Let's go then. Thank you for responding reasonably—that makes me more calm."

They entered the barn in silence. The moonlight permeated the air in a thick viscosity, like an element from another dimension, bas relief shadows re-shaping every surface. A barn owl glowed like an oval chunk of hematite on the apex of the barn roof. *Who-whoooo, who-who-who-who-whoooo!* she called to the albescent moon.

"You'll leave me behind if you're on Vladimir and I'm on Twinkle."

"I won't." Taffy went to Vladimir's stall. "Hey, boy, hey, my friend," he said softly, slipping his bridle on. "Midnight ride, eh? You up for that?"

Vladimir nickered softly.

Lori held Vladimir's reins as Taffy deftly saddled him, lost in her thoughts of wondering why Nathan behaved so oddly, amidst thoughts of worrying about Dawn. *Why had she left?*

"Why is Nathan so callous? Why do I have to argue with him all night about this poor girl? How can he not be worried about her?"

"Has to do mostly with him not liking changes that are not his idea," Taffy answered.

"But this is a girl, a person, a young human *life*. He can't just ignore her because her presence wasn't his idea! Goodness, what kind of mentality is that? This is a side of him I've never seen. I ... I'm very disillusioned."

Taffy slipped on Twinkle's bridle, then looked over his shoulder at Lori for a moment. "Don't be, Lori. Don't let this injure your love. Those of us who've lived with Nathan for years have learned how to make it work for us, and I know you can too. Because you're really sharp. Which, if I might be so bold, was a great relief to me. Beauty is pleasant, but intelligence is, ahm, much more important.

"I have to treat you with respect no matter what, you're the mistress. But I was delighted when I saw right away your kindness and wit. My god, Nathan is lucky to have found you. But he's good for you, too. He'll always be true, he's just got a couple corners that have never been knocked off. This event, this weirdness with the girl, has him feeling like he's not in power." Taffy finished cinching the saddle on Twinkle. "I'm the first to admit that he doesn't know what to do when the unexpected happens."

"I hear you, Taffy," Lori said as he gave her a foot up and she settled in the saddle, "and I'll take what you've said under advisement. But right now I'm having a hard time trying to make sense of his heightened negative focus on this girl, while he's just *blind* about Beau."

Taffy nodded as he hefted a saddle onto Vladimir. "It's a muddled story. And there are ... confidences."

"*Really?* Confidences. Well ...." Lori gave Taffy a studied look, but he kept busy saddling his mount. "The confidences of the dead, I believe, may be revealed. Especially when they threaten the lives of the living."

Taffy looked up, alarmed, at Lori. "*Threaten the lives?*"

Lori looked out into the dark night beyond the comfort of the barn. "I didn't know what I was getting into when I moved here, did I? Nathan brought me for a weekend before we got married to meet you and Mrs. Hinds, while Beau supposedly spent the weekend with a friend, which I'm sure Nathan arranged. Anyway, I've yet to see that Beau actually *has* a friend."

"*Umm* ...." Taffy made a begrudging, yet agreeing, sound.

"So why doesn't Nathan discipline and socialize his own son?"

"Because ...." Taffy deftly cinched the saddle. "Because Beau's not *exactly* his own son."

Lori gasped. "*What do you mean?*"

Taffy sighed the sigh of one who must engage in an unpleasant task. "What I'm about to tell you is a confidence that belongs to Nathan and Claire. If Nathan has not told you, then it's a frustration that I'm painted into a corner where it falls to me, but I will do it, because you deserve to have some insight about the strange legacy you've married into."

He paused, signed again, then carried on. "Claire and Nathan were high school sweethearts. Nathan, though sometimes silent as the oaks lining the drive, is loyal to the core. The same could not be said of Claire. After high school, she went to the university in Pullman, but Nathan had to stay here to take care of the ranch as his dad was in failing health.

"His whole world changed in one single weekend— *one single afternoon*—when he was only twenty. Clair came home from college to pay her respects to Nathan's dad in the hospital, and, as he lay there between this world and the next, she told Nathan she was pregnant, and that, even though the child was not his, would he marry her."

"*Goodness!*" Lori exclaimed. "And he said 'yes'?"

"Not at that moment. That was a hard time for Nathan. Hard for me, too. I loved that tough old nut, Nathan's dad."

"But ... where was Nathan's mother when all this happened?"

"Right there in the hospital, standing in the hall, gathering herself. When I arrived, we stepped back into the room, and Nathan's dad soon passed from this world." Taffy, frowning slightly, paused, patting Vladimir.

"Anyway," he continued, "Nathan said yes to Claire, and was suddenly running the ranch single-handed, married, with a baby on the way. His mother, also quite suddenly, up and moved back to England to live with her family."

"*Oh!* Why? Why didn't she stay?"

"She worked out the calendar in her mind and realized Nathan couldn't be the father. I'd already done that, too, of course. But I just let it be, as it was none of my business. Then his mother talked to me privately, telling me she'd decided to return to England, because of that fact."

"What did you say to her?"

"I said it didn't matter and it wasn't any of our business. She said it *did* matter, because she could not live in the midst of lies. She said if either of them had told her, she would have stayed, but she could neither live with trying to perpetuate the lie, nor confront them with the truth. She told me it would be easier to be out of the picture, sending occasional gifts and cards to the child, but she couldn't live the day-to-day deception."

Lori nodded, thoughtfully. "I can understand that. *Hmmm*, yes, I truly can." Lori reflected upon the mother-in-law she'd never met, nor even talked to. Nathan never spoke of her.

"Then," Taffy continued, "when Beau was about eight, Claire got cervical cancer, and, just—didn't fight at all. She passed so fast. We were in shock. Beau was *shattered*, poor little kid. I mean, he was already spoiled and overweight and difficult. It was like Claire knew she wouldn't be able to give him what he needed for long. But, as you've seen, Nathan has never been able to discipline Beau. Because, he told me, he wasn't 'really' his."

Lori made a disagreeing sound. "That's not right."

"I know. I told Nathan that Beau damn well really was his, and if he didn't parent him, the kid would become a monster. I told him he *had* to be parental. But he refused. Refuses."

"So, Beau doesn't know?"

"He does. But I don't think he understands. I was there when Nathan told Beau he was not his biological father. That was a year or so after Claire passed, so Beau was only about nine."

"Well ...." Lori shifted in the saddle, the information made her so uncomfortable. "That's ... that's quite a story, Taffy. *Why* doesn't Nathan tell me?"

"Ah! You know, Miss Lori, Nathan would rather eat raw frogs than get into an emotionally challenging talk."

Lori chuckled. "Have you seen him resort to the raw frog option?"

"Not yet. But if you try to bring all this up and offer him that choice, he'll no doubt take it."

Lori reached down and squeezed Taffy's shoulder. "Thank you, my friend, thank you. I can let sleeping dogs, *or frogs*, lie."

"*Ribbit!*" Taffy stood and—*somehow!*—leapt into the saddle, then turned Vladimir about.

"Stay here Lori," Nathan said, coming through the barn door. "If you're this determined, I'll go. Stay here, in case the girl comes back. I've got my phone, call me if she does." He took her in his arms down from Twinkle.

"Thank you, Nathan," Lori let go of her anger and held on to the 'it's about time' phrase that came to her lips. "You'll do a much better job of looking for her than I ever could."

Taffy got down from Vladimir, handing Nathan the reins. After settling in Twinkle's saddle, he looked down at Lori and winked, giving her his crooked, endearing, grin. Nathan mounted Vladimir and they passed out into the paddock, while Lori hurried ahead of them to open the gate. Nathan called to the dogs. Men, horses, and dogs headed out across the shadowy hills.

Chapter VII

Dawn:
Hands & Feet

I heard the bark of the dog I'd just met calling to the ones that were approaching. A conversation set up between them, then I heard men's voices, trying to quiet the dogs.

My new-found friend continued his noisy attempt to distract the posse dogs. Crouching in my little cave, I relaxed when it seemed my new dog-friend's efforts were successful, as the noise continued between dogs and men, but moved away.

One of the horses became nervous, neighed and stomped about heavily, and I recognized Vladimir. Then I heard Twinkle answer him. Yes, it was for sure Nathan and that little man, Taffy, who first found me transformed. They were looking for me. If they found me, I'd be x-rayed. And then what? I'd be taken away, far from my brothers, from Lori, from the land I knew. From home.

I recalled the one Eos who had been captured during metamorphosis, a hundred years in the past. She'd been put through so many tests, x-rays, injections, and studies, she died from the stress. It was a tragic deep memory that Eos shared, instilling a new fear that one must completely transmogrify without human witness.

I heard the horses move away to the ridge of the hill. The men had apparently decided to visit the little farmstead below, no doubt to ask the farmer if he'd seen me. But just as they passed the crest of the hill, one of the dogs, bringing up the rear, seemed to pick up my scent where I'd walked through the tall grass. He set up baying that brought all of them back near my cave.

The horses came close and stomped back and forth over my head, the dogs sniffing every inch of ground, howling and barking. I feared Vladimir and Nathan might fall through the roof of the small cave.

I nickered softly to the horses. They would hear me, but the men couldn't over the racket the dogs made. I told the horses I must be left alone for this night and the next, as Eos decreed.

All horses had at least a remnant of deep memory, all horses knew of Eos. I only had to give them a picture of Eos, and they did as I bid, becoming skittish and prancing off the roof of the cave, no matter how hard Taffy and Nathan tried to hold them in check.

"*Whoa, Twinkle, whoa!*" Taffy cried. "I've never seen Twinkle behave like this. There must be a goblin or something around here. Whoa, girl!" Taffy's voice receded as Twinkle took her head and galloped away across the countryside.

I couldn't make out Nathan's reply, but I could tell by the tone of his exclamations as Vladimir followed, head-strong, after Twinkle, he could not contain his mount. Vladimir's giant hooves beat a rolling thunder across the terrain, the dogs, hyper-excited, finally gave up their baying, and chased after the horses. Even the one who had set up the cry of discovery, trailed after the others.

Somehow, after all that, after so much unforeseen excitement and new experiences, I managed to fall asleep from sheer exhaustion. *I only had to get through one more night*, then I could return to Lori.

There would be a disagreeable discussion when I returned, but I didn't care. I just wanted to be where I felt safe. With Lori. At least now I had enough food to get through my transmogrification. I'd not have to leave the cave again, despite how cramped and lonely staying here might be.

* *

The next morning the sun beat down on the roof of the cave, making it a clay oven. I'd slept fitfully. I finally woke up realizing, as the aroma of tomatoes and peas rose around me, that I would soon have half-baked vegetables, if I kept them in the cave.

I peered cautiously through the curtain of grasses, and everywhere I saw bright sunshine and golden and green grasses. An incredible day, a day that made me feel like romping and kicking up my heels, racing full tilt across the earth. But no such activity would I indulge in today, no matter what form my body was in. Today I must lie low and conserve my energy, while my body completed the subtlest of changes.

I brought the food out of the cave, nesting it in the cool shadow on the western side of the cave. When the sun strode later in the day around to that side of the cave, I'd move what was left of my provisions back to the east side. I sat, crossed-legged in the tall grasses that towered over my head.

What a novelty to be entirely hidden by the beautiful grass. I laughed, then stopped short. That sound! That feeling! Altogether human. Horses did not laugh. We were aware of things that were ridiculous, but laughing, no, we did not laugh.

I laughed again, just to listen to the sound, so musical. Then I remembered I must keep quiet, or I'd be discovered—over laughing at nothing at all!

I remained sober the rest of the day, but reflected with pleasure on the discovery of laughter. I passed the afternoon watching a pair of red-tailed hawks swooping and diving and playing in the sky.

I closed my eyes, imagining what it would be like to climb on wings, to swirl and dive in the dizzying sky, the intense blueness, among the clouds, in the cold air, with the sun's warmth on my feathers. I pictured the small homestead below, the pretty little house, the red barn, the lush garden with its neat rows of produce, my friend, the beautiful black and silver dog, and the sleek chestnut roan quarter horse, in his paddock.

Then I became aware of another aspect of being human—I could imagine things I'd never even wondered about. I had enjoyed watching birds flying, but I'd never imagined what it might be like *to be a bird*.

Curious ... what purpose might this ability have? I wondered. Oh! The riotous, breakneck speed at which I was learning things, I understood even better why Deep Memory dictated it took at least three full days to transition. It wasn't just the body changes. There were these mind changes, too.

I nibbled at my food. The raging appetite had slowed. In fact, everything about me slowed, as I felt the puzzle pieces gently, almost lazily, fit into place. I was becoming myself. My human self.

I dared to creep over to the side of the hill and look down. A man puttered around in the garden, gathering vegetables. My dog-friend watched him devotedly from outside the garden's fence, his tail wagging in the grass. The dog didn't miss a single move his master made.

The man must be a very good person, I decided, as my smart friend would not be so loving toward someone who was anything less than good and kind. I stole back to my cave, happy just knowing the sweet dog and his gentle person lived below.

Later that afternoon, the dog came up to my cave and kept me company. I worried that the man would come looking for him, but the dog gave me a picture of the man lying down. He must be sleeping for a while during the day. That was good then. The herd always loved to take naps during the long afternoon.

As the day began to cool, the notion of napping grew upon me, as well. I carried my food back into the cave, and the friendly dog crawled in with me. We curled up, side by side and slept until I awoke with a start. From below I heard the man calling, *"Anubis, Anubis!"*

Ah! My friend was called "Anubis." He licked my face, then bolted through the entrance of the cave.

"Anubis," I whispered, listening to the dog swishing through the grasses as he ran downhill.

After he'd gone, the day melted fast amid a brilliant flow of colors from the bright sun. Magnificent! As Eos, I knew beauty, but now, with this human mind, human brain, I experienced more of this new way of sensing beauty as I watched the sun.

Brilliant orange and pink and red light melted onto the rows of plowed fields, the sunlight streaming into the upturned furrows. The young green grain reached up, in turn, to the life-giving light.

The wind shifted, the scent of the loamy earth receiving the evening light from the sun with the rapture of colors on the horizon, all came together like a grand music of nature, as the amazing colors ran like a river to the horizon. Rays of pink and orange shot up into the sky, weaving through the clouds, transforming them into colors I had never seen.

Then, suddenly, the sun shrank to a thin line on the horizon and, *blink!* disappeared. The colors, gone, the now-pale clouds drifted off, and night fell with a purple hue. Slowly stars began to show themselves in the clear, velvety sky, glimmering and shimmering.

I sat among the grasses, wonderstruck, the echoes of the bright colors such as I had never seen, accompanied by the shifting scents among the grasses, haunting me.

I knew, no matter how long I lived, no matter what wondrous things I was yet to see, I would never, never, *never*, forget this night.

The first night I knew what it meant, truly, to be human.

Chapter VIII

Dawn:
Crossing A Line

The beautiful evening turned dreadful. A chilling, heavy rain pounded down as morning approached. I sat morose and miserable in my little cave throughout the day, without appetite, longing to be back in Lori's home, longing to be warm, longing to eat something warm.

Then, as evening drew near, I felt the last of my changes click into place.

Finally! I felt unbearably cold, miserable, exhausted—even if I'd done nothing but sit in a cave for two days. Nothing, that is, except transform from one species to another. Gathering the few remaining fruits and vegetables, I piled them in the black bag and crawled out of my little cave, then plodded through grass that grabbed at my legs with wet, sticky little hands, while long vines wrapped around my feet—so difficult to keep my balance with only two feet!

I'd never in my life felt this cold and wet, right to the bone. Horrid feeling. I didn't care if everyone in that house yelled at me until the sun came up, if I could just get warm and dry.

Cresting the last hill, I looked down at the magnificent ranch and smelled the horses on the air.

The sight of the huge, pristine white, columned mansion, with the two rows of gnarled oaks along the driveway, their branches intertwined overhead, calmed me.

The horse house, stretched out long with stall after immaculate stall, the paddocks and corral—and the horses, several peeking out at the bleak day from their warm stalls, while others frolicked about in the rain knowing that they could go in and be warm and get dry any time they pleased—all beckoned to me.

This was where I belonged.

I ran down the hill in wild abandon, my hair flying, the rain streaming from my face, weeds and grass tearing at my clothes. I didn't care. I just didn't want to be alone anymore. I wanted to be near horses or people or both.

But as I came flying up to the house, I suddenly felt shy. What should I do? Just walk into the house? Somehow, that didn't seem right. Go back out to the barn and hope someone discovered me before long, just as Taffy had before? That didn't seem right either. Why couldn't Lori just be outside? But why would she be out here in this rain?

I walked slowly around the house to the back door, hoping to see someone. Anyone but Nathan. I knew Nathan didn't like me and I wasn't sure what he might do. I didn't trust him.

As I stood hesitating near the back door, it swung open and out stepped that horrid young man who had been with Nathan and Taffy the night they captured me and my brothers. He stuffed food in his mouth while pulling on a jacket, his shirt half in, half out of his jeans, his fat stomach sticking out between jeans and shirt.

I tried to step back out of sight, but he saw me. I didn't know he lived here, and I'd almost forgotten about him, given everything else I'd gone through since then. I was sorry to see him coming from Lori's house. But maybe he didn't actually live here.

"Hey," he said, talking around his mouth full of toast. "Hey, who're you? What're you doing here?" He walked up to me, fast. I glanced hopefully at the back door—maybe someone else would follow him.

"I ... I want to talk to Lori." I could tell, now that I was closer to him, that he was not a full grown man, although he was certainly big enough to be one.

He came up so close to me, I thought he meant to touch me. It made my skin feel like it was covered with flies. I shook, and took a couple steps back, but he moved up to me again.

"Lori? What do you have to do with Lori? Oh, I know, you're that naked girl in the barn. Trying to make guys crazy, huh?" He got an even uglier look in his eyes.

I stepped back again. Not only was there something about the way he talked and looked that frightened me, but he smelled bad too. Why was he here? He wasn't like anyone else in this house. They didn't smell bad and they weren't frightening in this way that I didn't understand. Nathan was frightening, but I understood that, because I came between him and his mate.

"I asked you a question! You trying to make guys crazy?" He grabbed my shoulder. "How come everyone gets to see the goods but me? Come on, give me a show."

He started pulling at me and I pushed him away. He went flying backwards into the house. He fell to the ground, and looked up at me, first with surprise, then anger. "*Damn!* You hurt me!" He leapt to his feet and rushed at me, grabbing my jacket, yelling, "I'll show you, you bitch!"

Right then, Lori poked her head out the back door. "Beau, what are you screaming at?" Then she saw me. She tore down the three steps toward me. I wasn't sure if she was angry with me for making this Beau-person yell, or if she was glad to see me. I braced myself, ready to run, as fast and as far as I could.

"Get your grubby hands off her, Beau! What the hell are you doing?" Lori flung her arms around me and hugged me. Her body was warm and soft, she was dry and she smelled wonderful. "You came back! I'm *soooo* happy to see you, I've been worried about you!" She led me toward the house.

"You're soaked, poor thing, out in this rain. Let's get you dry. You must be starved!" She gave Beau a terrible look as she walked by him. "You're in big, big trouble. I am so fed up with you. If you ever so much as look at this girl again...."

I watched Beau screw up his fat features in an ugly face. "What? What are you going to do to me?"

Anger poured off Lori as she hissed at him, "You dare to talk to me like that? You are not very bright, are you? You'll soon see what I can and *will do* to your life, you pathetic ... keep your distance from both of us ... do you hear me?"

"You're speakin' English."

"You'd better believe I'm speaking a lot more than that." The quiet fury in her voice was more frightening than her yelling. She knew something about what he intended toward me, and her unspeakable revulsion of him was not disguised.

But he grinned like he didn't care in the least and made what appeared to be a rude gesture as Lori and I went into the house.

"Look who appeared!" Lori called as we stepped into the back porch.

Mrs. Hinds looked up from her dish washing. "Lord, look at that poor bedraggled thing," she said about me. "Now, won't the boss be pleased to see her?" she added in a tone that seemed she meant the opposite.

"I'm sure he will," Lori agreed, innocently. I could see she was so happy to see me, she didn't care who said what.

"I'm sure she wants more than anything to be warm and dry, don't you?" she asked me.

"Yes, I do," I answered, surprising both of them.

"A full sentence! Can you talk now?" Lori asked.

"Yes, I can," I answered.

Mrs. Hinds and Lori exchanged a look. "Whatever it was, she must have gotten over it," Mrs. Hinds observed.

Lori shrugged. "Well, that's wonderful. You can tell us what you want to eat."

"Food." I had my eyes on a big, fluffy pie on the countertop.

"Not this, dear. The lemon meringue pie is for dinner. How about these?" Mrs. Hinds opened a pink cardboard box, and a sweet aroma floated out. I glanced at both Lori and Mrs. Hinds, and seeing approval on both of their faces, I took two handfuls of the sweet things inside, bit into one and an amazing gooey sweetness came out and ran down my face.

Lori laughed and even Mrs. Hinds chuckled, grabbing a couple napkins and wiping my chin. She turned and poured a tall glass of something white. "Those are better with some of this."

Then, with the food in hand, Lori and I ran up the stairs. Lori was giggling, and I found myself making the same sound, and the feeling that came with it was one of the best I'd ever experienced in my life.

Warm, in the house, with Lori, and Lori not liking that fat young human male, just like I didn't—and these amazing sweet things I was eating as fast as I could—I giggled again.

"Well, dear, donuts are not much of a meal." Lori took one of them from me and bit into it. "But they make a good celebration snack. We'll get you warm and dry and then have a lovely warm meal. How does that sound?"

"It sounds good." I watched as Lori bustled about, running a bath full of steaming water, which I understood now I could get into without hurting myself, and that warm water would feel very good. I wolfed down the rest of the donuts in my hands, while watching Lori.

"I'll be back in a few minutes, okay? You finish your high calorie snack." Lori left the bathroom and I heard her go downstairs.

I didn't want to be alone, so I followed her, but I paused on the stairs when I heard what she was saying to Mrs. Hinds.

"I want to tell you, Mrs. Hinds, quickly, before Nathan comes in, what I stumbled on when I went outside and found Dawn—Beau was trying to rip her clothes off."

"Oh, no, Missus, that can't be true."

"True and too true, Mrs. Hinds. We have to keep our eyes on him. Furthermore, he's off to reform school, or this marriage is in trouble."

"Oh, no, Missus, don't say that. You don't have to say that. I know Beau is sixteen different kinds of trouble, but the Boss will put the fear of God—and him!—in the brat. I can't imagine that Beau would really do ...."

Lori answered in a quiet, quivering, angry, voice, "I can imagine it, Mrs. Hinds. I've seen him looking at me like, well, just let me say I've only felt like that the time I got lost in a very unsavory part of Los Angeles, and got out for directions. I got directions, but they had nothing to do with finding my way to the freeway.

"I never wanted to have to say this to anyone in this household, but now, for Dawn's sake, I'm talking with you, Mrs. Hinds, woman to woman. Beau creeps me out! There's just ... something wrong with him. I'll not let him do anything to that poor traumatized girl, who's been through enough."

Mrs. Hinds sighed deeply, "Well, I still think you're over-reacting. But I'll watch him. I'm very good at watching."

"I know you are. I'm counting on you."

I turned and hurried back upstairs, relieved that Lori had feelings about that "Beau" person like my own. I went through my bedroom, stopping to touch one of the lovely oak leaves on the wall as I passed into my bathroom. The air was steamy warm, and I couldn't wait to get warm too. I started to pull off my wet clothes, when I saw the door closing behind me.

I turned and squealed in fright.

Beau stood behind the door, closing it, closing me in this little space with him. He had his shirt off, and that fat, white stomach ballooned, his skin creepy white and horrible.

I screamed now with a terrible, full-bodied, human scream.

Chapter IX

Lori:
House Afire

*L*ori turned from Mrs. Hinds and tore up the back stairs, down the hall, through Dawn's bedroom doorway, flinging the bathroom door open to see Beau being held at arm's length, Dawn gripping his shoulder, screaming with an unearthly cry.

"You're hurting me," he yelled as Lori stepped into the room.

"She's hurting you?! What ... what ...." Lori, shocked and furious, could not even form a sentence.

Mrs. Hinds, panting, crowded into the bathroom. "Oh, no," she said in a quiet voice filled with despair, while giving Beau a hard look.

Lori put her arm around Dawn. Mrs. Hinds glanced around the tiny room, went to the corner, picked up Beau's tee shirt and thrust it at him. "Get this on you, and get downstairs," she said in a rumbling tone like the very voice of God.

"She hurt me," Beau whined, pulling on his shirt, melodramatically rubbing his shoulder.

"She hurt you? Oh, you are sick. Get out of here!" Lori, much to her surprise, found herself raising her hand as if she would hit him herself. *"Get.   Out. Of. Here.* Before you *do* get hurt!" she whispered through gritted teeth.

Beau left, with Mrs. Hinds following him. She exchanged a look with Lori of despair and resignation.

Lori closed the door after them. "Are you all right, Dawn? Did he hurt you?"

"No. I'm not hurt. But ... he ... he ... wanted to ...." Dawn wrapped her arms around herself, "He was ... I don't understand. *He is a bad human.*"

Lori couldn't help a small, terse, sardonic chuckle. "You're right, Dawn. He *is* a bad human. Which is a mystery, as his father is a very good human."

"Is his father Nathan?"

"Yes."

"But the bad young human is not your child?"

"No. *Heavens, no!*"

"Hmmm …." Dawn said thoughtfully. "Nathan is not bad. But he is angry. He's angry about me."

"You're right again, dear Dawn. And that is yet another mystery to me. I don't understand his anger. But he and I are still getting to know each other. We've not been married a year." Lori shook her head, trying to release all the confusion welling up in her thoughts. "Oh, goodness, dear, there you stand, still soaking wet and freezing, and there's that lovely tub of warm water."

She poured some rose scented bubble bath into the tub and blasted the hot water on. Bubbles grew up in profusion.

Dawn giggled in surprise at the mountain of bubbles, and Lori grinned. "Bubble bath! *Fun!*"

"*Fun!*" Dawn agreed, pulling off her soaking wet clothes and stepping into the tub. She sank down into the bubbles with a big grin. "Warm!" She picked up a handful of the bubbles and pressed them to her cheek, a look of surprise overtaking her features when they disappeared. "Oh! I broke them!"

Lori laughed. "That's right! The bubbles break. Have fun playing with the bubbles. I must go for a few minutes."

"No. Don't go. That bad young man ...."

"You don't need to worry about him. Mrs. Hinds has him under her control, you can be sure." Again, a fury rose in Lori that she hardly knew how to contain. She noticed Dawn watching her closely.

Strange and unbidden, a picture of a glorious sunset came into her mind. She saw herself sitting quietly on a hillside, Dawn beside her, their shoulders lightly touching, sharing the red-orange-purple sunset. A delicious calm poured through her.

Puzzled, Lori turned and, closing both the bathroom door and the bedroom door firmly behind her, went down to the kitchen. Her uncontrollable fury had abated. But the anger remained.

Beau sat at the kitchen table, while Mrs. Hinds stood guard over him by the kitchen counter, a raging silence between them.

"Have you called Nathan?" Lori asked Mrs. Hinds.

"No. I'm just waiting for you, Missus."

"Yes. Well. Please call Nathan. I'm too distraught to talk with him at the moment."

"I didn't do anything!" Beau whimpered. "What's the big deal? She, that, bitc ...."

"Shut your smarmy, nasty, fat mouth," Lori warned. "Not a sound from you until your father gets here."

"I didn't ...."

Lori leapt at Beau and stood over him, rage surging off her. "*SHUT. UP.*"

Beau, cowering, *shut up.*

"Hi, Nathan," Mrs. Hinds said. "We ... have ... ahm, there's a situation here. You need to come home."

"What do you mean, a situation?" Lori heard him yell. "I've got a situation here, repairing downed fence."

Lori took the phone from Mrs. Hinds. "If you're not here, Nathan, in under half-an-hour, this son of yours will be on his way to juvenile hall." She disconnected the call.

"Oh, dear," Mrs. Hinds muttered.

"Oh dear is right, Mrs. Hinds." Lori strode up and back in the kitchen, refusing, now, to even glance at Beau. "Nathan's fence is down *right here in his home.*"

"Well, I can't argue that," Mrs. Hinds agreed softly.

The phone rang in Lori's hands, but she refused to answer it. The ringing hung heavily in the room while the three of them remained silent. Lori continued to pace back and forth, when, finally, a few minutes later, the truck came roaring up to the side of the house. Lori watched as Nathan and Taffy jumped out of the truck and hurried through the back door.

"All right," Nathan roared, "the house is not on fire." He looked at Lori, then Mrs. Hinds, then Beau. "This had better be pretty damn important."

"Dawn came back. Beau tried to rape her."

"That's crazy!" Beau protested.

"*Shut up!*" Lori shouted.

"What are you saying, Lori? Beau's a kid," Nathan looked from one to the other, utterly confused.

"Well, Nathan, your house is for sure on fire, and you sleep right through it. You just sleep right through it. This 'kid,'" Lori gestured at Beau despairingly, "this kid is ... is ... there's something really wrong with him, Nathan. Dawn was here twenty minutes, and I had to pull him off her twice."

Nathan scrutinized Beau. "What is Lori saying, Beau? What did you do?"

"Nothin' Dad," Beau sniveled. "Didn't do a damn ... ahm, darn thing. These crazy women. Even Mrs. Hinds, they're just ... just all went nuts. And that girl, she hurt me. *Twice!*" Beau nodded up at Nathan, obsequious.

"Mrs. Hinds ... *went nuts?* Yeah. Right." Nathan shook his head. "No, Beau. Not in a month of Sundays."

"*Urrr ....*" Lori growled at the implication that she and Dawn, however, may very well be nuts.

"You know what I mean, Lori." Nathan glanced at her, but his mystified attention was pulled back to study Beau.

"Yes, Nathan," Lori said, "your meaning is both clear and insulting. But, setting that aside for the moment, Beau must leave this house."

"*Oh!*" Nathan and Taffy exclaimed together.

Taffy, still standing by the back door, cleared his voice.

Everyone turned to him as though he held the holy grail.

"Don't look at me. I'm in shock too." He refused to even look at Beau, but Lori saw the pain in his eyes. She felt terrible that he had to be drawn into this family horror, although he'd known Beau his whole life.

Nathan pulled out the chair by Beau and sat. He looked up at Lori. "I need some details."

"I heard Beau yell, I stepped outside, and he was try-ing to pull Dawn's jacket off. He had the zipper in his hands, and she shoved him. I ran to Dawn ...."

"Why did you have your hands on that girl?"

"She came to me, Dad."

"*Oh. My. God!*" Lori stormed up and back in the kitchen. "You brazen, creepy liar! Why would she ... she's ... and you're ... I'm just ... speechless."

"Lori, I need to try to understand what happened," Nathan said.

"I told you what happened. Twice."

"Twice. Where's the girl now?"

"Taking a bath. She was soaking wet and freezing. I started running the bath in her room and came down to talk with Mrs. Hinds. Then we heard Dawn scream like ...."

"I never heard anything like it from a human in my entire life," Mrs. Hinds murmured.

"That's right. Nor I. I flew upstairs. There he was," Lori pointed a quivering finger at Beau. "In Dawn's bathroom, with his shirt off. With Dawn holding him at arm's length."

Nathan turned from Lori to Beau. "*Why? ... How? ...* Well, Beau, I simply don't know what to say. Why were you in the guest bathroom?"

"He is a bad human," Dawn said with calm assertion, as she entered the kitchen from the back stairs. She'd slipped on a pair of Lori's jeans and a soft orange silk blouse with billowing sleeves, her long fair hair, though still a bit wet, haloed her face.

A stillness hung, poised in the room at her intense *presence*, so different from the quivering, unsure girl of a few days before.

"He is not nice," Dawn continued, surprisingly calm. The calmest person in the room. "He has bad pictures in his mind."

"Well," Mrs. Hinds said, "there you have it. Doesn't get much clearer than that, I fear."

Taffy sighed heavily as if from a deep, dark well. "It's a troublesome day, Beau."

Beau looked at Taffy, an emotion crossing his features as if he finally understood the seriousness of his actions.

"What are you going to do, Nathan?" Lori asked.

"If what you say is true, I'll take him to juvenile detention myself." He turned to Dawn. "Did Beau try to touch you, twice?"

"No," she replied.

Lori gasped.

"He didn't try to touch you twice?"

"He didn't *try*. He *did* touch me. Outside, he pulled at my clothes. Upstairs, again, pulling at my clothes. And, his, skin. Not nice. Too much eating."

"He had his shirt off, in her bathroom, Nathan," Lori said. "Sneaking into her bathroom, so fast, too. We were in the kitchen for just a couple minutes, and then we went upstairs. He had to have practically run up the front stairs. Then the moment I left the bathroom, he went in ...."

"Give me the phone," Nathan said to Lori. "I'm calling your Aunt Louise, Beau, and you'd better hope to God she'll take you, because you're not spending this night under my roof."

Lori handed her phone to Nathan. He went down the hall and closed himself in a room. The rumble of his voice was soon heard. Lori looked from Taffy to Mrs. Hinds. She'd never heard of an "Aunt Louise." "Who's Aunt Louise?"

Mrs. Hinds shook her head, but was silent.

"Someone he's not talked to in nearly a decade," Taffy said.

Beau gave Dawn a terrible look. "This is all your fault! All your fault! What are you doin' here, anyway? It's not your home. Why're you here?"

"*BE QUIET!*" Lori demanded. "This is as much her home as yours. Wait. Let me correct that. It's now *more* her home than yours."

"*You!*" Beau yelled at Lori, jumping up. "*You* don't belong here, either! Everything was fine before you came. Everything was fine. *You ruined everything!*"

Taffy stepped forward, and though a full foot shorter, and considerably smaller than Beau, plopped him back into his chair with a shove. "*Quiet!* You're out of turn. Lori is mistress of this house. You really are not very bright." Taffy shook his head in disgust.

Even Mrs. Hinds spoke up. "You mind what Taffy says, young man. You're dancing around on very thin ice."

Nathan came out of the back room. "She'll take him. Mrs. Hinds, if you could pack some of his clothing, and, also, please, if you don't mind, I would very much appreciate you coming along with us, you and Taffy. I'll take the Mercedes. I'll not get out of the car when we get there."

He turned to Beau, but didn't look him in the eye, as if too distraught to even make eye contact. "Beau, take a shower and put on a decent shirt," he said in a low monotone. "I'll be waiting in the car." He stepped out the back door.

Lori looked from Mrs. Hinds, scurrying toward Beau's room, to Taffy, who followed Beau, also heading for his room.

"Looks like you'll have the evening alone with Dawn," Taffy said cryptically, returning her glance.

A few moments later, Lori heard the Mercedes pull up by the side of the house. Soon, Mrs. Hinds returned to the kitchen carrying a bulging backpack, while Taffy followed with a washed and properly dressed—strange sight!—Beau, down the hall and out the back door without a word nor a glance.

"There's soup simmering on the stove, Missus," Mrs. Hinds said from the back porch. "Those dinner rolls are ready to be baked. Twenty minutes at three-hundred-seventy-five degrees. Are you okay to do that?"

"Sure, Mrs. Hinds, I can do that." Lori wanted to wrest a bit of umbrage at the implication that she couldn't even run an oven, when she'd lived on her own from the age of fifteen, but, under the circumstances, she could not take offense.

Whatever was going on, it had an emotional undercurrent that didn't include Lori. That predated her presence in this household, altogether.

She moved to the kitchen window and watched them get into the car. Beau started to climb into the back seat, but Taffy directed him to the front, to sit beside Nathan. Mrs. Hinds slipped into the seat behind Nathan, while Taffy sat behind Beau. She raised her hand to wave at them, but not one of them looked up at her. No one spoke a word. No one looked around.

Lori felt the heavy silence among them, these people who were the only family she had, and wondered, what, beyond the current events, had the exploded hornet's nest exposed?

Chapter X

Lori:
Tell-A-Vision

*L*ori watched the Mercedes until it pulled onto the road, then she turned to Dawn. She'd not moved, still standing at the bottom of the stairs, a peculiar look of patience on her features.

"How are you?" Lori asked.

"So ... the bad human is ... is gone?"

"Yes. He's going—well, I don't exactly know where he's going, but, yes, he's gone."

"Good. Hungry."

Lori chuckled. "I'll bet you are. Let me turn on the oven to bake these beautiful dinner rolls." Lori reached to turn on the oven. "Oh! It's already on. I guess Mrs. Hinds was just about to put the rolls in. Good! We'll have a delicious meal in a few minutes." She scurried about setting the table for the two of them. "Come, sit, Dawn." She pulled out a chair.

"Yes." Dawn sat, watching Lori's movements with fixed attention.

Lori poured two glasses of fruit juice, then quickly tossed a salad together. She sat by Dawn and filled their salad bowls.

"Oh, I like this!" Dawn said, emptying her salad bowl. "Is it all right if I have more?"

"Of course!"

The timer for the rolls *pinged!* Lori brought gigantic bowls of soup and steaming dinner rolls to the table. They ate in companionable silence, Lori still processing the events, and Dawn, it appeared to Lori, very comfortable not talking.

"Good, Lori. I'm not hungry now," Dawn finally said when she had eaten more than Lori had ever even seen Beau eat at one meal.

"I'm glad of it, dear girl." She studied the nearly empty soup tureen. "I don't know what they'll have when they return."

"Oh!" Dawn exclaimed. "Did I eat too much?"

Her obvious alarm surprised Lori. "No, no! Goodness, no. This house is full of food! I was teasing."

"Teasing." Dawn frowned.

"Don't worry, sweetie." Lori stood, filled the tea kettle with water and put it on to boil. "Let's have tea and cookies in the living room."

"All right."

"Help me carry things." Lori loaded up a tea tray with all the necessary accoutrements, including a plateful of chocolate chip cookies.

Dawn pointed to the cookie., "They smell good!"

"They do!" The teapot whistled. Lori filled the teapot with aromatic tea, placed it in the china teapot, then poured steaming water into it.

In the living room, as Lori attended to the tea, Dawn strode around the room, looking at every detail, as if it was the first time she'd ever seen such things.

"He's not ... he doesn't belong to Nathan."

"What?" Lori asked, arrested mid-pour.

"Beau. He's not Nathan's ... foal."

Lori tried to laugh, but the strangeness of Dawn's accuracy took her mind. "Why do you say that?"

"Because Nathan ...." Dawn pulled herself up very tall, pulled in her ribs, threw back her shoulders, and marched around the room with a straight-legged stride. "He's like this."

Lori laughed at Dawn's spot-on imitation of Nathan's stiff, rather repressed, movement. "That's true. You've got him perfectly."

"And Beau, that Beau is like this." Dawn immediately—somehow!—transformed herself. She stuck out her flat stomach, slouched her shoulders down, pulled her head down between her shoulders, and shuffled around the room, sliding her feet in a lazy, halting fashion, an impeccable mirror of Beau's movement.

Lori, in nearly a paroxysm of laughter, delighted to have the dark mood lifted, cried out, "Oh no, Dawn, how do you *do* that? Perfect! *Soooo* funny!"

Dawn returned to herself, watching Lori as her laughter rolled away like a receding thunderstorm. "Ha-ha," she said. "Ha-ha," imitating Lori.

"Do I sound like that?" Lori asked, surprised.

"No!" Dawn shook her head. "You sound ... true happy. I ... I'm learning."

"You certainly are!"

"So," Dawn pressed on, "Beau is not the ... offspring of Nathan."

"But, Dawn, children often don't look like their parents."

"Not just 'look.'" Dawn pressed her index finger to the side of her nose.

"What? He doesn't *smell* like Nathan? That's just because Beau is a slob, and doesn't keep himself clean. Just now, when Nathan told him to take a shower? That's the first time I've ever heard him tell Beau to get clean. Mrs. Hinds and Taffy tell him all the time, and it's only because of their nagging that he's even remotely presentable."

"No. Not just unclean. Not his because of ...." Dawn shrugged in frustration. "Not his."

"Well," Lori paused, confused. Dawn was right, and that was the truth. "I guess, Dawn, you'll have to ask Nathan about that, as it's his business." She patted the sofa beside her.

"Come have some tea."

"*YES!*" Dawn sat down close to Lori, while she filled two delicate tea cups with tea. "Have a cookie." She gestured to the plate of cookies.

"Smells good," Dawn repeated, taking a cookie. She bit into it. "Tastes better! I like the ... cookies."

"You have a sweet tooth, don't you?"

"All my teeth are sweet, I think." Dawn finished the cookie and grabbed another.

Lori picked up the remote control and switched on the big screen television. A raucous game of basketball invaded the room.

"*Eeeee!*" Dawn squealed, jumping up.

"What!?" Lori jumped up with her.

"Those people!"

"It's television, Dawn. Just television. They're not real people." Lori turned off the volume.

"Not real? *They look like people.*"

"Yes. Well, they are. They *are* real people, they're just not really here, in this room. With us."

"Not here. But, look—*here.*"

"It's television. It comes through the air on like, waves, and then the television picks up the waves and brings it here. It's kind of like a light." Lori stepped to the wall and flipped the light switch off and on. "See?

But, with the television, it has the shape of things and people. You've not seen television?"

"'Tell-a-vision,'" Dawn repeated. "That's a good thing to call it. Or 'show-a-vision'—that would be better. It shows the vision of people not here." Dawn touched the surface of the big screen. "I've seen people boxes before, with tiny people in them. Tiny dogs, tiny horses, tiny buildings. I didn't know how they got everything in that box.

"Now here's one that's so big the people are almost real size."

"Show-a-vision. Very good," Lori nodded. "Much better name, actually. I've not thought about it, but you're right, this 'people box' is big enough for people to appear almost real-sized. Shall we see if there's anything that you find interesting on the show-a-vision?"

"Yes please. And another cookie?"

"Yes. Another cookie, of course." Lori began flipping through the channels while Dawn munched three or four more cookies and sipped her tea, not paying any particular attention to the fleeting images.

The image of a dance troupe flipped by on the screen.

"*Oh!*" Dawn exclaimed.

"The dancers?" Lori returned to the dancing.

"*Ohhhhhh!*" Dawn sighed as several of the male dancers took great and graceful leaps across the stage. She stood and moved to the side of the room, then took a couple strides and leapt into the air, her legs in nearly full splits, the orange blouse ballooning, her hair a halo of blonde light, arms extended in sheer joy.

She seemed to Lori to hang in the air for an impossibly long moment, landing gracefully on the opposite side of the room.

Lori smelled grasses, while there appeared a gauzy vision of rolling hills, passing in a moment.

"How ... how did you do that, Dawn?" Lori breathed, stunned and mystified.

"Jump," Dawn said. "Like the dancers."

"Like the dancers, and like something else, Dawn."

Dawn came and sat close by Lori again. "I'm very happy to see people jump. I'm very happy to get to jump, too." She ate another cookie.

"Have you had dance lessons?"

"Dance lessons?"

"You must have gone to a dance class to be able to just ... jump like that."

"No. No classes. Jumping naturally." Her attention was drawn again to the dancing. She got up and moved to the screen, touching the dancers as they moved. "I like the dancing on the tell-a-vision."

"So I see," Lori said, trying to argue herself out of what she'd just seen the beautiful waif-like girl do. "Would you like to take dancing lessons?"

"I think I might. Will I jump?"

"Yes. And pirouette and whatever else all the dance moves are called."

"That would be good, I think." Dawn remained silently attentive to the dancers until the program was over, then she came back to the sofa and sat by Lori. "Sleepy," she said, putting her head on Lori's shoulder.

"Of course you are." Lori retrieved a comforter and put it over the girl, then turned the lighting down and returned to the sofa. Dawn put her head in Lori's lap and immediately fell into a deep sleep, while Lori, finally alone with her thoughts, contemplated all that the day had held, with many things to wonder about.

When would Nathan return? What frame of mind would he be in? Would Mrs. Hinds and Taffy clue her in, or would they protect Nathan, and form a silent wall?

Would Beau return to this house?

And what about Dawn ....

Who were her people?

Would they ever come looking for her?

Should she actually look for a dance teacher for Dawn?

And ... *who was Aunt Louise?*

And the most burning, burning question of all ... how did Dawn perform that leap where—it was not an illusion—she had stayed airborne longer than the inflexible laws of gravity dictated?

With all these wonderments swirling about in her mind, Lori, too, fell into a deep, deep sleep.

Chapter XI

Lori:
Growing Apart

ometime in the night, Lori heard two car doors close, and then she heard the quiet chat between Taffy and Mrs. Hinds at the opposite end of the house as they came into the kitchen.

Lori felt guilty about leaving the kitchen in disarray, dishes sitting out, the remainder of the soup and rolls on the table. She hadn't intended to leave a mess, it had just turned out that way, with Dawn falling into a deep, and deeply needed, sleep in her lap, and she, herself soon fell asleep as well.

Plus, there was pretty much the same mess on the coffee table. But Lori loathed to wake Dawn, who still slept like a little rock at the bottom of a pond.

Lori looked at the clock. *One a.m.!* Where had they gone that it took this long?

"I'll get these dishes washed," she heard Taffy say in a slightly raised voice, that made Lori think Mrs. Hinds was headed to her room, but, instead, she stepped into the living room, turning the lights on.

"*Oh!*" she said, startled to see Lori and Dawn on the sofa. "Sorry, Missus. I assumed you were upstairs. Just came in here to see if you'd had tea."

"We did," Lori answered in a whisper. "I'm sorry to have left messes everywhere. It's not my way, but we got into a very interesting conversation, and then, poor girl, she just passed out here. I must confess that I did, too, right up to this minute when I heard the car doors close." She paused, then plowed on. "It's very late."

"Yes, I agree with you on that, Missus. And five a.m. comes very soon after one a.m."

"Indeed. I do believe, dear Mrs. Hinds, that everyone might sleep in. Well, except for us. Dawn and I must get up and make the three of you breakfast!"

"Oh, well ...." Mrs. Hinds said in a tone that left unspoken, "when elephants fly."

"It *is* just the three of you, right?"

"Oh, yes. Yes, indeed." Mrs. Hinds bustled about the coffee table, gathering everything up with a nearly mystical proficiency. "But I'll let the Boss fill you in on any details he wants to share."

To which Lori responded with her own, "Oh well ...." with her unspoken thought that he would do that, "when elephants fly."

Taffy came into the living room. "Still up?"

"No," Lori gestured to the soundly sleeping girl. "We both crashed out. I hate to wake her."

"I'll carry her up," Taffy said.

"Oh, goodness, no, Taffy. She's taller than you."

"Doesn't matter."

"You can't ...."

"He'll do it, Missus," Mrs. Hinds joined the whispering. "Oh, yes, he'll do it like nobody's business." She pulled out the coffee table while Taffy came around and gently picked up the girl, comforter and all.

"Light as a feather," he murmured, heading up the stairs.

"Light as a feather, maybe," Lori whispered back, "but long!" She reached out to pull Dawn's ankles back from the wall as they went up the stairs.

"She is that," Taffy agreed.

"You didn't hurt me," Dawn said.

"Goodness, no, dear girl, I wouldn't hurt you for the world," Taffy answered softly, surprise in his voice.

"No. You didn't hurt me. I was so scared, but you ... didn't ...."

They came to the landing. "Which room, Lori?"

"The Oak Leaf room."

"Ah, perfect. You did a beautiful job, painting those oak leaves."

"Thank you, Taffy. Dawn tried to pick them off the wall."

Taffy chuckled. "I can believe it, they're that real."

They came to the room where the door stood open, and the light in the bathroom on. Taffy gently laid Dawn on the little bed, pulling the comforter around her, while Lori stepped into the bathroom. The tub stood full of cold water, and the soaking wet clothes Dawn had been wearing lay in a heap on the floor.

She let the tub begin to drain and hung the clothes over a towel rack to dry, then turned out the light, shuddering at the instant replay of seeing Beau, shirtless, advancing on Dawn.

She hoped and prayed Dawn would not replay the horrible moment herself, but let it slip into forgetfulness. She came back out to pull up a chair by Dawn. Taffy looked down at Dawn. "She's a sweet, gentle soul," he said simply.

"Yes. She is that. I'm so relieved that her presence here doesn't make you upset, or whatever, like it does Nathan."

"Not possible. Like you, she brings grace and beauty to this house, and, however long she stays here, I will watch over her."

"Like you do me."

"Well. Yes." Taffy nodded.

"You were very late tonight."

"We had to go to Walla Walla. I don't know why Nathan didn't tell you that, but it wasn't my place to interfere."

"Of course not." Lori reached out and tucked the comforter more snugly around Dawn.

"Were you worried?" Taffy asked.

"Well, I confess, I wasn't, because I really did fall asleep so hard and fast, and didn't wake up until I heard the car doors close. But ...." She paused, "Where's Nathan?"

"Probably just doing some thinking."

As if on cue, they heard him steal up the back stairs and enter the master bedroom.

"All right, that's better," Lori whispered, more to herself than Taffy.

"I'll be off to bed," Taffy said, heading for the door. He turned in the doorway, "And you? ...."

"I'll sit here for a while. And let him have time to himself."

Taffy nodded, then ambled down the hall toward the back stairs.

Dappled shadows of clouds and oak branches danced across the walls, making her painted leaves come to life as the shifting moonlight flitted about the room.

In this private moment, Lori replayed the astonishing sight of Dawn's jump across the living room.

She needed to look again, in her mind's eye, at the sight Dawn not only moving in a superhuman manner, but where there had also faintly appeared a small and graceful palomino, imposed on Dawn's body as if they were, and at the same time were *not*, the same body.

So many strange things! Lori stood and went to the window. The oaks held their ground in the shifting, eerie light, familiar protectors.

Or, perhaps, more truthfully, familiars. *Her* familiars. "If you hear me, Spirits of ancient trees, please protect this girl. There's a lot I don't understand, and I give it up to you to keep her safe."

A breeze stirred, and the branches bowed. Lori accepted all of nature's response. Dawn would be protected by the same guardians who protected her—Taffy and the oaks.

She returned to her chair where she sat for another hour, quietly, as shifting energies flowed about her. Then she stood, brushed her hand across Dawn's forehead, and tiptoed down the hall to her own, vast bed.

Nathan, deep in a troubled sleep, mumbled something unintelligible, hugging the far edge of the bed. Too tired to change, Lori pulled off her jeans and flung them on the chair, then slipped into the opposite edge of bed, eventually falling into her own uneasy sleep.

*   *

*S*everal hours later when she awoke, Lori anticipated Nathan to be up and about his daily routine, surprised to see him still in bed. He appeared to wake up at the same moment.

"Good morning," she said cautiously.

Nathan looked over at her. "Good morning. Did you sleep well?"

"Not really. And you?"

"Same. Not well." He stretched. "Guess I'd better get at this day. That fence must get mended. I need to be able to turn some of the horses out to pasture there."

"Umm...." Lori uttered noncommittally. Then bravely forged ahead. "You were very late last night."

"Yes. I'm sorry I didn't tell you we had to go to Walla Walla. That wasn't thoughtful of me, and I do apologize. I ... I was preoccupied with the events of the moment."

"As were we all," Lori noted.

"Of course." Nathan sat on the side of the bed, his back to Lori.

She could feel him wanting with every fiber of his being to simply get up and get about his day—to move away from any conversation. But ... she had needs too, she argued with herself. "Who is Aunt Louise?" she blurted.

"Oh, that's right, you've never met her." Nathan glanced at Lori over his shoulder.

"Never met her? I never *heard* of her!"

"Well, I guess that's possible." He stood and ambled around the bed to the bathroom. "She's Beau's mother's sister." He closed the door, and Lori soon heard the shower blasting full force.

"Beau's aunt, on his mother's side. Very interesting, Nathan," Lori said sarcastically to no one. "Do tell me more. Why has his aunt never made an appearance in Beau's life since I've been here? Why have I never heard of her? Why won't you talk with me about last night? Why are you so emotionally unavailable? Why, why, why? Why am I continuing this—whatever it is. Not a marriage."

Yes, I am angry, she thought. She jumped up and pulled on her jeans, not knowing what to do or what to think, she stood, furious and immovable.

Nathan came out of the bathroom, a towel wrapped around his waist, sparkles of water on his shoulders, and Lori stepped back. Well, yes, there was *this* part—about how the sight of him pulled at heartstrings she'd not even known she had before she met him.

He was *soooo* gorgeous, and completely, innocently, unaware of the fact.

"Are you talking to yourself?" he asked.

"Ahm ... yes." She sat, taking a deep breath, trying to relax her anger. Trying to be present in the present moment.

"I've not noticed you talking to yourself before." He crossed the room and shed the towel, pulling on underwear, jeans and a shirt.

"That *is* a feature of talking to oneself," Lori smiled impishly.

Nathan let out a sound that was almost a chuckle. "You got me there."

Lori licked the tip of her index finger and made a mark in the air. "Lori, one, Nathan, zero."

Nathan half grinned. "Fair enough." He headed for the bedroom door. "See you this evening."

"But ...." Lori spoke up brazenly, not even knowing what she was about to say.

Nathan half-turned, reluctantly. "Yes?"

"I ... I want to hear about what happened last night."

"I spent the evening in the car, just as I said I would. You can ask Taffy and Mrs. Hinds what they did. I'm sure they'll tell you."

"But, why have I never heard of Beau's aunt? Why has she never been in his life as long as I've known you?"

"Well, now, Lori," the change in Nathan's voice let Lori know the pleasantries between them had disappeared, "that gets into troubled waters I'm not prepared at this moment to go into. Don't prefer it at any moment, and that's the truth.

"This whole mess is a huge upset, and it's all because of that girl. It's all because you refused to do what I simply asked of you. To let the police take care of her. Now look at all I'm having to deal with."

"My God, Nathan, are you really so heartless? It's just ... you're just ... I *don't know who you are.* But even more to the point, can't you see that this event, which you seem to think is all about you, is not about you at all," Lori fumed, pacing up and back alongside the bed, "this event diverts a train wreck that's been waiting to happen?"

"What do you mean?" Nathan closed the door and turned to face Lori. "What do you mean?"

"I mean, Beau is ... something is wrong with him, and you ignore him. You haven't socialized him, and he's just this unwashed, overfed mass of *mess.*"

"He's not that bad," Nathan argued.

"Have you really, really managed to not see the way he looks at *me?*"

"The way he *looks at you?*"

"Like he would jump my bones given the least opportunity."

"Oh, Lori, you're ... just ... wrong."

"No, Nathan. I'm ... just ... *right.* His behavior yesterday—goodness, was it only yesterday?—blew the lid off his creepy sickness, and now, I can only hope, this invisible, this un-heard-of, this unknown, aunt can save him from himself. And, frankly, from you, since you don't care about him."

"I care about him."

"Perhaps. But you surely have not cared *for* him. I pray his aunt will. And his uncle, assuming there's one in the picture."

"And there's the very weird rub to the whole situation."

"What do you mean?"

"I cannot tell you, Lori. But I will say, which will sound like I'm trying to defend myself, and maybe I am, I'll say that I tried to get Louise to take Beau after Claire passed, and she refused. I cited all the reasons you're blasting at me. I told her I was not equipped, psychologically, to raise Beau alone."

"What did she say?"

"She said I'd figure it out. She was wrong, wasn't she?"

"So it would seem." Lori couldn't help feeling sorry for Nathan, and even Beau, too. But, at the same time, her anger over the entire muddle, including the huge pieces she didn't even know about, kept her from voicing any sympathy. "You could have told me this—you *should* have told me this, long ago."

"I'm no good at talking about major emotional stuff, Lori. You know that."

"I do," she acquiesced, as he left the room, closing the door solidly behind him. I do, she thought. But it's one thing to believe you're marrying a man who is the strong, silent type. And it's another thing to discover you've married into a household with a pile of weird, dysfunctional secrets.

Chapter XII

Lori:
Little Blue

After Lori was fairly certain that Nathan had left the house, she wandered down the back stairs, anticipating finding Mrs. Hinds bustling about, and somewhat surprised to hear her soft laughter—a rare sound, Lori thought, trying to recall when she'd *ever* heard Mrs. Hinds laugh.

She stepped into the kitchen, surprised again to see Taffy standing by Mrs. Hinds at the sink as she peeled vegetables, his back to the sink.

"Lolling about the kitchen!" Lori exclaimed to Taffy. "I thought you'd be out with Nathan."

"He said he needed some time alone, and I'm all too happy to be accommodating."

"You've somehow managed to make Mrs. Hinds laugh, which is quite the feat!"

"I laugh," Mrs. Hinds said in her own defense.

"Other than this moment, your claim has never been proven."

Mrs. Hinds wordlessly wagged her vegetable peeler at Lori.

"But what's of primary import here, ladies and gentlemen," Lori said with exaggerated drama, raising a hand skyward, "is *what* has Mrs. Hinds in a mood jocular enough to actually utter audible laughter? *What*, Mrs. Hinds?"

She returned to the peeling of carrots. "I'm not telling."

"I pointed out to her," Taffy offered, "That, with the young man out of the house, her duties were cut in half."

Lori guffawed. "Oh, that's for sure!"

"Well," Taffy went on, "she replied that her duties were cut by two-thirds, and she hardly knew what she was to do with herself, with all that time on her hands. She made herself laugh. At which point, you entered the room."

"We're terrible to talk about him in this way ...." Lori began.

"I *said* I wasn't saying anything," Mrs. Hinds piped up.

"But, as I was about to say, the energy in this house will be very different in a good way, I do hope and trust."

"Amen," Taffy agreed.

"Still," Lori continued, "I'm wondering what transpired last night."

The mood became somber. "It was not pleasant," Taffy said in a quiet voice.

"No," Mrs. Hinds agreed. "But certainly insightful."

"Yeah," Taffy continued, "a bit too insightful. It's sad, but it is the way it must be. Poor little butterball, well, not so little anymore. But it was sad. A heart of stone would melt to see Beau look around him, and to get it that he really was to be left there, with those people, in that little house." Taffy shook his head, studying the floor, scrunching up his features into a frown. "'Twas hard when he began to cry."

"*He cried?*" Lori whispered, aghast.

"He did," Mrs. Hinds nodded. "No, it wasn't easy. But it truly is for the best all around. Louise will discipline him, she'll give him boundaries. And there's no distractions for him there, like you, Missus, and the girl."

"Well, what about his uncle? Was he not there?"

"He was there," Mrs. Hinds nodded. "Yes, indeed, he certainly was."

Taffy's phone buzzed. "Ah, the master calls. I guess Nathan has gotten some of his thinking thought. I'll see you lovely ladies this evening." He picked up a backpack and patted it. "Thanks for the lunches, Mrs. Hinds. I'm sure we'll be working the fence line all day."

Lori gave a little wave as he stepped out on the back porch, pulled on his boots and went out the back door. "So—what was that tone of voice, Mrs. Hinds, about Beau's uncle?"

The landline phone on the wall rang raucously, as any decent ranch phone must do.

"Goodness, it appears I'm not to ask this question!" Lori said.

Mrs. Hinds answered the phone. "Tanner Ranch." She nodded. "She's right here." She handed the receiver to Lori. "It's your doctor."

She stuck out her tongue at Mrs. Hinds, but took the receiver. "Hi Edna. What's up?"

"I've been trying to reach you, but you don't answer your cell phone. So I resorted to calling the landline. You missed your appointment to bring the girl in. Did the police find her people?"

"No, Edna. Sorry about not calling you. I haven't looked at my phone for, ahm, a couple days. The girl is still here. I apologize, I completely forgot about the appointment. There's ... there's a lot going on here." She decided not to tell her about Dawn's disappearance for a couple days, nor even about Beau's removal from the household. Edna would find out in due time. But for right now, Lori wanted to simply stay focused on the baby step in front of her.

"Let me reschedule the appointment," Edna said.

"Dawn's fine, Edna. Let's just leave it for the time being."

"Well," Edna paused, "I'm afraid that's not going to work. The police were here asking about my report on the girl."

"Excuse me, Edna. How would the police know to talk with you?"

"I gave a report to them after seeing her. Rather much required to."

Lori nodded, all right, that made sense.

"So, anyway, they're keeping tabs on the follow-up."

"I see. I'll get back to you later today after we've sorted out our plans here. I want to take Dawn into town to get her a few things and ... and the like."

Dawn stepped into the kitchen.

Lori nodded as Edna went on. She smiled at Dawn, and moved to her, taking her hand and leading her to the kitchen table, gesturing her to sit.

"All righty, Edna, I'll get back to you. Need to get off the phone, though. Talk to you later. Bye." She moved to the wall and hung up the phone with a shake of her head. "*Sheesh!* What's gotten into her?"

Mrs. Hinds shrugged. "She's a hoop jumper, Missus."

"How do you mean?"

"Give her something to be officious about, and she'll do a better job of it than anyone."

"I see." Lori paused and reflected on Mrs. Hinds' wisdom. Yes, Mrs. Hinds' experience with the doctor was considerably more than her own, as both the doctor and Mrs. Hinds attended to Claire during her illness and passing. "I'll keep your observations in mind, Mrs. Hinds. But she is very insistent that I take Dawn to see her. Supposedly the police are being rather a nuisance."

Mrs. Hinds chuckled wryly. "They can be that way sometimes."

"Do you think, Mrs. Hinds, that I should mention Dawn's .... ahm ... disappearance for those two days?"

"*No!*" Dawn, who had been quietly looking from Lori to Mrs. Hinds as they spoke, nearly shouted, startling both of them. "No," she said again with quiet insistence. "Are the police taking me away from you, Lori?"

Lori sat beside Dawn, putting an arm around her. "Not if I have anything to say about it, they will not. But we'd better do as the doctor says, to appear as agreeable as we can."

"I don't want to see her."

"I don't much either. But, what can we do? It seems like the simplest way to handle things."

"All right," Dawn agreed, though apparently not happy. "Hungry," she added.

"Of course!"

Mrs. Hinds brought her a bowl of steaming oatmeal, topped with brown sugar.

"What is this?" Dawn asked, frowning into the bowl.

"Oatmeal," Mrs. Hinds answered. "It's good for you."

"Oh." She cautiously tasted it. "*Ohh!* Too hot, but, yes, good."

"Ick," Lori said.

"Hmmm," Mrs. Hinds returned to the stove. "The girl has more wisdom about some things than you, Missus."

Lori laughed. "I'm all right with that. I'll bet she's smarter than me about a lot of things, aren't you, Dawn?"

"No," Dawn said, her focus upon the bowl of oatmeal. "You are very smart and kind. Like Taffy."

Mrs. Hinds made a low growl at the stove.

"Well, what about Mrs. Hinds?"

"She is also very smart, but more ...." Dawn growled, imitating the sound Mrs. Hinds had just made. "She is most kind. But different."

"True," Mrs. Hinds agreed. "I am growly-kind."

Dawn took her bowl to Mrs. Hinds. "More, please."

"You eat like a farmhand," Mrs. Hinds said, pleased, filling Dawn's bowl nearly to the brim.

"That's her biggest compliment, Dawn," Lori observed. "Okay, I have some research to get to. You don't happen to know if there are any dance instructors nearby, do you, Mrs. Hinds?"

"Dance instructors? Are you going to take dance lessons?"

"No. I believe Dawn might have an aptitude for dance. We watched a dance troupe last evening, and she was completely mesmerized. Then she demonstrated an astounding raw talent."

Mrs. Hinds looked at Lori over her shoulder where she stood washing dishes at the sink. "Or maybe she's taken dance lessons, and it's a clue about her ... where she's from."

Lori nodded thoughtfully. "I asked her if she'd taken dance lessons, and she said no. She seemed amazed to learn that dance was taught."

"Could be amnesia."

'Well," Lori pondered the suggestion, "you may be right. All the more reason, I suppose, to find a dance instructor, to see if they know her, or know of her. Her talent is amazing."

"Really?" Mrs. Hinds actually put the pan she was washing back into the sudsy water and turned to look at Dawn. "Interesting." Lori watched Mrs. Hinds' eyes close down as if contemplating a series of thoughts. "Very interesting." She returned to washing the pan.

"What was that?" Lori asked.

"Just thinking. Anyway, to answer your unspoken question, there does happen to be a rather famous dance teacher in Ellensburg. She's well-known among dancers and was famous when young. She retired from performing and came out here, as I've heard you say, between 'No' and 'Where' to teach."

"Oh, dear. You've heard me say that? That's private self-talk, dear Mrs. Hinds."

"Well, then, you must say it privately, not stomping up and down the living room like a caged filly."

"Sorry. Really didn't mean for you to hear that."

"Well, you're not wrong."

"So, about this dance instructor?"

"Madame usually trains dancers from around the age of five, or students who have been dancing since five. She very rarely, if ever, takes on older students."

As if suddenly waking up to the conversation, Dawn piped up, "Dancing? Dancing!" She jumped up and pirouetted around the kitchen table, swirling faster than they could even see her features, her hair fanning out like a giant, animated sunflower. Then, when she came back around the table to her chair, she calmly sat again and continued devouring her oatmeal.

"What was that? Goodness, raw talent? An understatement. I think Madame is likely to be interested in teaching Dawn. My, my!" Mrs. Hinds exclaimed.

"That's good to hear. Come upstairs, Dawn, when you're through eating your way through the kitchen, and get changed. I'll get myself ready, and make some calls to organize our day."

*　*

Finally Lori and Dawn were on their way into town. The sun came out bright and cheerful, and Lori found herself in a delightful frame of mind.

She had a mission, she had something to focus on, something she could do for someone else. The pull of purpose filled her with satisfaction, and she felt deeply happier than she'd felt in a long time.

"Apparently we're very fortunate to have gotten an appointment with Madame Colette today, as her assistant said she never has same day availability. But she had a last minute cancellation for a private lesson. The student had an emergency appendectomy. I guess that would keep a person from getting to a dance class." Lori chuckled softly at the whole mystifying chain of events.

"Is that funny? A person in pain?"

Lori cut off her chuckle mid-breath. "No, no dear girl. Of course not. That's not funny in the least. It's ahm, hmmm, I don't know how to explain it. But, you're right it's not funny, and I do pray that the student is not in pain."

Lori found herself re-thinking the *joy* of purpose, coupled with the *responsibility* of purpose, as this stunningly impressionable young girl role-modeled or questioned her every thought.

"Anyway, we're to be at her studio at four this afternoon, and the doctor's office at two ...."

"I don't want to do that."

"I know, Dawn. But what must be done, must be done. I'll make sure the appointment is short and sweet. Just keep your mind on meeting Madame Colette, and taking dance classes from her." She pulled into the parking lot of the little town's only shopping mall. "In the meantime, let's spend a lot of Nathan's money, getting you your own clothes, clothes that you like."

"I like your clothes, Lori. Beautiful colors, and everything smells so ... *nice!*" Dawn rubbed her shoulder to her cheek. She'd insisted on staying in the rumpled orange silk blouse. Lori let her, intending to get her into something new and less disreputable before either of the afternoon appointments.

She parked near *Cyber-Style*, a shop jam-packed with cutting-edge clothes and accessories for teenagers. Lori loved what they carried. Although most of it was too young for her, she'd often discovered an accessory she couldn't resist. Lori jumped out of the car, but Dawn refused to move. "Come on, Dawn," she waved, smiling, chomping at the bit to buy the beautiful girl pretty things.

"Too many cars," Dawn said, not moving.

Dawn's strange alien behavior struck Lori once again. "It's all right. See, people are getting out of their cars ... the cars stop for them."

Dawn cautiously opened the car door. "I don't like it," she said, stepping out.

Lori took her hand. "You're safe with me. I will not let anything harm you, Dawn."

Dawn visibly relaxed. "All right, Lori. I am safe with you. You will not let anything harm me."

Lori stopped, hearing the tone of Dawn's voice, as if reciting a sacred statement. With ingenuous innocence, Dawn put herself in Lori's hands. This guileless and *strange* girl had just made a contract of Lori's sincere, but casual, comment.

Sensing Lori's hesitation, Dawn turned to face her. "And I will not let anything harm you, either, Lori, if it ever happens that you need my protection."

"Oh, my, Dawn," Lori whispered, then fell wordless. No one, not even Nathan, *no one* in her life had ever said, in so many words, that they would protect her from harm. She found herself deeply moved and near to tears. Not only because she'd never heard these words, but even more, because of the depth of sincerity that this young girl uttered them.

Lori gathered herself. "I trust such a moment never arrives my dear. But thank you from the bottom of my heart for your kindness." She sighed, feeling a release of a tension she didn't even know she'd carried. "Let's go shopping!"

"Is it fun?" Dawn asked as they scurried across the parking lot and into the mall.

"Sometimes. It's fun when you find something you love."

Cyber-Style was the first shop they came to when they entered the mall, filled to the doorway with adolescent girls of all shapes and sizes. Almost all of them, as Lori had noticed before, too thin or overweight. All were pierced, tattooed, and with many colors of hair. Dawn stood out like the only teen not a member of this tribe.

Maybe, Lori thought, this was not the best place for Dawn.

Thumping music blared in the small shop, and Dawn leaned near Lori. "It's very loud. Is that all right?"

"Sure," Lori grinned reassuringly at Dawn. "We can take it for a little while."

"But why is it too loud?"

"Because all these girls like it."

"*Really!*" Dawn looked around as if stunned. All the girls chatted animatedly with one another, checking out clothes, grinning and laughing, in their element. "But *why* do they like it too loud? It's difficult to talk and to be heard."

"Hmmm ... honestly, Dawn, you ask an excellent question, but I don't know the answer. Why *do* they like the music too loud? I'll have to research it. Are you miserable?"

"No. It's interesting. If it's not harmful to be in this noise, I can handle it."

"Good!" Lori nodded. "Let's see if there's anything you like here, okay?"

"Yes," Dawn agreed. "Let me look at the too many things here."

They wandered around the crowded little shop, clothing and accessories jam-packed into every nook. Lori pulled out a few shirts and blouses and jeans and leggings and dresses from the racks, and put them back. Dawn got the idea, and started looking through the racks of clothes.

Soon she came to Lori holding two hangers. "Now we exchange money for these?"

"Is that all?" Lori asked, incredulous.

Dawn nodded.

"Well, first you try things on, and decide which you like the best, and we'll get those."

"I see. Can we do that now? I think the noise is making me tired."

"Of course, Dawn. I'm sorry you're not enjoying the music."

"Music. It's music. Are you enjoying it?"

"Yes," Lori said candidly. "I must confess, I'm rather much enjoying the music, its volume, all the pretty and strange things, and all the happy girls."

"Then we'll stay."

"Not necessary. Let's see if any of these clothes we've picked look good on you, and then we'll go somewhere else, all right?"

"All right."

Dawn dutifully tried on all the things Lori had picked out, but didn't seem to care for anything. And last, she tried on the orange and peach colored flowery silk blouse and dark brown leggings that she'd picked out. "I like these, Lori," Dawn reached out and touched her reflection in the three-way mirror. "Can I wear them now?"

"Sure thing, pretty girl." They emerged from the fitting room and stood in line at the cash register. After paying, they stepped out of the raucous little shop, Dawn looking much the same coming out of the shop as when she went in.

Lori, however, to her own surprise, emerged with a gigantic shopping bag, stuffed with leggings, a couple scarves, a hat, multi-colored socks, a couple pairs of ear-rings, and a beautiful little box, that had no purpose other than beauty, that she'd spied in the show case.

"I love my new blouse, Lori," Dawn crossed her arms and ran her hands down the silk. "My own blouse, yes?"

"Oh yes, your very own beautiful silk blouse. How it was even in *Cyber-Style*, I don't know. It's as if you con-jured it up. Completely out of place there. But it's beau-tiful and suits you perfectly."

"Thank you, Lori. I didn't know if it was right for me."

It's *very* right for you." Lori linked arms with Dawn and they strolled along the mall, looking into windows as they went. "But, jeez, Nathan will kill me for buying all the stuff I got for myself. But I just couldn't resist."

Dawn came to a halt. "*Kill you! No!* We must take these things back!"

"Not literally, dear. I just mean, he'll complain. That is he *would* complain if I showed him what I got. But I won't." They continued their meander.

"You will hide it?"

"Not exactly. He never notices things like this, any-way—typical guy."

"Typical guy," Dawn parroted. "So ...." Suddenly, Dawn stopped dead in her tracks, mid-sentence.

Lori followed her gaze, surprised to see she was tak-en by something in the toy store window. "What is it, Dawn? Do you see something you like?"

Dawn went up to the window and put her hand out to pick up a little stuffed horse, her hand collided with the glass, she was so transfixed by the stuffed toy.

"The little horse?"

Dawn nodded, looking very much as if she would cry.

"Come on, then, we'll get you the little black and white horse." Lori led Dawn into the store, thinking there'd be other toys to take her attention, if this one small stuffed animal so affected her.

But Dawn looked at nothing around her, going straight to the window. She made a strange almost panting sound when she saw that the back of the window was enclosed and not accessible to her. She looked at Lori in distress.

"Don't worry, we'll get it for you, sweetie."

"May I help you?" A short, pudgy, twinkly-eyed man with a cricket-like voice asked.

"Hi!" Lori smiled down at him. "Yes. I believe my friend would like to have the little black and white spotted horsie in the window."

"But of course. Come with me." He danced away on tiny, elfin feet, wearing little elfin shoes with upturned toes from which jingly little bells dangled and jangled.

Lori started to follow him, still linked with Dawn, but she refused to move. "Come along, Dawn. The funny little elf is getting your horse."

"But the horse is *here!*"

"I'm sure there are others. Let's follow him and find out."

The little man had been chatting away to Lori, and turned, surprised to see she'd not followed him.

"Just a moment, we're coming."

Reluctantly, Dawn let Lori lead her away from the window. They went further into the interior of the store, and then the little man pointed to a shelf out of their reach, where a row of twenty or so little black and white stuffed horses stood, lined up, forefoot by fetlock.

"Oh!" Dawn exclaimed, alarmed. "So many!"

"But you only want one, right?"

"I see. Yes. I only want one."

Lori watched as Dawn looked at each horse in turn, apparently rejecting each, one after the next.

"They are beautifully hand-crafted stuffed animals," the elfin salesman pitched, "from, oh dear, it eludes me at the minute. But they are each individually hand-crafted. No two alike, as you can see."

"Yes, I see that, now that you mention it," Lori nodded. She hadn't noticed, but she anticipated that Dawn would insist on having the horse in the showcase, for whatever personal, secret, reason.

"No, Lori. The one, *there!*" Dawn pointed, her hand quivering, toward the front of the store.

"I am so, so very sorry to trouble you, you are the most kind toy store sales person I've ever met, but do you think it's at all possible to trade one of these beautiful little horses for the one in the front window?" Lori pled, charming the elfin sales clerk.

"I do believe," he said with a smile, "I can accommodate two such beautiful girls as you." He reached for a pole with a clamp on the end, retrieved the horse from the end of the row overhead, then jingled and jangled his way back to the front of the busy store, the little horse captive in its noose. "Excuse me, pardon me, coming through," he called as he went, with Dawn immediately behind him, and Lori dragging up the rear.

Everyone stepped aside, delighted with the spontaneous performance.

At the front window, he handed the pole to Lori, "If you would be so kind as to hold this for a moment."

"Certainly," Lori agreed, taking the pole. Dawn stuck to her like glue, watching every move of the tiny salesman with quivering intensity.

Th elfin man opened a small door to the window, then took the pole from Lori, reached it through and released the suddenly promoted horse in place, then clamped the device around the neck of the preferred horse, and pulled him into the store. Releasing him from the clamp, he handed the horse to Dawn.

"Oh," Dawn sighed, a single tear coursed down her cheek. "Thank you, Mr. Elf, you are very nice."

The toy store employee giggled and even, Lori saw, blushed a bit.

"You are most welcome, dear girl."

As Lori looked from Dawn to the little horse she held close, she saw the single tear fall onto the horse, right on the beautiful white blaze down his nose, and to her complete amazement, the little horse shook its silky mane and looked up at Dawn.

Transfixed, she continued to stare at the stuffed animal, but it did not move again.

"Shall we pay for the lovely horsie?" the little man asked, bringing Lori out of her stupefaction.

"Of course," Lori agreed, involuntarily shuddering.

Again, she followed the little man with his now empty pole in hand, as Dawn hugged her side. She paid for the horse, thanked the toy store helper, and they stepped back out into the mall. Suddenly Lori felt overwhelmed by the noise and lights and crowd.

"Let's find a quiet place for lunch. How does that sound?"

Dawn hugged the little horse close. "I like that. It's noisy and too ...."

"Too noisy, too many people," Lori said.

"Yes."

They made their way to *Earthbound* at the end of the mall, quiet, with subdued lighting, where Lori's favorite lunch was a wonderful sprout and avocado sandwich on freshly made whole grain bread, and the restaurant's special blend tea. Here it was *quiet*.

"Oh, Lori, it's nice here," Dawn said as they stepped inside. "Smells like the field ...."

Lori inhaled deeply. "It does! It really does. It smells like an open field of grass."

A young waitress came up to them, "Two in your party?"

"Yes, just two. A quiet booth would be so lovely."

"Of course."

When they were seated, Lori looked across at Dawn and her little horse. Dawn put the horse down on the table, and it sat, then curled up as Dawn patted it.

Was it mechanical or some sort of fake fur covered robot? Lori dug out the sales receipt. Nineteen dollars and ninety-five cents, plus tax. Not mechanical and not a robot at that price.

*   *

After their wonderfully relaxing lunch, after watching Dawn pet the little horse while it remained unmoving during the entire meal, after trying several approaches at conversation only to have Dawn reply with a beatific, wordless smile, after asking Dawn if she could hold the horse and Dawn shaking her head, asking quietly that Lori please not touch the little horse right then, Lori finally looked at her watch and realized they must leave for their appointment with the doctor.

"We have to go, Dawn, or we'll be late."

"Oh! Sad. It's very nice here. I like it," Dawn answered softly.

Lori nodded. "I like it too, I feel quite calm now. But! We have appointments to keep."

Dawn gently picked up the little horse, cuddling him close. "If we must."

Lori paid and they headed back out to the parking lot. As she stuffed her *Cyber-Style* bag in the trunk then got in the car, she found herself thinking about that giant shopping bag filled with expensive items, none of which gave her the pleasure and joy of the one simple item Dawn chose from the depths of her heart, instead of superficial whimsey.

They soon arrived at the doctor's office. "Here we are, dear."

She looked at Dawn, who continued to hold the little horse close. "You'll have to leave the stuffed animal in the car, Dawn."

"No."

"Yes, Dawn. You can't hold onto that horse when the doctor wants to check you over."

"Why not? Why not, Lori? I don't see any reason why I can't hold him. That doesn't make sense."

"Well, Dawn, the horse is a toy for a small child. Now, for reasons I don't entirely understand, Edna is looking for something to be wrong with you. If you, a nearly grown young woman, go into her office clinging to a stuffed animal, she'll diagnose you as having ... of being ...."

"Of something wrong with my mind?"

"Yes, dearest Dawn. Of something not quite up to the level it ought to be. And ...."

"And she'll insist on more tests to prove there's something wrong with my brain?"

"Yes, Dawn. You've captured what I'm trying to tell you, perfectly."

"Well, that's a problem then. I must hold him for a little while longer for ... for his soul to ... to ... stick."

"So, you believe," Lori gasped, "that, somehow, the little horse is alive?"

"In a way. Not with his own life, but with another ...."

Lori looked nervously at her watch. "I can't make sense of what you're saying right at this moment. We're late now. Can I hold him then, instead of you?"

Dawn giggled. "Since you're older, won't you look even *more* like something is wrong with your brain than I would?"

"Impeccable as your logic may be, Edna can try to put me through all the tests in the world, and I'll either do them, or refuse. But you—it's different. The police are involved."

"Only I can hold him for a little while. But I *must* do so." Dawn got out of the car holding the little stuffed horse. "I'm sure it'll be all right."

Lori got out of the car and followed Dawn, who was calm and not arguing in the least about being here. Strange! She thought she'd be fighting Dawn tooth and nail to go into the doctor's office.

"Hi, there!" Edna's receptionist greeted, grinning with a huge, fake, toothy grin. "The doctor will be with you in a moment. Please have a seat." She gestured to the expensive but uncomfortable looking chairs along the wall.

Moments later, Edna herself ushered them into her office.

"Good to see you, Lori and *Dawn*. That's a perfect name for her, Lori, isn't it? Dawn. Let's chat for a few minutes." She gestured for Dawn to sit on the exam table. "Why not sit here, Dawn, while I check your blood pressure and the like."

Dawn sat where directed, and calmly answered all the doctor's questions about how she felt. Yet Edna made no reference to the little stuffed horse on Dawn's knee, that she kept her hand on the entire time.

"Can you tell me anything about your people?" she asked as she felt along Dawn's back and her shoulder blades.

"No people."

"Everybody has people, dear."

"No. No people. Only Lori."

"Well, you just met Lori. And she's very good to take you in. But she's not your relative."

"No people," Dawn repeated. "No pain. Nothing wrong with my body, nothing wrong with my brain. We can go now, yes?"

"All right, dear. Why don't you go back into the outer office, while I talk with Lori for a few minutes."

Dawn nodded and, cradling her little horse, left the office.

"What Edna, *what* is buzzing through your mind? I can practically see the bees," Lori asked when they were alone.

Edna chuckled. "Can't pull any wool over your eyes now, can I? There is still something anomalous about her bone structure, and I'm inclined to insist that you have the x-rays I previously prescribed."

"She looks perfectly fine to me," Lori insisted, still a bit boggled that the doctor made no mention of the stuffed toy Dawn refused to have out of hand.

"Well, Lori, that's why I'm the doctor. I'm referring you to Dr. Baduna for the x-rays. I'm calling him right now to make an appointment that works for you."

After confirming an appointment that Lori begrudgingly nodded assent to, Edna asked, "How are Nathan and Beau?"

"Oh boy, Edna, you sure know how to hit the tough spots."

"What do you mean?"

"They're both fine. But ... Nathan took Beau to live with his Aunt Louise last night."

"Really?!" Edna exclaimed. "That's ... interesting."

"Yes. Well, he has become more and more of a challenge, and he finally, just crossed a line."

"Well. Well, well."

"What's in all those wells?"

"Well!" Edna chuckled, "Sorry. That one just escaped. I'm not at liberty to say. But I surely do hope it works out for everyone. Poor Beau, sad ... sad."

The phone rang, which shook the doctor out of her reverie. "I'd better get that. I squeezed Dawn in this afternoon, mostly to get you to become serious about getting those x-rays."

Lori stood, grateful to be leaving.

As she reached the door, Edna asked, "By the way, Lori, have you ever heard of Eos?"

"What?"

"Eos."

"No. What's that? Some sort of disease?"

"Oh no, most decidedly not."

"What does it have to do with me ... or Dawn?"

"Probably nothing. Talk to you later." She picked up the phone, nodding dismissively to Lori.

Dawn jumped up as soon as Lori entered the waiting area. "We're through here?"

"Yes, dear. Now, to the fun part of the day." They stepped through the door into the warm sunshine. "How beautiful!"

"It is," Dawn agreed.

They got in the car and Lori started the engine, but she paused before pulling out of the parking space. "How strange that Edna not only didn't mention your little stuffed horse, she didn't even seem to see it."

"No. She didn't. I put a thought shield over him."

"A thought shield?"

"Yes. To make him invisible."

"I see." Lori fell silent for a moment. "No, I don't see." She pulled into the flow of traffic. "Now then, let's see if I can find Madame Colette's studio. It's in an area I've never been. I must suggest, though, Dawn, that you'll not be able to show the dance teacher your amazing talent while holding onto the little horse."

"It's all right now. I want to hold him, but he can stay in the car."

Lori shook her head. It was all more than she could take in.

Chapter XIII

Lori:
Madame Colette

Strangely, even her GPS couldn't find the address of Madame Colette's studio. They drove around and around a block where the address claimed to be, but the number was not to be found. In fact, there were no numbers on the edifice of any building or store front the entire block.

"This is beyond vexing," Lori finally said, tired, frustrated and becoming just a bit angry at all the confusion suddenly thrown at her. It was a seedy part of town that she'd never been to, and she didn't feel comfortable, not in the least. What seemed particularly strange was that there were no people around. She'd ask *anyone* for assistance, if only there was someone to ask.

"There," Dawn said. "It's there." She pointed at the most rundown doorway of all.

"Oh, no, Dawn, that doesn't make sense. It's completely awful. Why would a renowned teacher be in an uninhabitable location?"

"It doesn't look that bad to me," Dawn protested. She pointed to a recessed doorway. "There."

Lori found a place to park nearby. "Let's put your little horse in the trunk."

"Not necessary. He'll be fine here." Dawn placed him lovingly on the car seat and closed the door, heading for the doorway she'd pointed out.

"Wait just a minute, Dawn. Don't go running off without me."

Dawn paused on the sidewalk.

Lori scurried up to her. "I hope you're right, Dawn. We're a few minutes early, but I suspect if we're even one minute late, we'll have lost our audience with her majesty." Lori couldn't help a bit of sarcasm in her voice.

"Why do you not feel friendly about her?" Dawn asked.

"No, no, I feel friendly. It's just, she seems not very ... ahm, flexible."

They came to the obscured doorway, and sure enough, she then saw black numbers of the address on a black wrought iron gate. "And, she doesn't make it easy."

"She wants smart people," Dawn observed transparently.

"That appears to not include me," Lori laughed as she shoved on the wrought iron gate, which let out a screech like a tormented owl that abruptly cut off her laugh. "*Yikes!* Well, dear Dawn, I hope she's worth it. This is quite an audition, and the two of you haven't even met yet.

"Oh!" Lori gasped as the wrought iron gate gave way to a door, and the door gave way to a beautiful, aromatic, light-filled, flower-filled, garden.

"*Well, wonders and more wonders!*" Lori whispered.

"Yes. Wonders and more wonders," Dawn agreed, inhaling deeply.

They followed a little stone path meandering by a small fish pond, the path strewn on both sides with small flowers in a riot of colors. Lori couldn't have named the flowers, no matter what the prize, but she could say for sure that they were just about the sweetest flowers she'd ever seen or smelled.

Across the garden a narrow, wrought iron stairway led to the second story. There seemingly being nowhere else to go, as the garden was entirely enclosed, they climbed the antique stairs.

"Oh, Lori, so wonderful!" Dawn whispered, hurrying up the stairs, nearly flying.

Or, Lori thought, maybe she *was* flying. No rules of logic, nor of the three dimensions, seemed to be in application since Dawn had come into her life.

When Lori arrived on the landing, she paused to take in the surroundings. Next to her ran a wrought iron filigree railing. She stepped to it and looked down at the beautiful garden. As she studied the beauty and amazing colors, she became aware that some information came into her subconscious, as if there was a pattern in the flowers, but she couldn't bring it into her conscious mind. She tried to shake off the impression in order to simply appreciate the peaceful beauty. But it wouldn't quite leave.

Then, studying the second-floor level where she stood, she noted that the wrought iron railing on the balcony ran all around the four sides of the second story of buildings, the entire block.

Everywhere she looked, there was light and beauty. The interior courtyard was day to the buildings' exterior night.

Dawn passed through a doorway, and Lori hurried to catch up to her. If Madame was as fussy as everything thus far seemed to imply, Dawn's odd first impression could be damaging.

Lori passed through the doorway and stopped in wonder at the diaphanous, light-filled, space. Skylights above let in flowing natural light, which reflected off two walls of mirror.

Dawn stood in the center of the space, captured in the light.

From what seemed a great distance, a petite woman with regal bearing approached, a silken floor-length wrap in shades of blue and purple flowed out around her graceful movements.

Lori moved to stand near Dawn while the woman came nearer, every step she made a study in grace and power.

She smiled warmly as she came up to them. This was not the person Lori expected to meet. That person was taciturn and difficult. This person was warm and curious. "Hello," she extended her hand to Lori, while studying Dawn. "I'm Madame Colette."

Lori took her small and delicate hand, animate, as if a bird had come to land in her palm. "I'm Lori Tanner, and this is my young friend, Dawn."

Madame Colette took Dawn's hand. "Lovely to meet you, my dear. Let us go for a walk, shall we?"

Lori watched Dawn closely while the two of them interacted. "Oh, yes, please. I would like that very much."

Madame Colette looked over at Lori. "Yes, me too," Lori agreed. "I would enjoy walking," she said, even as she wondered where they would walk. Were they to leave this lovely space and go down to the street? Or would they simply promenade around the dance studio, seeing themselves in the surrounding mirrors?

They moved toward the far end of the room where Madame Colette had first appeared. There, she took them through a doorway, and they entered another space nearly identical to the one they just left—radiant sunlight pouring down upon them like a benediction from the ceiling of skylights.

Lori waited for Madame Colette to say something, but, for the moment at least, she appeared to be focused on walking rather than talking. Finally, Lori screwed up the courage to attempt conversation, from her position behind Dawn and Madame Colette, walking abreast in front of her.

"The garden, Madame Colette, what a wonderful surprise, entering upon it from the gritty street. It's beautiful."

"It is, isn't it, I say with a degree of immodesty. I have a gardener who helps me, but I do most of the planting and maintenance myself. It has very precise demands."

"Does it?" Lori asked, trying to picture the beautiful little flowers with raised and demanding voices.

"Discipline. As all things in the three dimensions. To be effective, to be beautiful, to be meaningful, to be all that anything can be, there must be discipline."

Lori mulled that philosophy over, trying to find an argument she could politely voice. She didn't like the thought of it, that everything had to be "disciplined." But thinking about the exquisite garden below, she knew discipline certainly must be a large component of its crafted and inspiring perfection.

And there was no arguing that dance required discipline.

"Though I want to argue against your point, I fear I cannot. However, I'm not inclined to entirely agree either, for some reason."

Madame Colette responded with a tinkling laugh. "Your honesty contains its own reward," she replied.

They had progressed across the second mirrored dance studio. Madame Colette opened the door before them, and they entered a third room identical to the first two.

"Goodness," Lori exclaimed, "How many rooms does your studio have?"

"There are sixteen," Madame Colette replied. "I own the block. On the second level, there are four studio rooms per side."

Lori paused in her walking, while Madame Colette and Dawn continued on. "You ... own the block."

"That's right."

Musing, Lori caught up to them. "So you own all the shops."

"I own the buildings, yes. I rent the storefronts to the various shopkeepers."

"Goodness." Lori couldn't think of a single other thing to say.

"I'm now teaching the third generation of my first students," she said as they turned a corner, passing through yet another door.

"You're teaching the grandchildren of your first students," Lori observed simply.

"That's right. That's why I have so many studio rooms. Each age group and level of accomplishment has their own room. The first room is for auditions, and for the potential new student. A few advanced students are rehearsing for a production in the last rooms. We won't bother them."

Madame Colette stepped through a door that led to the railing outside. They stood looking down at the garden.

"Beautiful," Dawn sighed.

"Yes," Lori agreed, "so beautiful."

"Oh!" Dawn gasped.

Madame Colette chuckled.

"There's ...." Dawn pointed.

"Yes. Very good. We won't spoil the surprise, though, will we? We'll let Lori see it for herself."

"Yes," Dawn agreed.

"*Harumph!*" Lori exclaimed in fake exasperation. "I had a sense that I saw a pattern when I first looked down. But, then, the impression wouldn't come clear. Now, I don't see anything at all."

"Visions come when they're needed," Madame Colette recited.

"Who said that?" Lori asked.

"Well ... *I did!*" She laughed her little tinkling chortle. "I'm quoting *me*."

They returned to the first studio room via the exterior walkway, the riot of sweet aroma from the garden below rising up to them.

"Like being a god, with the offering of the scent of the flowers rising up," Lori mused.

"Lovely observation," Madame Colette agreed.

They stood silently at the railing, meditatively appreciating the sight and trilling water sound of the garden.

"Let us go into the studio," Madame Colette finally said.

The reason they were here in the first place came back to Lori. What would Madame Colette's response be to Dawn's raw talent? But perhaps what she'd seen the previous night was a fluke. Or perhaps it was an illusion of her own tired mind. Perhaps what she thought she saw had not happened at all.

And the pirouettes of this morning, with Mrs. Hinds as witness? Impressive, but, again, perhaps not as unusual as Lori thought.

They stepped inside. The light, slightly shadowy, yet more golden, slanted as the afternoon sun moved to the west. It stole about the studio, seeming to look for a place to rest, then found Dawn. She glowed.

"What, Dawn, do you know about dance?" Madame Colette asked.

"Nothing. I saw it on the tell-a-vision. I may have seen it before, I'm not sure. But on Lori's very big 'not-real' box, the people did this."

Dawn took a flying leap, just as she had the previous night, except now the ceiling did not constrain her. She jumped impossibly high, again there was the strange sense that she defied gravity, staying at the very zenith of her jump unnaturally long, legs in a stunning split before gracefully coming to the hardwood floor.

Did Madame Colette see, as Dawn hung high above in her poised position, the faint image of the silvery palomino that Lori, once again, believed she saw?

"*Eos*," Madame Colette whispered. She turned to Lori. "Do you mind if I have a private chat with Dawn?"

"I ... I'm not sure."

"It'll be all right, Lori," Dawn said.

Why, Lori wondered, did she suddenly feel as if she were the child and Dawn the adult? Dawn and Madame Colette went into her office at the far end of the dance studio.

Lori wished she could hear their conversation. But she knew, if she'd insisted on joining them, the conversation would not be the same as it now was with just the two of them.

More than anything, she wanted to know what "Eos" was, having heard the word twice in one day. She had a strange sensation that she *was* familiar with it, while at the same time, she had no clue. Much like looking down at the garden—she sensed *something* there, *something* her mind saw, but it refused to float up into her conscious awareness.

Lori sat in one of the chairs lined up against the wall, patiently waiting for Dawn. Through the window in the office door, though at a distance, Lori saw the look of joy radiating from Dawn. Madame Colette had accepted her as a student. But something more passed between them—they put their heads together as if sharing a profound secret. Then they came out of the office.

"I'm happy to say," Madame Colette announced, as they approached Lori, "that I would love to work with Dawn to help her develop her raw talent. Ideally, she would have three dance lessons per week."

Lori gasped.

"Will that be a problem?"

"I believe it will be a serious problem with my husband, who is the source of income."

"I'm prepared to reduce my fee significantly."

"Thank you, Madame Colette, that's very generous, I'm sure. And then the other complication is ... he'll not be agreeable with me being gone that much for something ... that ... that doesn't have to do with me."

"I see, I see," Madame Colette said thoughtfully. "Well, let us begin with two lessons per week, and see what might arise regarding the third."

Lori nodded somewhat feebly, reeling from the shock of bringing Dawn to even two lessons per week. What had she been thinking?

"It is necessary for a new student to work closely with the teacher, to make sure proper habits are set from the beginning," Madame Colette continued. "Bad habits can take over quite readily, and then the dancer not only does not have the best form possible, but she may injure herself, or stress her body."

"Oh goodness! Well, yes, that makes perfect sense. We'll have to do what we can to assure Dawn gets all the training she needs. We'd better work out the schedule, then, for the immediate future, and," she glanced at her watch, "oh dear, we're late for dinner. We need to get on the road. I want to recruit Nathan to the plan, not alienate him before he even hears about it."

The three of them returned to Madame Colette's office and hovered over a calendar for another fifteen minutes, Lori becoming more nervous with every passing minute.

Finally, Lori and Dawn made their way back down the winding wrought iron stairs and hurried across the garden. As Lori opened the door, they turned to glance up at Madame Colette, who stood watching them, and waved. She smiled, returning their wave. Lori then opened the creaking wrought iron gate. A bevy of little girls in leotards came pouring through from up and down the road, like a flutter of exotic butterflies.

The previously empty street had become animate with beautiful, graceful little girls and their mothers, equally graceful and beautiful. Probably, Lori thought, they were young women who had come in leotards at another time for their own lessons from Madame Colette.

Giggling, Lori and Dawn hurried to the car.

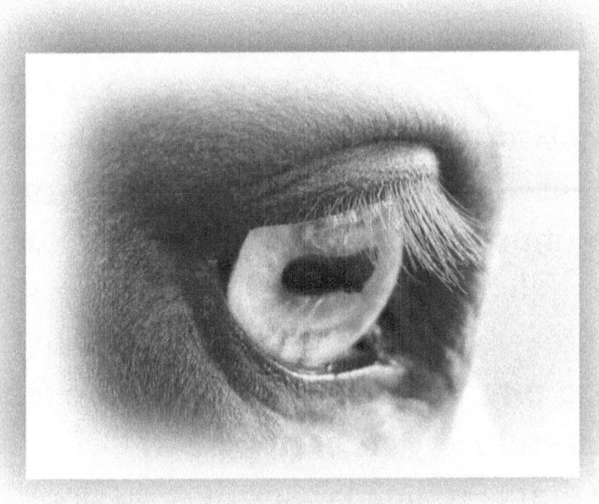

Chapter XIV

Lori: Animation

When they came to the car, Lori saw Dawn's little spotted horse standing on the seat, unmoving, watching the window attentively. She unlocked the doors and Dawn lovingly picked up her little horse.

"He's standing," Lori observed. "And he looks very...."

"Yes. He was concerned that the little girls would take him. A couple of them saw him and became so excited, that a bunch of them crowded around the car."

"Oh dear ...."

"He's all right."

"Yes," Lori said, starting the car and pulling out of the parking space, with the street, once again, completely empty of people, although filled with cars. She worried that the little girls saw the horse moving, which they must have, to have become so excited.

As she pulled onto the road, she called Mrs. Hinds. "Just want to let you know we're running late."

"That's a pity. I've set up dinner in the dining room and Nathan and Taffy are ready to eat."

"In the dining room? What's the occasion?"

"Just a whim I had. Sort of celebrating the, ahm, less work around here."

"I see." Lori almost added, "The Beau factor," but kept it to herself. Dawn might not understand what she meant and think Beau had returned to the house. She heard Nathan and Taffy come into the kitchen, and she and Dawn were half-an-hour late.

"Don't wait for us, Mrs. Hinds. Please feed those hungry men. I apologize, but it's been a most, *most* profoundly interesting day. I'll tell you about it later." She disconnected the call and glanced over at Dawn. "We're in deep do-do now."

"What does that mean?" Dawn asked, caressing the little horse, who still stood, but appeared to be much less tense.

"That means Nathan is ready to eat dinner, and we are not there."

"And he's not happy that we're not there?"

"That's right."

"But we were with Madame Colette. And, well ... we were with *Madame Colette!*"

"I know dear, but Nathan most assuredly will not care about that." Lori paused. "Or, rather, he *will* care, but in a way opposite to what we'd like."

"Oh," Dawn said softly. "We must not tell him about her, then," she murmured.

Lori pulled onto the highway, a straight shot home now, and, if nothing unforeseen occurred, they would be home in twenty minutes. "As much as I wish I could agree with you, we can't hide something as conspicuous as my taking you *somewhere* two or three times a week."

"You're right." Dawn snuggled her horse and Lori could have sworn she heard the softest of whinny.

"We'll just ... hope for the best," Lori added, unconvinced.

"Yes. But Lori, Madame Colette! She ... she ... is ... very special."

"I see that. In many ways, yes, she's amazing and unusual."

"Amazing and unusual," Dawn repeated reverently.

"What did the two of you talk about?" Lori dared to ask.

"I can't tell you everything right now. I'll just say there are no accidents. No accidents. Even when it looks like things have no meaning, or that they happen by chance, no. They happen for a reason."

"Madame Colette said that?"

"Yes, but I already knew that. Although some things seem very, very bad, they always have a purpose."

"I can't argue that bad events do often have a purpose. For instance, Beau doing ... what he did to you, which was very bad, got him to his biological aunt, which, I'm sure, is much better for *him*, and much better for our household."

"Yes," Dawn said somberly. "But, Lori, the happy, *happy* part is—*I will be Madame Colette's student*. I'll learn to use this body in the most beautiful way. Everything else seems ... small."

Lori glanced at Dawn and nodded. Despite the strange way she expressed herself, it *did* seem that meeting Madame Colette played a significant role in the unfolding of her life experience.

"There's home!" Lori gestured. The ranch, still miles away, spread out before them. Its gigantic oaks, tiny at the distance, lined the drive in front of the formal, Doric-columned house, looking like a doll house, with the long, elegant, horse barn to the west, surrounded by its sparkling white corral—a postcard-perfect picture.

"Look at Vladimir and Twinkle and the other palomino, they're watching for us!" Dawn exclaimed.

"I can't even see them. The other palomino? That would be Goldie."

"Goldie. Yes, perfect, that's her name."

"Yes. It is perfect for her. I *still* can't see them. Why do you say they're watching for us?"

"Because they are."

"They wouldn't even know we're gone."

Dawn gasped incredulously. "You ... you ... don't know that they know we're not home?"

"I'm sure they don't know, much less care."

"Oh, Lori, I'm surprised! I never would have thought you believed horses were that stupid."

"I don't think horses are stupid. I'm forever telling Nathan he treats his horses as if they're stupid, when they're so bright. But I don't think my coming and going would be of any, I guess I'd say, 'interest' to them."

"Goodness!" Dawn murmured. "Of course they know when their people are around and when they are not, and when they're returning. That's why the three of them are standing at the corral."

"What about the other horses?"

"The others are out to pasture, where Nathan and Taffy repaired the fence, except for the two horses in stalls in the barn. I don't know why Nathan has them there. They'd like to be out with the others, of course."

"Of course!" Lori said. She suspected she was being just a tiny bit sarcastic. She drove into the driveway and up to the garage. Vladimir gave them a loud *"neigh!"* making her aware that he certainly did acknowledge their arrival.

Not even bothering to take the time to pull into the garage, she jumped out of the car. "Let's hurry inside, Dawn."

"All right." Dawn waved to the three horses who had come as close as they could to her in their paddock. A series of whinnies from the three ensued.

"Yes, yes," Lori laughed. "We know, you've been watching for us! We're home, safe and sound, don't worry. Now all we have to deal with is the wrath of the lord of the manor. Scary enough."

"Don't be frightened, Lori. You must be brave."

They stepped onto the back porch.

"Oh, I'm brave, Dawn. And I have a few tactics up my sleeve I can pull out, if I must."

They entered the kitchen where Mrs. Hinds stood at the sink, watching for them every bit as much as the horses had been.

"I got here as fast as I could," Lori protested Mrs. Hinds' unhappy look.

"Yes. Well …."

"'The Boss' is not happy?"

"Not one bit."

"Where is he?"

"At the table. He refused to begin eating. Everything at the table is untouched. And cold."

"I'm very sorry, for your sake, Mrs. Hinds, having been so thoughtful as to put together a formal dinner for us. But regarding his royal highness …." She broke off. "Let's wash our hands, Dawn, and, without further ado, join the men for dinner." Lori washed her hands at the kitchen sink.

Dawn set the little horse down on the counter and washed her hands. "Will there be loud words?" she asked.

"I doubt it," Lori answered. "Though there will probably be unpleasant words, and not nice energy."

"I will take Little Blue upstairs, then."

"Little Blue?"

"The little horse."

Lori nodded, but frowned. "All right, but come down *immediately*."

Mrs. Hinds gave Lori a questioning look, but Lori just shook her head as if to say, I'll explain later.

As Dawn ran upstairs, Lori was torn whether to go into the dining room, or wait at the bottom of the stairs for Dawn to return. She decided to head into the dining room to attempt to diffuse her husband's ill humor. They had the important business of Dawn's dance lessons to discuss, and she must get Nathan in a receptive frame of mind.

Not easy in the best of circumstances.

"Let's go through, Mrs. Hinds. Dawn will be down in a moment."

Mrs. Hinds nodded, but said nothing as she followed Lori into the sumptuous walnut-paneled dining room.

Nathan sat silent at the head of the table, frowning, Taffy to his left in a cocoon of meditative calm.

"Sorry to be late, Nathan," Lori apologized.

"Where's the girl?"

"She'll be right down. Why didn't you go ahead and enjoy Mrs. Hinds lovely meal?"

"Because of the very reason, Lori," he said with disdain, "that Mrs. Hinds went to the trouble of a formal meal. It would be disrespectful not to have all the members of the household sit down together."

"I see. Well, no, I don't. Not wanting to speak for Mrs. Hinds, who is in every way extremely capable of speaking for herself, I dare to suggest that she would have been fine with you having the meal in a pleasant frame of mind, rather than this stormy visage you're sharing with us."

Lori glanced at Mrs. Hinds, who stood by the sideboard waiting to bring the re-warming dishes to the table. She remained mute as the Sphinx. Her secrets, her mood, her thoughts she would not tell, her look said.

Dawn flew into the room, bringing in light and breathy energy.

"Thank you for coming right back down, Dawn." Lori gestured to the empty chair beside her. "Come here and sit by me."

As Dawn sat, she smiled sweetly at Nathan. "I'm very sorry we're late. Even when Lori knew we'd be late, she drove very carefully. I've seen many people drive extremely recklessly, for no reason."

Taciturn, Nathan made no reply.

"You make an excellent observation," Taffy dared to pipe up. "We'd rather have you safe and a tiny bit late, than unsafe and even later."

"Anyway, apologies have been offered," Lori observed. "And now, dear Mrs. Hinds, if you would be so kind as to bring what you're hovering over, and then join us." She looked around the table. "Wait! I don't see a place set for you."

"Oh no, Missus, I don't sit at table. I have too much jumping up and down and running to and fro to do."

"Not acceptable," Lori insisted. She stood and went to the breakfront, gathering a set of dishes which she placed on the table, then she opened drawers until she found the silverware. "Obviously I've never done this," she giggled. Finally finding the tableware, she set a place for Mrs. Hinds, while Mrs. Hinds stood by, flustering.

"The 'Missus' requests your presence at table, Mrs. Hinds." Lori moved to stand by her. "Now, which of these dishes go where?"

"Oh, dear, please sit down, Missus. I can't think with you hovering."

"All right." Lori sat while Mrs. Hinds scurried about, bringing the serving bowls to the table.

"Now please sit," Lori demanded.

"I was to serve," Mrs. Hinds protested.

"Nonsense, we're perfectly capable of serving ourselves."

Mrs. Hinds reluctantly sat.

"Lovely," Lori smiled around at everyone. "Now, let us pass the food and have a genteel chat. It's a delight to have dinner in the dining room. Most thoughtful."

"But *why* are you late," Nathan demanded.

"Oh, dear, dear Nathan, please, let it go. There have been numerous times when Mrs. Hinds and I have sat waiting dinner for you. Even, sometimes for *hours*."

"That's different. We're working. There's no excuse for you being late when all you're doing is gallivanting around with a teenager."

A sputter rose to her lips, but stunned to silence, Lori couldn't even let the sputter escape. As she reflected on the day, the amazing, unbelievable, miraculous, peculiar, paranormal, life-changing day, she could voice no response.

The day flowed over her—from the unlikely experience of Dawn finding clothes much like her own in the teen clothing and accessory shop, to the beyond-extraordinary acquisition of the little black and white horse now named "Little Blue," assisted by the elfin toy store employee, to the strange interaction with her doctor, to the absolutely explanation-defying environment of Madame Colette's " block of buildings" and numerous, gigantic, studio rooms, and the mystical, aromatic garden below—through these swirling thoughts, Lori remained speechless.

Nathan nodded, seemingly satisfied to have quelled her, finally taking the bowl from her that she held out to him.

The frozen smile left her face as she said in a low but firm voice, "I do not know who I married."

Silence prevailed, except for the click and clank of serving silver against serving bowls.

Finally, Taffy dared to speak. "That's a lovely blouse you're wearing, Dawn. Big beautiful flowers, it suits you very well."

"I love my new blouse," Dawn replied. "Lori took me to a shop with a lot of girls and, ahm, the 'music' loud. I thought it was noise, but Lori told me it was music. And she let me have this very beautiful blouse, and some new things ... what are they called?"

"Leggings," Lori offered.

"Yes, leggings."

"You went to *Cyber-Style*, and found a classy blouse like that?" Taffy asked incredulous.

"Yes," Lori answered, "we did. But, Taffy, how do you know about *Cyber-Style*? And an even more compelling question, how do you know what they have in the confines of that extremely 'girls only' environment?"

"I know many things," he answered cryptically, tapping the side of his nose.

"Indeed."

"Did you meet Madame Colette?" Mrs. Hinds blurted in a rush of courage.

"Yes!" Dawn answered, rapturous.

Everyone turned to look at her, but she said nothing more.

"To say she's impressive, Mrs. Hinds," Lori replied, "is to make an immense understatement. However, describing her is another matter altogether. I can say she is petite, beautiful, wears flowing clothes, and has a beautiful smile. But beyond that, I become a bit stumped.

"Do you know anything about her, Mrs. Hinds?"

"Not really, no. Just, a bit like what you're saying—that she defies description."

"She owns the entire block where her studio is located, which is on the second floor. It's a most unassuming block, even rather dark ...."

"Not really dark," Dawn added.

"Not dark to Dawn. It seems it appears different to her than to me, but I dare say her vision is probably closer to the truth. Anyway, in the center of this block of buildings is an amazing flower garden, with fabulously aromatic flowers. There's a small fish pond and little winding walkways."

"Charming," Mrs. Hinds said, enchanted.

"Very, very charming," Lori agreed.

"Who are you talking about?" Nathan asked.

"A dance instructor," Lori answered. "A famous dance instructor."

"Are you intending to study dance?" Nathan asked in surprise.

"Not me. Dawn."

"This girl?" He waved his butter knife at Dawn.

"Yes," Lori answered quietly, "this very girl. This unnaturally talented, homeless girl. Yes. *This very one.*" She leveled a gaze at Nathan daring him to pick up the gauntlet.

"Over my comatose body," he replied, locking Lori's gaze.

"*If you insist!*"

Taffy burst out laughing. All eyes turned to him. "Sorry, *sorry!* I know this is a serious conversation. But, Boss, your wife is armed and dangerous. You haven't asked for my advice, but here it is anyway: don't engage in battle. It ain't worth the blood being drawn."

Nathan hesitated, sighed, the furrows of his frown deepened. "We will take this up later, privately, Lori."

"Oh, goody, can't wait," she answered, holding back no shred of irony.

"It's enough to be dealing with being short-handed," Nathan continued, "I don't need all this drama added to my life."

"*Beau?*" Lori exclaimed. "You refer to Beau as a 'hand'? All he's ever done is break things."

"The things he breaks, I can repair. But another pair of thumbs I cannot make."

"That's true," Taffy agreed. "Beau has no ability to reason on his own, but when Nathan tells him to do something, he does it. He's a world champion klutz, but he's also strong."

"Goodness!" Lori exclaimed, "There must be a high school kid who would love to work on this ranch, Nathan. I'll write the ad: 'The help is wonderful, though the boss is a bit of a curmudgeon.'"

In an effort to cover her snigger, Mrs. Hinds exclaimed, "Jude. Jude Jenks. He might be perfect."

"The Jenks boy?" Nathan shook his head. "He's just a little kid."

"He's a year older than Beau, Boss. I saw him with his mother grocery shopping a couple weeks ago, and I honestly didn't know who he was. So I asked, 'who's this great strapping lad?' And his mom says, 'you know who this is, it's Jude.' 'Oh my,' I says, 'he's grown considerably since last I saw him.' 'He's done that, it's true,' his mom says." Mrs. Hinds paused. "Well, to be honest, I must say he's become quite attractive, too, though I kept that comment to myself."

"Why, Mrs. Hinds?" Lori asked. "Why would you say he's tall but not tell his mother he's handsome?"

"Oh, well ...." Mrs. Hinds drifted off. "Anyway," she finally continued, "his mom said, 'he's looking for work if you know of anyone who needs a strong hand and a good heart,' and I said I'd keep an eye out. Shall I give her a call?"

"If you'd like," Nathan answered in brusque monosyllables.

"Well, I'd very much like," Taffy added. "Just about lost my hand today in that wire tangle."

"Oh, no, Taffy," Lori cried in true alarm. "That's not acceptable."

"I heartily agree," Taffy crinkled up his face smiling at her. "Don't worry Miss Lori, I'm a tough old bird. It takes more than that to remove me from commission.

But, as the Boss says, another pair of thumbs is worth more than gold on a ranch."

*   *

Somehow ... *somehow*, I made it through dinner, Lori thought later as she and Dawn sat side by side in Dawn's room on the bed, scooched up against the wall, poring over an over-sized book on the history of horse dressage.

She felt particularly sorry for Mrs. Hinds, whose obvious if unspoken desire was only that everyone get along. Just—can't everyone get along?

But all too often, the unspoken reply was "*no!*" Lori prayed with all her heart that this attractive, tall, high school kid would fill Beau's work shoes, which could not be much of a challenge, given Beau's laziness.

Lori chatted with Dawn, while the stuffed horse, "Little Blue," slept by Dawn's side. Lori silently continued to stress over learning that an absent Beau posed a serious problem on the ranch. She'd not had the slightest clue that this could be, having only seen Beau work hard at not working, including failing almost every class in school to the extent that he might not graduate from high school.

Which presented another hope Lori held out for Beau living in his aunt's home—that she'd discipline him enough to get him to graduate high school. He wasn't brilliant, but he was certainly smart enough to get through high school.

What worried her was the possibility of Beau returning, but risking injury to either of the men running the ranch was not an option—with or without her threat to render Nathan comatose.

Chapter XV

Dawn: Midnight Foraging

The next morning, as I tiptoed past Lori and Nathan's room on my way downstairs to find something to eat—the raging hunger having come over me again—I could hear them arguing. Quietly, talking, but without love between them. It made me sad. And more than sad, because I knew they were arguing about me. I thought about leaving, once again.

But ... where would I go? That was the biggest problem, and so, once again, I decided to stay, at least until I learned more about life as a human.

I reminded myself of what my mother had instilled in me—not in human language, but in deep memory. There were no accidents, and as long as I was attentive and intentional, what I must do would always become clear.

I came into the kitchen, relieved to see the room empty and the lights off. I had the room—and the food—to myself.

The dinner had been delicious, but with the bad emotions between Lori and Nathan, I'd found it almost impossible to eat.

I opened the refrigerator and took out the leftover yams and tossed salad. Perfect! Sitting at the kitchen table, I didn't even bother to find a utensil, which I still found awkward to use. I wasn't quite sure how to use them. I watched Lori and tried to do what she did. But when I did that, I didn't get enough to eat!

I dug into the cold yams, sliced neatly and covered in butter and spices. The lovely platter of orange root was soon gone. Then I started on the salad, enjoying a handful of the chilled greens, when Taffy came into the kitchen.

"Whoa! It looks like you didn't get enough to eat last night!" he chuckled.

"No. Unhappy Lori and angry Nathan made me ...." I rubbed my stomach. "Everything feels upside down."

"It's the same for me too. I came sneaking out here to do just what you're doing. Had my mind on those yummy yams, but I guess you beat me to them."

"*Oh!*" I cried. "I ate your food! I am bad."

Taffy laughed. "No, you're not at all bad. There's *tons* left over from last night." He opened the refrigerator and stuck his head in. "Let's see, Brussels sprouts and these delicious beets." He brought them to the table. "I think this will do me. But, if you don't mind, I believe I'll use a plate and some silverware."

"I don't mind. Especially if you don't mind that I use my hands. Is it terribly awful to not use that?" I pointed at Taffy's fork.

"Well, honestly, Dawn, it *is* pretty awful."

"But it's slow. I don't understand how to use it."

"Let me show you." He got a plate and another fork and started to give me instruction in the use of the fork. Soon we were giggling over all the ways he made up how to *not* use a fork.

"*What* is going on?" Mrs. Hinds demanded, flipping on the bright overhead lights and giving us a stern look.

"I'm teaching her how to use a fork," Taffy said, looking guilty.

"And how to *not* use a fork, too," I added.

"So I see. Eating all my leftovers, and I meant to make a lovely stew for lunch." But she brought a plate and fork to the table and joined us, filling her plate with salad, beets, and Brussels sprouts.

"Too much emotional stuff last night. Didn't have a good dinner," she muttered.

"Us too," Taffy nodded. "I believe there are more of your prize winning dinner rolls, too, if I'm not mistaken."

"In the breadbox." She waved her fork at it. "Your hand isn't broken yet, you can get them."

"You bet!" Taffy brought the rolls to the table. "Speaking of broken hands, are you going to call Jude's mother?"

"I am. That's what I came out here to do, when I discovered thieves in my kitchen."

"It's a bit early to be calling," Taffy observed. "Not for the likes of us ranchers who get up mighty early in the morning, but for other folks, it's a bit early."

"Yep. I intended to start breakfast, then give her a call. I had it in mind to see if Jude might even come over this morning, before you and the Boss were out on the land."

"Good thinking, Mrs. H. What a godsend if he works out." Taffy lowered his voice to a whisper, "I don't want Nathan thinking he has to have Beau back."

"Amen to that," Mrs. Hinds agreed. "Amen, twice."

"Me too," I added. "Amen twice. That means something like 'let it be true,' right?"

"It does." Mrs. Hinds nodded. "Let it be true."

We fell dead-silent as we heard footsteps on the stairs.

Nathan entered the room. "What have we here?"

"Sorry, Boss," Mrs. Hinds stood and took her plate to the sink. "We got into a wee hours snack."

"Weird. Well, I just came down to work on that saddle that needs repair, before breakfast." He headed for the back door. "Carry on," he added without looking back.

"You don't want to join us in a debauchery of leftovers?" Taffy asked.

"Not really, no." He pulled on his boots and stepped out the back door.

"I feel sad about him," I whispered.

"Well, so do I," Mrs. Hinds said.

"Ay, as do I," Taffy agreed.

"I hope he can become happy. But I think it won't happen as long as I'm here," I added.

"You *do* ruffle his feathers," Mrs. Hinds agreed. "But, dear girl, his feathers are already ruffled. So more or less ruffling doesn't make much difference."

"But, if I were gone ....?"

"You're here," Taffy said firmly. "And, as long as you need a home, here is where you're staying."

"*Yes!*" Lori exclaimed, startling us by silently entering the room. "This is Dawn's home for as long as she'll put up with the lot of us, most especially Nathan. I cannot understand the extremes of his acting out. He's behaving as if *he's* homeless."

"As I've said before," Taffy said, "he needs to rule his roost. Or believe he does. Mrs. Hinds and I make loads of decisions around here that he doesn't even know about, and have been doing so for years—things his father put in place that are never even addressed. But we're happy to let him think he makes all the decisions."

"Very true," Mrs. Hinds nodded. "I don't need the well-oiled machine I've developed with his fingers in every pie, to mash up a couple metaphors." She did a double take. "Sorry, Missus, that sounded very disrespectful."

Lori shrugged. "It sounds perfect to me. Please continue running this place as you have been. I'm sure *I* don't care to put my mind on every nut and bolt you both have carefully screwed into place."

"I like how you think!" Taffy chuckled. "All right, let's find out about that young hunk, with the beauty and strength of Superman."

"Yes, let's." Mrs. Hinds pulled a tiny slip of paper from her pocket, went to the phone and dialed a number.

"Is she calling about Jude ....?" Lori asked.

"Yes," Taffy nodded. "Fingers crossed that he hasn't found a job, and that he's just dying to work like a dog for, probably, very little pay."

*   *

We did a spontaneous happy dance around the kitchen when Jude agreed to come over shortly to discuss possible employment. Nathan came into the kitchen carrying a saddle, in the middle of our dance.

"What in the name of anyone's god is going on in my house, all of a sudden?" He looked at each of us, seeming very confused.

"This girl dancing," he pointed at me, "all right. First of all, she's a kid, and secondly, supposedly, she *can* dance. *But the rest of you! ....*" He shook his head, and no more words came.

Mrs. Hinds got out the griddle for pancakes. "We're celebrating, Boss. Jude is coming over this morning to talk with you about possible employment. He'll be here at eight-thirty sharp. It ... inspired a happy dance."

"A happy dance." Nathan took the saddle into a back room. "Call me when breakfast is ready. Or when the kid shows, whichever comes first."

"Breakfast, first, of course, Boss," Mrs. Hinds called after him, then turned to make a face at us. "*We bad!*" she whispered.

"*Verwy, verwy bad,*" Lori whispered back.

*   *

lthough I felt somewhat confused by the exchange between Lori and Mrs. Hinds, I loved the merriment—I'd always been the first to frolic in the morning, which was how I came by my name. Deep happiness came over me, knowing someone would soon arrive who could help Nathan and Taffy.

Even if that work was to keep fences tall and strong —fences were the one thing cayuse hated. *Fences!* Tearing apart our beautiful home.

I took my mind off the dark thought, a thought I could do nothing about, and thought about dance, instead. Beautiful, lovely dance.

And, even more important, the amazing secret Madame Colette had told me. I wished I could tell Lori, but the time was not right.

A wonderful, warm aroma soon filled the kitchen, as Mrs. Hinds did her cooking magic, and I was perfectly happy to sit at the table—*again!*—and enjoy her pancakes, covered in a sticky, sweet, liquid.

Eos - 192

"You're the best cook anywhere," I exclaimed around a mouthful, glad Taffy had given me the "fork lesson."

"Well, now, that's not objectively true," Mrs. Hinds said, with a big grin.

"Pretty darn close to it," Taffy agreed, putting away a pile of pancakes of his own.

"Don't know what we'd do without you," Lori added, biting into her one little pancake.

"Why don't you eat more?" I asked, mystified by the little pancake on her plate.

"Got to keep my girlish figure. I can't pack it away like you can, dear."

"*Oh!*" I said, shocked. "Is it possible to eat too much?"

"Well, I can. However, I think I just may indulge in another pancake, because they are *scrumptious*."

"Oh, geez," Mrs. Hinds blurted, "I forgot to tell Nathan breakfast is ready. You-all in my kitchen while I'm cooking makes a muddle of my mind." She scurried down the hall and poked her head into the room where Nathan worked on the saddle.

The three of us heard their quiet exchange, and Mrs. Hinds soon came back into the kitchen. "He'll be a few minutes, just getting to a place where he can put his project down. He's amazing with that saddle work, I must say. I thought for sure that thing would be sent to the saddlery, but he's done beautiful work on it already, and he's just started."

I saw Lori look down at her second pancake and shake her head, just a tiny, little bit. I reached out and patted her hand. "Enjoy your pancake, Lori. This sticky stuff will make you happy, like it did me!"

Lori giggled. "All right, I'll try it!" She covered her pancake in sticky liquid and took a big bite. "You're right, I feel utterly delighted."

The phone on the wall clanged, and Mrs. Hinds answered it. "Tanner Ranch. Hi there … sure, she's right here, hang on." She nodded to Lori, "It's Mr. Wise."

Raising her eyebrows in surprise, Lori got up to take the receiver. "What's he want with me?" Lori whispered.

Mrs. Hinds shrugged as Lori took the receiver. "Hello? … Oh! That's very sweet of you, we'd love some. In fact, I think I might ride over later to get them … sure, that works. See you soon, bye!" She turned to us. "He has a bumper crop of peaches and wants to give us some."

"Peach cobbler!" Taffy exclaimed.

"You can count on it," Mrs. Hinds said. "And if he gives us enough, I'll put up a few quarts. The Boss loves peaches!"

"He does?" Lori returned to the business of finishing her pancake. "I didn't know that. Anyway, I've not gone for a ride in a long time, and it might be fun, Dawn, if you and I rode over to get Mr. Wise's peaches. What do you think of that?"

I hesitated, but everyone looked at me with smiles like they expected me to jump up and down with delight, although that was not at all how I felt. "Oh, yes, it might be fun," I murmured.

"Goodness! Not the response I expected," Lori said, surprised. "Are you afraid of horses? No, that doesn't make sense, you're very close to the horses. And the little stuffed horse ... no, I'm confused. Would you rather not go? I'm fixed on riding over to Mr. Wise's, now that I got the idea in my head. But you don't have to go if you don't want to."

"I do," I said quietly. "I want to go with you to get the peaches, Lori."

Lori shook her head. "Sorta strange, dear girl." She finished her pancake with a flourish, then took her dishes to the sink. "I'll change into some riding gear. When you're through eating everything in sight, Dawn, come up so I can get you in some riding clothes."

"Riding clothes," I repeated. "All right. But I'm not going to eat everything in sight. I think I'm almost full."

The door to the back room closed, and Nathan was heard coming down the hall.

"Glad to hear it," Lori said as she scurried up the stairs. Then she called back, "Oh, Taffy, will you be able to help us saddle up?"

"Sure, Lori."

I exchanged a look with Taffy, sad because I knew Lori hurried upstairs to avoid Nathan.

Taffy returned my sad smile. His frown alarmed me, showing his real concern about this household. And I, myself, the biggest part of the problem.

Chapter XVI

Lori:
Jude's Blue Volkswagen

When Lori and Dawn came down in western riding outfits, western jeans and cowboy-styled shirts, Taffy, lingering in the kitchen waiting for Jude to show, whistled.

"You ladies take the show!"

"I like these clothes," Dawn said. "They're beautiful, and this ... what is it?"

"Cotton," Lori answered.

"This cotton feels very comfortable."

"Yep," Taffy agreed. "I love my cotton cowboy shirts."

"Let's get saddled up." Lori stepped onto the back porch and pulled on her cowboy boots. "Here, Dawn, try these on."

Dawn joined her and pulled on the boots Lori handed her. "Well, they seem a little small."

"Do they hurt?"

"No. I can ... it'll be all right."

"We'll have to get you some proper cowboy boots before long, but if you can ride in those today ...."

"Yes. I'm fine."

"Where's Nathan?" Lori asked.

"He went back to work on the saddle until Jude comes," Mrs. Hinds said.

"Oh, yes. I should know that without asking. Ready, Taffy?"

"Ready and waiting."

They made their way to the horse barn. In the paddock were the three sentries who had welcomed them home the previous evening, Vladimir, Twinkle and Goldie.

"Who do you think is good for Dawn to ride," Lori asked Taffy as they entered the paddock.

"I was thinking Twinkle, and maybe you'd ride Goldie."

"Sounds good."

"No," Dawn said.

"No what, dear?" Lori asked.

"I would not climb onto Twinkle." As she spoke, Twinkle came up to her and put her muzzle right in Dawn's hand.

"But she likes you," Lori said.

"Yes. And I love her, too. But I won't ride her."

Goldie had now come up to Dawn, too.

"What about Goldie?" Lori asked.

Dawn put her cheek against Goldie's muzzle. Finally she said, "Not Goldie, either, no." She patted Goldie under her forelock. "She is Twinkle's grandmother."

"She is," Taffy said, shocked. "How do you know that?"

"She just told me. There's another horse who would really love to be taken out for a ride. It would be all right for me to ride him. He's in the barn." Dawn headed for the barn.

Taffy and Lori exchanged a shrug and followed her, the three horses padding along by them.

The long horse barn smelled of hay and straw. The morning light slanted through the wide barn doors, curling up on the straw on the floor of the stalls, golden and warm in pools like yellow cats.

Dawn moved along the row of stalls to the very end. There, stretching his neck out of the stall, watching Dawn with intensity, a pale brown horse nickered.

"There he is," Dawn said happily.

"Carlton?" Taffy exclaimed. "He's not much of a ride."

Dawn hurried up to him and hugged him. "He's a lovely horse. My goodness," she said to him, "they really don't see your beauty, do they?"

"He was a fairly decent show horse in his prime. But, well, he's past his prime now."

"He's a good horse. A hard-working horse. He hates being stuck here and ignored. He's got a big, huge, heart."

"Hmmm," Taffy uttered noncommittally. "Are you saying you want me to saddle him up for you to ride?"

"He's the *only* horse I'll ride," Dawn affirmed.

"Well, then, Carlton, my man," Taffy said, coming over to give him an affectionate pat, "looks like you're in commission again. Let me get the gear."

"I'll ride Twinkle then," Lori said. "Do you think she'll mind?" she asked Dawn, with a twinge of teasing.

"Oh, no. She's your horse. She loves it when you ride her."

"But she would mind if you rode her?"

"Not *exactly*. But *I* would mind."

"I see," Lori said. "Meaning, I haven't a clue what you mean."

"I know, Lori. But I believe eventually, you'll understand."

Taffy and Lori saddled the two horses.

"This is quite impressive," Taffy noted as he saddled Dawn's mount. "The last time I tried to put a saddle on Carlton, he resisted so much, I gave up and saddled one of the other horses. It kinda decided me to retire him. But right now, he's docile as a kitten."

"Yes. He's sorry he acted out that day. He knows that's when everyone started ignoring him. But he had a stone in his shoe. He was hoping you'd check his shoes, but you didn't."

Taffy contained a small gasp. "Well, I hope you're wrong. I'd feel terrible if that was the truth. Let me check his shoes now, just to be on the safe side."

"The stone worked loose shortly after that," Dawn said. "But you'd already decided he was not to be ridden."

After Taffy checked Carlton's shoes and all was ship-shape, he started to put a bridle on Carlton.

"Oh, no, just a halter is fine. He doesn't need that bit in his mouth. He'll do just as I ask, won't you, my friend?"

Carlton made a rumbling sound and nodded his head.

"Oh!" Taffy and Lori exclaimed.

"She is truly a horse whisperer!" Lori said softly to Taffy.

"Yes," Taffy answered simply. "I've never seen the like."

At that moment the three of them turned to see a little blue Volkswagen come in the driveway.

"Must be Jude," Taffy said, trading the bridle for a halter and slipping it onto Carlton. "All right, you're both all set, let me give you a hand up." He gave Lori and Dawn a hand up into their saddles, and they all ambled to the house as Nathan stepped out of the house and a tall, gorgeous young man unfolded from the little car.

"My goodness," Lori said softly, "Mrs. Hinds wasn't lying."

"Yes, but let's see what he can do," Taffy responded.

"Of course."

Mrs. Hinds came through the back door behind Nathan, and everyone gathered around the little car.

"Nathan, this is Jude Jenks," Mrs. Hinds said. "I believe you've not seen him in years. The last time he was but a wee thing, but, as you can see, he's grown considerably. His mother says he's a serious, attentive worker, always ready to learn."

"My mother is right," Jude said, extending his hand to Nathan, smiling a radiant smile framing perfect teeth.

Nathan took his hand, and, Lori could tell, sized him up. He seemed to like him on sight—that was very reassuring.

"We'll go inside and have a talk," Nathan said. "But first, let me introduce my household. You already know Mrs. Hinds, who runs the household. This is my wife, Lori, on our prize palomino, Twinkle."

Lori reached down to shake Jude's offered hand. "Very nice to meet you, Jude. I hope it works out that you become a helpful member of our merry band."

"That would be excellent, I agree," he answered, bestowing his smile on her.

"This is our guest, Dawn," Nathan went on. "Much to my curiosity, she's on Carlton, who's been retired for a couple years now, so ... that's strange." He turned to Taffy. "Why did you ....?"

"She was adamant to ride Carlton, Nathan."

"Yes. My choice," Dawn nodded.

Jude took Dawn's hand, and smiling up at her, paused. "Very pleased to meet you, Dawn."

"Thank you," Dawn answered, taking her hand back, appearing confused.

"And this," Nathan said, gesturing to Taffy, "is my right hand man, Taffy. As a rule, what he says, goes."

Jude turned to Taffy and warmly took his hand. "I've heard about your prodigious knowledge of ranching."

"*You have?*" Taffy asked, stunned.

"Yes. And, as I'd love to learn everything there is to know about horse ranching, it would be a special privilege to work with both you and Mr. Tanner."

"Let's go sort that out," Nathan said, heading back inside without further ceremony. But at the back door, with Jude, Mrs. Hinds, and Taffy lined up behind him, he turned and waved to Lori. "Have a great ride."

"We will," she replied, sounding surprised. Then she and Dawn ambled down the drive and onto the shoulder of the road.

Chapter XVII

Dawn: Mr. Wise

A deep fear washed over me as a car sped by us on the road. It moved into the far lane as it passed, but still, I couldn't help being frightened.

Carlton, sensing my fear, put a picture in my mind of turning at the corner a short distance ahead.

Lori turned in her saddle to look back at me. "We'll only be on this awful road for a short distance," she called, repeating Carlton's reassurance. "People know this is horse territory, so they're generally very careful. We'll turn at the first corner, up there." She waved. "Then it's a quiet gravel road the rest of the way."

"That's good. I didn't like that car going by so fast."

"Don't worry, Dawn, Carlton is a very patient horse, he has never been one to spook."

"Twinkle is very good on this road, too," I said.

"Yes, she is." Lori reached down and patted Twinkle. "She's an excellent and beautiful horse. She and Vlad are the best animal friends I've had in my life."

"Oh! Twinkle is sooo happy to hear that, Lori!"

Twinkle whinnied loudly, performing a spontaneous little dressage two-step.

"My goodness, Twinkle!" Lori exclaimed, her voice full of wonder. "I'm speechless!"

I was relieved to leave the busy highway when we came to the corner and turned onto the quiet gravel road.

"Now for a lazy stroll!" Lori circled back to ride by me. "Such a fabulous, beautiful day, full of peaches and cream—in the sky, and on the dinner table tonight, too."

"Peaches and cream," I repeated.

The soft clip-clop of Twinkle's and Carlton's hooves against the gravel fell like a cozy blanket around us. A meadowlark on a fence post trilled her amazing song. Lori, much to my astonishment, imitated the bird's song perfectly.

"How did you do that?" I asked.

"Like this." Lori again whistled the meadowlark's call.

"That's so, so … *beautiful*. How did you learn to imitate that bird?"

"I sat out on the hillside one afternoon, and the meadowlarks were all around me, singing. So I began to practice their song. Finally, I had it figured out."

"That's quite special to be able to do that," I said, still in awe.

"I'll teach you sometime, if you'd like."

"Yes. Please."

"What do you think of Jude?" Lori asked, changing the subject abruptly.

"He seems very nice," I answered, somewhat surprised and uncomfortable with her question. "He made Nathan happy. That's the most important thing. If he can provide his thumbs so no one gets hurt, then Beau won't have to come back."

Lori glanced at me. "Everything you say is true. But I mean, what do you think of Jude—for yourself? He's about your age. And you don't have anyone else around who is about your age. Just all us old folks."

"You're not old!"

"No. I'm not, but I'm not your age either—and Jude is. He could be your friend."

"Yes. No. I mean, I have a lot to do and to think about right now. I'm not missing having a friend my age. I think right now, I'm supposed to work with Madame Colette. So … another person feels like … like too much."

"I see," Lori said. "You are a strange little bird, yourself."

"I am? Why do you say that?"

"Because any ordinary girl would notice Jude from a mile away. Would be saying, oh, my, he's ... whatever it is girls are saying about a gorgeous boy these days."

"Well, yes, I guess he is very nice looking. But I didn't think about it. I'll give it some thought, if you really believe it's important for me to. Anyway, I suspect I'm not an ordinary girl."

"No, Dawn, you are not ordinary, that's a fact. And you're right, dance and Madame Colette *are* important to you." Lori gestured to a little house in the distance. "There's Mr. Wise's farmstead! He's such a nice man. All alone since his wife died. But he always seems cheerful enough, growing his garden, tending his fruit trees, and riding his big old white roan horse, Arion."

Looking where Lori pointed, I saw the little house whose garden had provided me with food while I hid on the hillside in my tiny cave. So it was Mr. Wise's vegetables that helped me get through the trying time of my transformation.

"Oh!" I exclaimed, when I saw Anubis, my special dog friend. I knew he'd run to me the moment he recognized me. And, sure enough, right then, he flew from Mr. Wise's yard and down the gravel road toward me.

"*Anubis! Anubis!*" Mr. Wise called, to no avail.

"Oh dear," Lori said, worried.

"It's all right, Lori. He'll not do any harm." I slipped off of Carlton as Anubis rushed up to me, tail wagging, leaping about with cheerful, affectionate barking.

"Hi, Anubis," I said, kneeling down to hug him.

"We'd better get off the road," Lori advised, looking up and down the road anxiously.

"*Oh!* Of course, I'm not thinking." I said. "Let's go to your master, Anubis. Come along."

We came to Mr. Wise's driveway and hurried off the road. Then I knelt down and gave Anubis a proper hug.

Mr. Wise hurried up to us. "I've never seen him act like that! What has gotten into you, Anubis? *Heavens!* Such behavior."

Lori slid off Twinkle, and extended her hand to Mr. Wise. "It's so good to see you!"

"Yes. It's been too long. But tell me, who is this lovely young woman?"

"This is my friend, Dawn. Dawn, this is our kind neighbor, Mr. Wise."

"Timothy, please," he smiled at me and shook my hand. "No formality needed around here!" He led us into his yard. "You can tether your horses to the fence."

"Sure." Lori took the reins of both horses, wrapping them about the fence post. "The horses won't go anywhere, they're such docile friends."

"I've not seen that gilding in a few years. He looks great!"

"I know! Poor guy, he was more or less retired before his time, I guess. But Dawn bonded with him on sight, so he gets to strut his stuff again."

We stood admiring the two horses for a few moments.

"He's beautiful," I insisted, softly.

"He really is," Lori agreed.

"That palomino is looking pretty sharp, too. That's Twinkle, isn't it?"

"Yes," Lori said, surprised. "It's Twinkle. How do you know?"

"Oh, I've got an eye for horses." Timothy held a finger to the side of his eye, grinning. "I used to be fairly close with Nathan's dad."

"Really?" Lori said. "Nathan has never mentioned that."

"He was just a kid. His dad would come over and chat with me, especially when he was having a problem with a particular horse. Every now and then he'd bring Nathan, but, like I say, that was when he was little."

Lori and I followed Timothy through his back yard and out to his orchard. "Well, here we are. Bumper crop of early ripening peaches. They are *sooo* delicious! It's a good thing you told me you were riding over. I had the peaches in a bushel basket, not the best thing to carry on horseback."

He gestured to a large backpack sitting on the ground next to an empty basket. "I put them in this backpack I rarely use. You can drop it by any time, no hurry."

"More to the point, Timothy, you can pick it up when you come over for dinner, in the very near future," Lori answered. "We'll get Mrs. Hinds to make a peach cobbler. Taffy was already dreaming about that, the minute he heard peaches were on their way."

Timothy chuckled. "Well, thank you for the invitation, that would be lovely. Although I talk to Mrs. Hinds on occasion, I haven't seen her in, *hmmmm*, a good while. Strange how time gets away from you."

"Too true!" Lori nodded.

As they chatted, Arion, the big white roan horse who had been nearly as friendly to me that night as Anubis, came plodding up to see what was going on. My attention was drawn to him, and Timothy followed my gaze.

"Ah, Arion, come to check out what's happening, have you?"

We wandered over to the corral to take turns giving the good-natured horse a forehead scratch. "He's a good horse, and a special friend, but probably not long for this world. He's one of the oldest horses in the territory."

"You've been wonderful to him," I said, looking into the horse's eyes. "He loves you deeply."

Timothy raised his eyebrows and cocked his head, but said nothing.

"She's seems to be rather a horse whisperer," Lori said.

"Well, if he's telling her that, it warms my heart. I know there've been times I didn't pay much attention to him. You know, when life takes over and you can barely think about what you have to do for yourself."

"He understands," I answered, seeing the pictures of a pretty woman coming out and petting him, laughing in the yard, and walking out on the land, hand in hand with Timothy. Then there were pictures of Timothy alone, and Arion was very sad.

"It'll be *sooo* hard to say good-bye to him, I must admit." Timothy turned away from the fence and sighed. "Well, let me give you some vegetables from the garden, too, as long as you're here," he said, his voice wavering with emotion.

"Oh, you needn't," Lori protested. "You've been generous enough."

"Nonsense. These cucumbers and tomatoes are going to go to waste if you don't take them." He stepped into the garden and handed a few of each to Lori and me.

Hands full of cucumbers, he waved to a corner of the garden. "The strangest thing happened a few nights ago. I don't know what went on, but there, in that corner, a bunch of produce was pilfered, clearly by a human, not a raccoon or opossum, as they typically leave a big mess. No, things were neatly picked. I don't know how they got away with it, given that Anubis will set up howling at the least disturbance. He's a great watchdog. And Arion will whinny if people come about, too. So ... it's just really strange." Timothy frowned.

"I don't mind, you can see I've got way more garden than I need. I can't break the habit of gardening for more than one. But I sure wish I knew how they got away with it. Anubis wakes up if a leaf falls." Timothy shook his head, bending over the cucumbers, chuckling.

Lori exchanged a look with me, and I could not hide my guilty expression.

"I'm sure," Lori said, "whoever took your produce needed it and is truly grateful."

"Well, I hope so. I'd have given it to them, gladly, and even more." He stood and put his hand to his lower back. "I can bend, and I can stand. But going from one to the other is tricky." He stepped through the little garden gate, closing it behind him.

"Let's see if there's enough room in the backpack for these veggies."

We returned to the backpack under the peach trees. Timothy stuffed the vegetables into it. "Tight fit, but I think they'll go."

"Oh, yum, Timothy," Lori said. "There's nothing better than vine ripened veggies. I'm looking forward to dinner tonight!"

We wandered back to the tethered horses. Lori got on Twinkle and Timothy handed the backpack up to her. She slipped it on, then he handed her the reins.

Seeing that we were about to depart, Anubis started barking and jumping around me. I got down on my knees and gave him a great hug, looking up at Timothy. "When you come to dinner, will you bring Anubis?"

"He'd consider it a rare treat. Maybe I will, since the two of you are such great friends!"

I climbed onto Carlton and we made our way to the gravel road, waving to Timothy and Anubis.

Chapter XVIII

Lori:
Dinner with Jude

"At least we won't be late for dinner," Dawn said as they turned onto the unpleasant, but, at the moment, empty, highway.

Lori laughed. "Good point! No, we won't be late and we come bearing delicious gifts."

As they rode up to the barn, Taffy came out, arms loaded with tools.

"Good timing!" Lori took the backpack off and handed it to him.

Taffy put the tools down and took the backpack.

"Full of peaches, and vine ripened tomatoes and cucumbers," Lori said, climbing off Twinkle and heading for the barn, Dawn following.

Taffy gently hugged the backpack. "All for me!"

"*Ah-hum*," Lori exclaimed. "I think not!"

In the barn he helped them unsaddle the horses. "It'll be a super supper!"

"It will, indeed. How is it that you're here at the barn instead of out on the fence line?"

"Had to get some tools."

"What about Jude?" Lori patted Twinkle's muzzle after removing her bridle. "Good girl!" she murmured.

"It went great. He's out there with Nathan now. He brought work clothes on the off chance that he might be put to work. Well, he's *been put to work*. Already proving to be invaluable, although I hope we don't drive him away with the hard work. Nathan expects a lot, and Jude's just a kid. Anyway, I gotta get back out there with those," he gestured to the pile of unceremoniously dumped tools. "I'll see you later, I hope with Jude still in tow."

"Dawn and I will charm him so much, he'll never want to leave."

"Now, there's a plan! That'll work for sure." Taffy retrieved the tools, jumped into the truck and headed back out onto the land.

"I ... I don't think I can 'charm' that boy, Lori," Dawn said anxiously. "I don't know how to do that. And ... I ... I'm not sure that I want to."

"Oh dear!" Lori put her arm around Dawn's shoulders. "I was teasing. I mean, I probably *will* charm him, because it's just my nature. But, no, you don't have to do anything other than be your sweet self. You can leave the active charming to me."

"All right. I will." She got a curry comb and stroked Carlton from his neck to his flank, his eyes half closed in contentment. "But, Lori ...."

"Yes, Dawn?"

"Tomorrow. Tomorrow I go to my first dance lesson, I go to Madame Colette, don't I?"

"Yes! Tomorrow, your first real dance lesson. Are you excited?"

"Very, yes. I'm very excited to have Madame Colette teach me what she knows. But ...." she paused.

"Go on ...."

"I'm afraid Nathan will ...."

"Nathan will nothing. Not to worry, my girl."

"Have you told him about my lesson tomorrow?"

"I told him Madame Colette was looking forward to working with you. But I couldn't get him to appreciate who she is or what that means. So ... I stopped talking to him about it."

"I see," Dawn said, brow furrowed.

"Don't worry, Dawn. You are to study with Madame Colette as long as you and she both want to. It's a fantastic opportunity. But we can't expect a farm boy to under-stand such things."

"But Nathan is smart," Dawn defended.

"He is, I won't argue that fact. He's brilliant—in his own world. But move him away from it, or just try to even a hair, and he ... well, he won't budge. This has been my experience."

"Hmmm," Dawn muttered. "But I've added a lot of confusion to his life, *all of a sudden*. I think that would be difficult for anyone."

Lori gave her a studied look. "You are wise beyond your years, young woman!"

*   *

*J*ude stayed for dinner.

Lori fluttered around him smiling and teasing, which he took shyly but good-naturedly. She insisted that he sit next to Dawn while she and Taffy sat across from them, with Nathan, as usual, at the head of the ta-ble, and Mrs. Hinds at the foot, closest to the kitchen.

"So! Nathan and Taffy didn't scare you away with their slave labor?"

"Not at all," Jude smiled deferentially to Nathan, and warmly to Taffy. "No. It was a great day. I learned a lot, and I love to learn. My biggest concern was that my lack of knowledge might frustrate them. They need someone who can work spontaneously, and I just don't know enough yet to do that. I'll be really happy when I can."

"Didn't frustrate me in the least, Jude," Taffy fairly crowed. "You learn lightning fast, and I was pleased." He turned to Nathan, who nodded.

"Yes. No complaints. You took in what you were told, without endless repetition. Unlike someone else who shall remain nameless at this meal. I'd like to rest in a few moments of contentment, having spent a productive day, dinner on time, and all members of the household present." He raised his glass, filled with water, his preferred beverage during a meal. "Well done, household!"

"Yes, indeed," Mrs. Hinds raised her glass, and everyone followed suit. "Well done."

"Nathan! That was lovely." Lori smiled at him sweetly. He looked at her, not quite smiling, but not frowning, seeming bemused.

"We had the most charming visit with Timothy Wise today," Lori continued. "Goodness, he was chatty. He told me he and your father were good friends."

"I believe that's true," Nathan said without further comment.

"Yes. He has a beautiful black and silver German shepherd, named Anubis, who took to Dawn like she was his long-lost friend. She has an amazing way with animals, I must say."

"She does," Taffy agreed. "Poor old Carlton has a new lease on life. You should have seen him, Nathan. All proud and holding himself high. It was something to see. Lori said she's a horse whisperer, and I have to agree."

All eyes were on Dawn with an expectation that she say something. She remained silent for a few moments, then blurted out, "His name is actually 'Steed.'"

"Whose name?" Lori asked.

"Carlton. A person named him Carlton. But that's not his name. His name is Steed."

Lori and Taffy chuckled. "That's quite a name for him, Dawn," Taffy said, eyes twinkling. "But it's a bit much, isn't it?"

"Not at all. He doesn't understand, nor do I, why he's always been sort of ... looked down on. He's of good breeding, he's intelligent, he has good form, and he's good-natured. So, that name, it's just wrong for him."

"Well ...." Nathan began.

"Some woman named him," Dawn interrupted. "It was always wrong."

"I was about to say that he was Claire's horse, and she named him," Nathan continued. "I never asked her why she named him that ... that doorman's name. We just went with it."

Lori burst out in a guffaw, "Doorman's name! Perfect, Nathan, you hit the nail on the head. Well, I believe that settles it. Regardless of what that horse's name may be of formal record, we shall call him what Dawn says is his real name. We shall call him 'Steed.'"

"Very good," Taffy raised his glass. "Second cheer of the evening—to Steed!"

"*Yay, Steed!*" they cheered.

Jude turned to Dawn. "That's amazing—how did you learn to communicate with horses like that?"

"Oh! It's not ... I don't think you can learn it. It just comes naturally. I mean, for me, it's as easy as talking to a person. Easier, actually."

"Oh! Disappointing. I was hoping it was something you could teach me."

"No. I can't teach you." Dawn put down her fork and sat uncomfortably.

"Are you staying here for good?" Jude continued. "I mean, will you be at my school this fall?"

"Ahm ... I don't know. We haven't talked about ... about any such thing." She looked at Lori, begging to be rescued.

Lori smiled engagingly at Jude. "We've not come to any decisions about future concerns. Perhaps we'll consider home schooling. Would you like me to be your teacher, Dawn?"

"You already are," she said simply.

"Aww, so sweet."

"No. Just ... truth."

Jude looked from one to the other of them, but his eyes rested upon Dawn, attentively.

Chapter XIX

Dawn:
Thunder, Lightning, Dance!

All I wanted was to go to my dance lesson. I didn't want to say or do the wrong thing to cause that not to happen. I didn't want to make Nathan upset. I didn't want to be asked questions that had answers I could not know.

I didn't want anyone to be upset with me. If I could have my true preference, no one but Lori would even talk directly to me. I felt completely happy to sit at the table and let everyone else converse, letting the sound of their chatter pour over me like the tall grasses did when I was a little foal lying next to my mother, napping, the grasses waving overhead, relaxing me with their soft language.

Why, I wondered, did I say that about Carlton's real name?

But, I reminded myself, it went well. Carlton was Carlton no longer, and he'd be happy to be called his real name, the name given to him by his mother, many years before.

As delicious as the dinner was, I was delighted when Mrs. Hinds finally brought in her beautiful, warm, peach cobbler, topped with something called "ice cream"—shockingly cold, while strangely wonderful.

But, oh!, it made me uncomfortable how that boy, Jude, looked at me. He wasn't horrible like Beau. No. Quite the contrary. He looked at me with curiosity and intelligence. But he tried to see into me where I didn't want him to look.

Only Madame Colette knew my secret, and I knew that was how it must remain.

*　*

A tremendous summer thunderstorm rolled in when we wandered outside after dinner to wave good-bye to Jude. He folded his tall body into his little car and headed home.

A cold breeze came up, and with it, distant thunder. Lightning danced while the thunder pounded on the horizon, and the storm rapidly flew across the hills toward us.

"Wow, Nathan, it'll be a whopper!" Taffy said.

"Looks like it. We'd better get out to the barn and batten down the hatches."

"How far does Jude have to drive, Mrs. Hinds?" Lori asked, worried.

"You read my thought," she answered. "Not far, but he's driving right into it."

The wind raised a sudden blast of cold around us, and Mrs. Hinds and Lori and I scurried into the house, while Nathan and Taffy ran toward the barn.

"Do you need any help?" Lori shouted after them.

"No," Nathan called back. "Just get in the house and stay dry. It'll open up any second."

As if that was a command to the heavens, the sky opened and dumped buckets of water on us. Though we were only a few feet from the back door, we got soaked.

We ran inside, freezing and giggling.

"*How dramatic!*" Lori cried.

"I'll get a pile of towels." Mrs. Hinds hurried down the hall, doing the one thing she complained of most when other people did it, tracking water on her nice, clean floor. She immediately returned with a giant pile of fluffy towels.

"Look at my floor," she complained.

"We didn't do it!" Lori laughed.

"And it's a good thing, too!" Mrs. Hinds handed us each a towel. "Take your shoes off before you go traipsing through the house."

"I'm barefoot," Lori said, holding up a wet foot.

"So am I," I said.

"All right. Well, get changed into dry clothes and bring the towels down. I'll make some hot tea for everyone."

The thunderclaps hit above the house as if a herd of cayuse ran in the hills of the storm clouds directly overhead. I cried out, not because I feared for myself, but because I worried about my herd, hoping they had found shelter in this storm that came up so fast. Were they being pelted by the cold, driving, rain, terrified by the close thunder, in danger from the lightning strikes?

"It's all right, Dawn," Lori said as we ran up the back stairs. "We're safe in our cozy home."

"Yes. But all the animals...."

"What a soft heart you have. I'm sure, dear, that they know how to protect themselves and have found safe, dry places to hide out. They probably have known, by instinct, for hours that this storm was coming. And we humans, thick as bricks, are taken by surprise."

"Yes. You're right." I then wondered at my own lack of knowing that the storm was coming. Lori was right, the herd always did know when the weather would change. How disturbing to realize that not only was my deep memory gone, but even my basic senses were nearly nonexistent.

I went into my room and changed into what Lori called "pajamas"—soft and fluffy—my favorite clothes, even though Lori said they were for bed. I wanted to crawl into bed right now with Little Blue, and quietly try to be with my herd. I didn't want to be around people at all right now. I didn't want tea. I didn't want to be warm and dry.

I wanted to be out there, with them, wherever they were, but *together*.

I hugged Little Blue and put him back on the bed. "I'll be back soon," I whispered. I dutifully headed back toward the stairs, and heard Lori on the stairs in front of me, while Taffy and Nathan came through the back door, stomping and exclaiming.

At that moment, the electricity went out in the whole house, and Mrs. Hinds, Taffy and Nathan all said, "*Ohhhhh!*" together, as if trying to sing.

Lori, in the dark on the stairs, burst into laughter. "Bad music, everyone!" She continued down the stairs, and I, feeling that the darkness gave me a moment to myself, sat on the stairs, listening to the commotion, wondering what they would do.

"Get the flashlight."

"Got it. Get the lanterns, Taffy."

"Okay. Need another flashlight."

"Right. There's one in the doodad drawer."

Everyone bustled about, and soon I saw a stream of firelight faintly on the wall of the stairway. As I watched, the light took on form, and the forms became a herd of cayuse—it became *my* herd. They leaned together under a sheltering rock. I knew that rock, I'd been there when young, in a thunderstorm much like this one, close to my mother, who wrapped her neck around me, keeping me safe.

"You are safe, little Dawn, I'm here," Mother had thought to me. "We're all safe under this sheltering rock. See the pretty lightning? But, little foal, don't ever stand under a tree in the lightning. That can be dangerous."

I remember shuddering from fear when the thunder crashed overhead, and my mother had said, "That's the clouds hooves, running across the sky, just like we do across the land. The big clouds are having fun, running across the sky. The lightning breaks the clouds open, and down comes the rain. The rain makes the grass we eat grow, and fills our little ponds full of fresh water."

Lori's voice broke in on my meditation. "Where's Dawn? Did she not come downstairs? Oh, dear, I'll bet she's terrified. Give me that flashlight, I'll go up and get her."

I shook myself out of my trance. "I'm here, Lori. I'm coming down." I stepped into the kitchen, where the oil lamps on the table made the kitchen glow, warm and cozy.

"Okay, we've got light, I'm changing out of these wet clothes," Taffy said.

"Me too," Nathan headed for the stairs.

"Come back for tea. I got the water boiling before the electricity blew, and the tea is steeping," Mrs. Hinds said.

"Sounds great," Taffy said. "If the electricity doesn't come on soon, I'll get the generator running."

Lori helped Mrs. Hinds set the table for tea, while I stood aside, feeling awkward.

Lori glanced over at me. "Are you all right?"

"Yes. I … I'm … yes, I'm all right."

"You're not afraid of the thunderstorm, are you?"

"No. I mean, not really. But, will I still be able to go to my dance lesson tomorrow, if the wind is blowing and there's lightning like this?"

"Not to worry. I won't let a little old thunderstorm keep you from your big day!"

I sighed relief as Taffy returned to the kitchen. And then Nathan soon came downstairs. We all sat together in the lamplight, drinking tea, listening to the wind and thunder, flashes of lightning making the room bright for a few seconds, casting crazy shadows on the walls.

"Shall I fire up the generator, Nathan?" Taffy asked.

"No rush. Reminds me of when I was a boy, just my folks and me, in the kitchen of the old farmhouse, the storm tearing around outside. We were cozy with our kerosene lamps. No generator to fire up." Nathan smiled into the firelight. I saw the little boy he'd been, feeling safe with his parents.

I looked at Lori looking down into her cup of tea, some deep, deep thought taking her attention.

*　*

few minutes later the lights popped on, the mood shifted, the coziness dissipated, and we all soon made our way to bed. Lori walked with me to my room, and tucked me in.

"That was clever of you to change into your pajamas."

"I like them. My pajamas are my favorite clothes. I'd wear them in the day, but you said they're only for sleeping."

"That's true, they're for sleeping." Lori looked around on the bed. "Where's your little horse?"

"He's here, under the pillow. Maybe the thunderstorm frightened him. I ought to have closed the curtain." I pulled Little Blue out from under the pillow and kissed him on his forehead. "I'm sorry I wasn't here, Little Blue." I felt a great tiredness sweep over me and I curled up, holding my little horse. "I sleep now. Little Blue and I sleep."

Lori kissed both me and Little Blue on the forehead. "Yes, sleep little girl and little horse. Tomorrow is a big day!"

*　*

Eos - 230

he storm still beat about the house in the morning. Although no longer flashing lightning, and no more crashing clouds, the rain pelted and the wind blew.

By the time Lori and I came down for breakfast, Nathan, Taffy, and even Jude, too, were already outside riding the fence in the heavy rain, looking for damage.

"I hope they don't find anything significant," Mrs. Hinds said. "It'd be a nasty day to do fence repair."

"It surely would," Lori agreed. "It's bad enough that Dawn and I are heading into town."

"You're not really going into town in this pelting rain," Mrs. Hinds exclaimed, waving at the kitchen window.

"We sure are. It's Dawn's first lesson with Madame Colette, and we dare not miss it. She did a lot of juggling with her schedule to fit Dawn in, and we'd better be there, or suffer her disapproval. Maybe even dismissal."

"That would be a shame!" Mrs. Hinds said.

"It would, especially since it means so much to Dawn. Doesn't it?"

"Yes," I said simply.

"Oh, dear, I just had a thought," Lori said.

"What?" I asked, anxiously.

"You need a leotard for dance. Why didn't I think of that? Didn't Madame Colette say anything about what you'd wear, or any other gear you might need?"

"Yes. She said for me not to worry about what to wear right now. She said she wants to see where I fit in, and then, I guess I'll need certain things. Whatever it is, I hope it's like pajamas."

Mrs. Hinds and Lori laughed. "I doubt she'll have you dance in pajamas. But we can hope that it's comfortable." Lori stood and looked out the window at the blowing wind and rain. "I think we'd better get on the road. I'd rather be early than risk being late. With all this water, there may be flash flooding on some of the roads.

"Oh! And I have that stuff in my trunk I bought the other day. I completely forgot about it, given all the unnecessary drama around being a few minutes late. I'll go out and get it while you get ready to go, Dawn."

"I'm ready. I just need to put on a jacket and something on my feet. What should I put on my feet in this wet weather?"

"There, you see, we need to get you a rain coat and boots. All the more reason to get on the road." Lori ducked out to the car and brought the shopping bag in. She poked around in it. "Well, this is fun stuff. Here, Dawn, why don't you have this shoulder bag?"

"What will I do with it?"

"Put things in it."

"I don't have anything to put in it." I felt confused. I didn't want to make Lori unhappy, but—what would I put in this big bag?

"You could put Little Blue in it, if you wanted."

"Oh!" That made me happy. "I like that. I was going to leave him, but I could take him in this bag."

"You could. Here, take this scarf, take both of them. You can put them in the bottom, for bedding. And then, if you need some color, you can pull out one of them and throw it on."

"I don't imagine Little Blue would like it if I gave them to him to lie on, and then took them away."

"I think if the occasion called for it, he wouldn't mind."

Mrs. Hinds stood at the sink, washing a few dishes. "Little Blue? Am I missing something?"

"Dawn's little stuffed horse that she got the other day when we went to the mall. She named him Little Blue."

"And a stuffed horse needs two designer silk scarves to languish on in the bottom of a designer bag?" Mrs. Hinds asked.

"Doesn't every stuffed horse?" Lori asked cryptically.

"Not in my world," Mrs. Hinds answered.

"I'll go get him right now." I hurried upstairs.

"All right, but hurry back. I'm ready to go."

We were soon on our way, with Little Blue safely between us in his new portable stable.

Lori pulled into a parking lot a few miles away. "Let's see if we can get you rain boots and a rain coat here at the farm store, so you don't end up sopping wet when we get to Madame Colette's."

"I like the way this store looks," I said. "There's pictures of horses all over it!"

Lori looked at the building as if she'd never seen it before. "Goodness! You're right. I never noticed all the horses."

"Maybe they have a raincoat with horses on it."

"Hmmm, that seems unlikely. I'll be happy if we can simply find something that fits you and keeps you dry."

Soon we returned to the car, me wearing my wonderful new rain coat and boots covered in brightly colored, stampeding, horses.

"I love, love, *love* my new coat and boots that keep the rain off me!" I said as we got in the car, thinking how much I could have used them when I was out in the field in my little cave. I looked at the strangely colored—but beautiful!—horses, running across the coat. "Although red and blue and purple horses are not real, I still love these horses."

"Yes." Lori nodded. "But a stuffed horse that moves on its own is not real, either. And yet, one sits on the seat between us."

"Little Blue." I reached into the bag and petted him where he lay, contentedly, on his warm scarves.

When we came into town, the streets were flooded and Lori had to take three detours. I became more and more anxious that I'd be late, but by the time we arrived at Madame Colette's, we were still half-an-hour early. I sighed in relief.

"We're so early!" Lori said, "But, as I said, that's much better than being late."

"Let's go in!" I started to jump out of the car.

"Wait, Dawn. We might be interrupting."

"It's big up there, we can be somewhere, quiet as little mice."

"Perhaps."

"I don't think she'll mind."

"Well, button up, we'll see if the door's open."

I carefully wrapped the shoulder bag inside my new coat.

"Aren't you leaving Little Blue here?"

"No. He can come with me in his new home."

We jumped out of the car and hurried through the black iron gate and the garden door, then dashed across the garden to the winding stairs. The flowers shimmered in brilliant colors, and smelled even more fragrant in the pelting rain.

"Careful," Lori called to me as I flew ahead of her up the winding stairs. "The metal might be slippery."

But I was at the top of the stairs before Lori finished her sentence. I turned and watched her as she cautiously came up the stairs, holding the hand rail.

"You don't want to go tumbling down the stairs. That would be the end of your dancing career before it's begun."

"I don't want a dancing *career*. I just want to dance!" I went into the studio, while Lori followed close behind.

The gigantic, high-ceilinged room echoed with emptiness, except for the rain beating against the sky-lights, accompanied by the drumming thunder.

Moved by the energy in the room, I gently set Little Blue's home on the floor, flung off my new raincoat and boots, and began to dance to the rhythm of the thunder and the rain. I leapt higher and higher, turning and twirling, filled with joy and wonder at this new, light, *incredible* body that did as I asked it to do.

Chapter XX

Dawn: Dance!

The pounding rain began to slow and the thunder moved into the distance. As it did so, my dancing slowed too. I finally settled on the floor, imagining myself to be one of the flowers outside in the garden, wet and refreshed by the life-giving rain.

A burst of applause broke out from Madame Colette and her students, who had quietly come into the studio. I jumped, startled, so completely in the space I'd created with my movement, I had no idea they'd come into the studio.

I leapt up from the floor, intensely embarrassed. "I'm so sorry, Madame Colette!" I pointed at the skylights. "The music of the rain and thunder...."

"Don't apologize, my dear. Spontaneous art is pure art. Your few minutes of unrehearsed expression of your soul has taught these students more than a week of lessons from me. Never, *ever* apologize for following your heart."

Madame Colette turned to her students. "Take in what you saw, and aspire for yourselves to so love what you do, that the room may fill with people, and you don't even know it.

"All right now, off with you, I'll see you in a couple of days."

The room rapidly emptied, but as the students left they each came up to me and said something kind or amazing about my dance.

I stayed where I stood, more and more awkward and embarrassed, hanging my head, wishing I was not there. Finally, *finally,* Madame Colette, Lori, and I were alone in the huge studio.

"You must change how you feel, Dawn," Madame Colette said, coming up to me. "Dance is an art you share. It's a way to raise the human soul to new levels of awareness. By awe are we made more than we were. You produced awe among a group of advanced, extremely talented, but somewhat self-centered, somewhat entitled, dancers.

"This is your calling. It's what you share. It's not your place to be ashamed."

"I'm *not ashamed!*" I protested. "But ... I am ... I'm confused that my moving, just, moving as I feel it, would make them experience awe. I'm sure every one of them can dance better than I can, because you've been teaching them. And it feels like, it seems I must be sort of ... I don't know. I don't know how to say it."

Madame Colette fluttered her beautiful hand as if to erase my words. "You must accept that you have a raw— but rare—talent. You are a dancer's dancer. What you do naturally, another dancer may take years and *years* to perfect and never really *quite* have it.

"I say again, it's not your place to challenge or criticize your special gift. It's your place to share it. To treasure it, to protect it, to nurture it, yes. But not to judge it. And not to hide it.

"All right, enough preaching from me. We'll now go to another studio." She led Dawn through the door.

I glanced at Lori over my shoulder, surprised that Madame Colette didn't even seem to know she was there. We went through two more studio rooms, and stopped, finally, in a room smaller than the others. Chairs faced a big white board on one wall.

"This is where I teach dance history, dance form, dance aerodynamics, human anatomy, and, well, whatever else I teach." She laughed lightly. "Let us sit."

I sat.

She began where she left off when she had taken me into her office the last time. "Dear little Eos, you've recently transmogrified into human form, just as Eos have done for thousands and thousands of years. Just as every Eos *must* do, one time at least, whether they want to or not."

"Yes," I nodded, still mystified. "But ... *how do you know that?*"

"I'm coming to that. But first, I must get some understanding about what is troubling me. You seem not to know certain things that all newly transformed Eos *must* know. You're strangely naive. Fabulously talented, yes. And smart. But ...."

"I'm lucky to have Lori, aren't I?"

"Very, very fortunate indeed. There are no accidents."

I gasped. "That's ... that's the truth my mother always taught me."

"And now we come directly to my most important question—where is your Eos influencer? Your mother or whoever was to share with you in deep mind what you must know after transmogrification to make your way, and *to survive*, in the world of humans?"

"My ... my mother ... my mother was shot by those horrible humans, those terrible men driving across the hills, chasing us and ... and ...." The strange human tears began to flood from my eyes like the rain hammering against the skylight, as the memory overtook me. I had not felt my grief like this since that day, when my brother and I had mourned over our mother's body until the herd pulled us away by force. In the herd's deep, shared memory, I felt their gratitude that only one had been taken from us. But my grief ... I now could release it as never before, with these tears.

"*Oh!*" Madame Colette exclaimed. "*Daphne!*"

"Yes! Daphne. *My mother!*" Stunned, I stopped crying, amazed. "Yes. How ... how ....?"

"I just had a flash of deep memory. I saw her. *Daphne!* She was a student of mine, years and years ago. I've wondered about her. She was, well, she was much like you. Somewhat more reserved, but a remarkable talent."

"You ... *you taught my mother when she transitioned to human!* So my being here with you now ... *oh!* There surely are no accidents! And Lori ...."

"Lori is the instrument of fate. Of Serendipity. But Dawn, how did you come to be with Lori?"

"I was drawn to their ranch. I *knew* that to transform on a man's property was very dangerous—for me, for my brother, and for my near-brothers, who were my overseers. But *I couldn't help myself!* I brought them close on the night before solstice, and Lori's man and their other man, that little horse-man, and that terrible boy-man, and their dogs, they came out and captured me and my brother and three near-brothers. They brought us down to the horse prison.

"The next morning Lori came out and talked to us, and I knew why I was there. She didn't have any deep memory, of course, but I knew she would take care of me and not let those men do anything bad.

"Then I transformed and with these," I raised up my hands, "so very strange at first! With these I was able to let my brother and my near-brothers escape. If not for Lori, where would I be? You are so right, Madame Colette, I know nothing!"

Madame Colette shook her head sadly, and a tear escaped down her cheek as she took my hands in her own. "Oh," she whispered very softly, "I am so sad to hear about my beloved student, your mother. And I am sad for you, too, poor, dear, little Eos. *Ah!* It is a challenge men have always given us!"

"*Us?*" I asked, shocked, leaning nearer to Madame Colette.

"Yes. Us. Dear Dawn, I, too, am Eos. I've chosen to stay human as there's such a heart-breaking need among humans to understand and grow love. A daunting task, it's true, but worth it when one sees the heart of a student open like a beautiful rose as they learn to love themselves, love their talent, and share that love in movement.

"Then—to feel an audience open in awe, to feel their hearts move. This is my work. That's why I lectured you about not being shy, about letting your work shine, without excuses or an unnecessary modesty. Don't ever get in the way of your talent. Your talent has work to do!"

"*My talent has work to do!*" I whispered, so stunned, relieved, happy, and even mystified to be with another Eos. We sat quietly together for a few minutes, Madame Colette holding my hands. We shared a little deep memory, as much as we could with our delicate human minds.

"Deep memory," I sighed, as even then, the pictures faded.

"Yes. A little," Madame Colette agreed. "That's what I miss most. Shared memories, shared thinking, shared knowing. *Ah!* One can feel quite lonely! I've been thinking I might return to my herd, next summer solstice."

"*Oh!*" I exclaimed, shocked. "If you do, I will go with you."

"I don't think I will now, though, since you're here. We could both go back, it's true. But ...." She paused, contemplating. "I believe we have work to do *here*. Yours has just begun. And mine is not complete."

"All right then. We'll stay. But ... do you think we could visit my herd?"

"We can. I visited my herd once in human form. But you must know, it is quite painful."

"It's painful *not* to see them."

"It becomes less painful over time. But, yes, to be truthful, it's painful either way. However, now, my dear, I am not alone!"

"No. And you won't be. It's so good that I will have you to teach me. I never know what to say to Lori. What do I tell her, or not tell her? She's already seen something I think I ought not to have let her see, but I didn't know ...."

"What is that?"

"We went to a huge place where all the things to buy are together. And all the cars are together outside—very scary to walk among all those cars."

"*Hmmm*, the mall."

"Yes. That's what she called it, yes. Inside, she took me to a very noisy place. Hurt my head, but she liked it, so I tried to like it too. She let me choose this clothing, and keep it for myself.

"Then we left there. I was so relieved to get out of that noise! We were walking and there ... *there*, Madame Colette, in a window was a tiny Blue, *exactly like my brother*. There. Behind a big sheet of glass. I went into shock when I saw him, so tiny and in that big place with all the humans rushing up and down. Oh! I couldn't understand it! I still don't exactly. The people seemed to want to be there in all that madness and noise.

"I can't imagine ever saying, 'let's go to the mall.'" I shuddered. "Anyway, Lori thought it was wrong for me to want the tiny Blue. She called him a 'toy,' and said I'm too big for a toy, or something like that, that didn't make sense.

"But I know Blue, and I know there are no accidents, and I know Blue figured out a way to come to me. The little horse has Blue's exact markings and, most especially, *his blue eyes!* But I also knew, in that noisy place where I couldn't even *think*, I couldn't tell Lori about Blue.

"I refused to move. I refused to take my eyes off the little Blue. So Lori took me in the toy store to get him for me. But there was a wall behind him. Then the funny little man-not-man, the little gnome .... I could see that humans didn't see the real him, not even Lori could see him. I could see they don't believe in gnomes—so the gnomes must disguise themselves, but he wasn't disguised! He was a gnome pretending to be a gnome. So funny, isn't it?"

Madame Colette laughed at the image of the gnome pretending to be a gnome. "It is *very* funny!"

"Anyway, Lori and the gnome with the funny things on his feet, tried to make me take another one of those horse toys on a shelf. The gnome said, 'oh, ho, each of these horses is different! No two are the same!' He made a very big deal about each of the little horses being different. Why would they be the same? I don't understand that either. But anyway, only the one in the window was Blue. Well, of course! *Only Blue is Blue!*

"I put in my heels again, and Lori, because she's so loving, made the little gnome get me the small Blue from the window, and he put a different horse in the window.

"My brother Blue came into the little horse toy when I called to him, because I need him. And now the 'stuffed horse' as Lori calls him, is animate with Blue. He stands and sits and sleeps, and keeps me good company, because he's attached to Blue's soul.

"I was terrified for the herd last night, with the lightning, and the wind, and the terrible blowing rain, but Blue showed me the herd was safe under an overhanging rock. So I could sleep. Because I didn't want to be unhappy and worried. I wanted to dream about being here, with you today, at my dance lesson.

"But we're having some other sorts of lessons, aren't we?"

Madame Colette smiled at me. "Well, yes, everything we consider develops who you are, as a creator of beauty, peace, joy and happiness. But, tell me, Dawn, has Lori seen Little Blue do anything animate?"

"Oh, yes. She's seen him do *everything* animate."

"And what does she say?" Madame Colette asked, concerned.

"*Ahm*, she said, 'there's a lot of strange things going on, and Little Blue isn't the strangest.'"

"Well, then, I guess that's all right. There may be a lot of things she doesn't know, but she's very perceptive. Now, though, I fear we must return to the main studio, where my next class is gathering."

We stood and Madame Colette gave me a hug. "I'm so happy, little Eos, that serendipity, through Lori, brought you to me. The human family is hungry and thirsty for the beauty, grace, and wonder that your talent will allow them to experience."

"With your instruction, I know what you say will be true."

When we returned to Lori, I saw her standing in the corner, holding my bag and raincoat, smiling at the girls in white leotards and pastel tutus, warming up at the bars. I noticed them admiring themselves, or criticizing themselves, in the mirrors.

Madame Colette sighed as we came into the room and approached Lori. "Ah! prepubescent girls. The most difficult to work with, even when very talented. All criticism and fragile ego. But someone must take them through the troubled waters of this age."

Lori smiled. "I believe it must be you, Madame Colette, you have such a strong, yet kind, presence."

I slipped on my boots and Lori handed me my raincoat. Then she handed me Little Blue's home.

I took it and peeked inside. I held it open so Madame Colette could see.

"Ah, there, Little Blue!" she said softly.

"You told her about your stuffed horse?" Lori asked, unable to keep surprise out of her voice.

Madame Colette smiled at Lori. "Interestingly enough, he did come up in the conversation. She was telling me about her experience at the mall."

"Oh, well, to be truthful, I'm fairly certain Dawn did not think much of the mall until we stumbled upon this little horse, and then we had a quiet, lovely lunch at *Earthbound.*"

Madame Colette nodded. "Yes. She said something to that effect. Well, I must attend to this group of preening swans. I'll see you in three days, Dawn."

I waved as Lori and I moved to the door. "Yes. Seeing you is the only thing that will get me through that day," I said.

Madame Colette gave me a puzzled look, then turned her attention to her class.

Chapter XXI

Dawn:
Chocolate Chip Cookies

"It doesn't seem as though you had a dance lesson," Lori said. As we dashed to the car, the rain picked up again.

"She took me to a classroom where there were chairs with a surface to write on ...." I made the shape with my hands.

"Desks," Lori suggested.

"Desks. And a big white board on the wall at one end of the room. She said that's where she teaches dance history and human anatomy, and, ahm, some other things.

But mostly, we just talked. We ... we got to know some important things about each other."

"Bonding," Lori said quietly, attention on the rain-driven road.

"Yes. Bonding."

"Why does she need to bond with you? Are you not simply another student?"

I felt an emotion come from Lori I didn't like. I'd not felt this emotion from her before. But ... *Oh!* It was like the emotion Nathan felt about me! It was ... *jealousy!* I didn't know what to think of Lori being jealous of Madame Colette. Why would she have that feeling?

"I ... you ... why are you jealous of Madame Colette?" I finally blurted.

"I'm not jealous!" Lori retorted in an angry voice.

Silence fell between us, with only the slam of the windshield wipers banging back and forth, as if her emotion had crawled out onto the window.

"No. I'm not truthful. You're right, Dawn," Lori finally said so soft, I almost didn't hear her. "Let me think for a few minutes, while I consider my inappropriate emotion."

I sighed, relieved. Lori's outburst frightened me, and I didn't know what to do about it. But *this* Lori, now considering her emotions, was the Lori I knew. I quietly let her contemplate her feelings.

The rain began to let up, and the windshield wipers calmed down as well. Finally, Lori said, "I think it has to do with my mother disappearing when I was about your age. I'm sorry to say it seems to have sort of broken something in me. I think maybe I don't trust friendship with women. Or even girls, apparently. I admit I'm confused by this emotion. Goodness, *sooooo* unlikable! And just ... wrong! I'm truly happy, Dawn, that we found Madame Colette for you to study with, and that she sees who you are.

"But I think I felt I'd lose you, because why would you want to be with me, when there's this amazing woman, who sees and understands you? You'd prefer Madame Colette, of course.

"Quite frankly, I'd prefer Madame Colette to me, *myself!* So, there!"

"No. No. No. Lori, *no!*" I protested. "Madame Colette is amazing, but you ... you're ... there's no other Lori. You're my Lori. I bonded with you on sight! You took care of me. You put clothes on me. You fed me, and I was crazy-hungry. You combed my hair, so pretty and put that little," I made a gesture at my hair where she had put the little clasp in the braids she'd made. "So gentle, so ... outside of yourself, just caring about me. Lost Dawn. Sad, lost Dawn. You took me, and put beautiful clothes on me, and fed me and ... well ... that's all. That's everything. And you knew my name! You called me by my name!

"I'm very, very fortunate and grateful to have Madame Colette and Lori care for me. I feel close to Madame Colette in a certain way. But nothing can come between you and me, between Dawn and Lori. Don't be afraid, don't be angry. Don't be jealous. Be ... Lori! Don't have that feeling for Madame Colette that Nathan has about me. It's soooo, ahhh, *hard* to be near."

"*Oh!*" Lori gasped, "Yet more insight!" She reached over and took my hand. "I say again, dear Dawn, you are wise beyond your years."

We drove the rest of the way home in a warm, contented silence.

*   *

"*L*ook, there's Jude's little blue bug," Lori said as we approached the house.

"Jude's bug?"

"His car."

"Then it's a car, not a bug," I said.

Lori laughed. "It's a car, it's a bug, it's two things in one!"

I looked at her, somewhat curious and confused.

"*Ah!* Where have you been, strange girl, that you don't know a Volkswagen?" Lori asked.

"Out there," I answered honestly, sweeping my arm toward the hills.

"Out there." Lori repeated, pulling into the garage. "Well, now you're in here!"

"I am," I said gleefully. "Look, this is a big house for the cars!"

"Oh, you haven't been in the garage, have you?"

"Garage. No."

We got out of the car and went into the house, down the hall to the kitchen.

Mrs. Hinds was busy, stirring up something that smelled sweet and lovely.

"Oh, Mrs. Hinds!" Lori said, "Chocolate chip cookies on a cold and stormy day—*perfect*!"

Mrs. Hinds smiled at us over her shoulder. "I thought the weather called for it."

"We came through the house for the cars, and didn't get wet!" I exclaimed.

"So I see."

"Jude's bug is here," Lori said. "I wouldn't expect to see him on this dreary day."

"Oh yes, he came right after you left. He's been out in the barn with Nathan and Taffy the whole time. They're working on repairing tack, I believe. I'm not sure, I didn't listen too hard."

"That's news!" Lori teased. "I thought you listened very closely to everything everyone said around here."

"No. Indeed, no, Missus. What I accidentally overhear is generally a lot more than I care to know. You can't tell secrets about things you don't know."

"Goodness," Lori exclaimed, "It's my day to be close to wise women. But, tell us, Mrs. Hinds, tell us a secret about something you *do* know."

"My lips are sealed," Mrs. Hinds retorted.

"What is a 'secret'?'" I asked.

Lori took some cookie dough right from Mrs. Hinds' mixing bowl.

"Get your grubby fingers out of my cookie dough."

"*Urg!* You make a good point. I haven't washed my hands. At least my cooties will be destroyed when the cookies are baked."

Mrs. Hinds stopped stirring and looked at Lori. "You're in a fine mood."

"I don't understand what's going on," I said quietly.

Lori sat down by me. "Secrets are things you know that you must not tell anyone. If you do, they are no longer secrets. And cooties are imaginary germs. They're not real."

"I see," I said, frowning. "And so ... what are germs?"

"Oh, *goodness!*" Lori exclaimed.

"Germs are things that are *not* imaginary," Mrs. Hinds answered. "You can't see them, but they can make people and creatures sick."

"Oh," I said. "I understand that. It's like, don't drink the water at *that* watering hole, it's the wrong color, and will make you sick." I thought for a moment. "So, there are germs in it."

Mrs. Hinds nodded. "That's a way to look at it, yes."

Right then, Nathan and Taffy and Jude came onto the back porch, stomping the rain off their feet.

"You done for the day?" Mrs. Hinds called to them.

"Yes, Mrs. Hinds." Taffy came into the kitchen, washed his hands at the sink, then snuck his hand into Mrs. Hind's mixing bowl and took a giant hunk of cookie dough.

"Will everyone kindly keep their fingers out of my of cookie dough! I won't have anything to cook."

"Cooked or raw, it's so darn good!" Taffy protested.

"Excellent! We got a good day's work done," Nathan said, coming into the kitchen, followed by Jude. Nathan pulled out a chair and sat opposite Lori. "This kid's a wonder. We got more tack repaired in six hours than I'd have gotten done in six weeks if I took all those bits and pieces that needed repair to the saddlery."

He turned to look at Jude, who still stood in the doorway. "You're a natural, Jude. If you never went to school another day, you could make a tidy living, just repairing tack. It's a lost art."

"Don't go telling him to quit school, Boss. What will his mother say?" said ?

"No, of course not. I'm just making an observation."

"Don't quit school," Lori advised somberly.

"I won't." Jude answered. "I'm going to the university. I've already received a scholarship to study animal husbandry and ranch management."

"Perfect!" Lori exclaimed. "Bright *and* beautiful!"

Nathan gave Lori a puzzled look. "What's gotten into her?" he asked no one.

"I don't know," Mrs. Hinds said. "She seems a bit drunk."

Nathan looked at Lori, surprised. "You been drinking, my beautiful bride?"

"No, I have not! I'm just in a playful mood. And it appears you are too, my beautiful bridegroom," she laughed.

They exchanged a look of affection, then I saw Lori look down, seeming confused.

"I smell chocolate chip cookies!" Nathan abruptly declared. "And I want my share!"

"Coming, oh master!" Mrs. Hinds turned from her mixing bowl and bowed to Nathan.

Jude and I stood on opposite sides of the kitchen looking back and forth at the strange, but, I guessed, playful interaction.

"Do you think we're safe here?" Jude asked me.

I giggled. "I'm not sure. They *are* acting strange, but they don't seem dangerous."

Everyone burst out in laughter.

"Good to know," Nathan said, still chuckling. "I'm not dangerous. I was beginning to think perhaps I was!"

"Sit down you two," Mrs. Hinds waved her spoon at Jude and me. "Cookies and milk for everyone!"

"*Yay!*" We all cheered.

Just when we got settled with our milk and cookies, the phone on the wall jangled noisily as if it thought everyone was in the barn.

Mrs. Hinds jumped up and answered it. "Tanner residence. Yes, she's here." Mrs. Hinds covered the mouthpiece and whispered, "For you. Your doctor. She's called *three times* today!"

"What the ...." Lori took the receiver. "Hello, Edna, what's up? Yes, we have our appointment. Next Monday. Well, I'm certain you don't need to be there. Why are the police contacting you, Edna? Why don't they call me?" Lori's voice became more exasperated. "And, Edna, why aren't you calling me on my phone, instead of bothering poor Mrs. Hinds, who's busy enough without fielding my calls. She's not my secretary.

"Yes, Edna, I am a 'bit *testy*.' We are in the midst of a family moment, laced with chocolate chip cookies, and I'd like to get back to it. So, bye for now. And, please, from now on, leave messages on my cell phone." She hung up without a further word.

"Oh, my!" Mrs. Hinds exclaimed. "I guess you told her!"

"I guess I did. But, what in the name of ... of ... of hot chocolate chip cookies is *up* with her?" Lori asked everyone and no one in exasperation.

"She has the nuisance gene," Nathan said, biting into another cookie.

Mrs. Hinds giggled nearly uncontrollably. "She ...."

"Never mind, Mrs. Hinds," Nathan warned, giving her a warning look under his brow.

But Mrs. Hinds continued right along. I began to see the reason for her saying she didn't want to know secrets, because they might not remain secrets. "She had her little cap all set for Nathan. And then you came along, Lori."

Oh! I thought, that woman doctor wanted Nathan for her mate? *How strange are humans?*

"*REALLY!*" Lori said. Coming back to the table, she stood behind her chair looking down at Nathan. "No one ever tells me anything. Is this true, Nathan?"

"Well, probably more true than false," he said, refusing to make eye contact with her.

"*Ack! I will not* have a doctor who, who hates me, and who ... *ack! Such an unpleasant thought.* Why didn't you tell me?"

Nathan shrugged. "It was none of my business who you chose for a doctor, especially since there's only two within a reasonable distance."

"It's very distasteful and ... and ... *inappropriate.* In any case, why is she taking it out on poor Dawn? Now I don't believe anything Edna says. She's called every day, saying the police are nagging her about Dawn. But why would they do that? Wouldn't they just call me, or come by here, and see for themselves that the girl is alive and well?"

"And the girl is happy," I added.

"And happy ...." Lori paced back and forth across the kitchen. "Edna just said she intends to come to our appointment with this Doctor Baduna on Monday, for that stupid battery of x-rays they're both insisting on. Why? There's nothing wrong with Dawn. Nothing's broken. She's not in pain." She stopped pacing and looked at me. "You're not in pain, are you?"

"No," I answered, "I'm not in pain."

"Quite the contrary, she's moves like an angel. Like a real, true angel, flying through the air in supernatural jumps. She had advanced students gaping in awe today."

"*Hmmmmm....*" Mrs. Hinds said reflectively.

"You took her to a dance class without confirming it with me?" Nathan asked.

Lori returned to standing behind her chair, and looked at Nathan across the table. I saw anger grow in her eyes. "Yes, Nathan, I did. I did, indeed. I had the unmitigated gall to do something without your express approval. I had the unmitigated gall to behave like an adult, who is capable of thinking, all by herself. *Imagine that!*"

"Yes?" Nathan said, beginning to sound angry himself. "And who's paying for these lessons?"

"Let me think that through for a few moments," Lori said, her voice becoming low. "Let's see. I live in the state of Washington, which is a fifty-fifty state. I've not spent any money to speak of in several weeks. A human being who needs attention comes into the home where I live, that, according to the laws of the state, is one-half mine. And I invest a tiny, paltry, amount of my half of this estate in the happiness and development of said homeless person."

Then Lori raised her voice. "My God, Nathan. You really know how to completely suck the joy out of any moment. I think you're particularly well-suited for Edna. May you both be happy." She turned and stormed upstairs. We all heard her banging around in the master bedroom, then she stomped down the hall past my room.

And then a door slammed with noisy finality.

Chapter XXII

Dawn:
Jude

athan looked at everyone around the table, each in turn, and finally his gaze rested on me. "I guess I'd better approve of your dance lessons."

We all tittered nervously.

"Good idea, Nathan," Taffy nodded. "Look at these two kids, you and the Missus have their ears pinned to the backs of their skulls, scared breathless." He smiled

at me, then Jude. "Don't worry kids. They're just prac-
ticing for roles in the local theatre."

"Really?" I asked, amazed.

"No, not really, dear Dawn. They are two people, each used to having their own way. They're showing us a good lesson on the value of flexibility. That is to say, how damaging it is when you refuse to have it. On pain of possible dismissal, Nathan, I believe the missus has won this round. It has not hurt you one little bit to let this beautiful girl explore her potential."

Nathan looked at Taffy and nodded slowly. "You're right, Taffy. You. Are. Right." He paused for a moment, then he said, "Did you make that crow pie, Mrs. Hinds, I'm ready for some now."

"Naa, Boss, not after cookies. It's all right. Everything will be all right," Mrs. Hinds affectionately reached over and patted his hand.

I didn't like the thought of anyone eating crows, but I would ask about that some other time. At this moment, I wondered at all the things Mrs. Hinds must know about Nathan's life. More, and a lot more than Lori, I could see.

*   *

*L*ori stayed in the room beyond my room for the next two nights. She didn't even come in to sit with me and Little Blue. I knew she wasn't angry with *me*, but she was, for sure, angry. She didn't even go down to meals.

I couldn't imagine this intensity of anger toward anyone I loved. But I knew Lori felt deeply hurt, and I guessed she expected Nathan to go to the room next to mine and talk with her. She hadn't heard his apology at the dinner table and his permission for to me to have dance lessons. But, we all noticed, he refused to go to the room down the hall.

Because of the unhappiness everywhere in the house, I, too, stayed in my room. Every time I looked out the window that "bug-car" was there. If only it wouldn't be there, I'd go downstairs and talk with Mrs. Hinds. But Jude made me self-conscious and uncomfortable, and I didn't want to encounter him. What ought I say, or how should I behave around him?

On the morning of the third day, Lori came to my room and knocked. I opened the door a tiny crack. See-ing Lori, I flung the door open and threw my arms around her.

"I miss you!" I said.

"I miss you too, Dawn," she said, but her voice didn't sound quite right. "We've got to go get those stupid x-rays today. Here, wear these sweats." She handed me a big, soft, pile of pale grey fabric. "I know sweats are not beau-tiful, but if you wear them, you won't have to change for the x-rays, and I want to get in and out of there as quickly as possible. Especially if Edna shows up."

"All right." I took the "sweats"—a strange name for clothes. "I don't care what I wear, just as long as we get in and out fast, like you say. And then, to Madame Colette."

"Yes. And then Madame Colette."

I sighed, relieved. I'd been worried that Lori would not take me to Madame Colette's studios. And then, of course, I would have to discover how to get there by myself, because I'd made a commitment to Madame Colette, and, whatever went on in this household, the word between two Eos came before and above anything and everything. For Eos, it was law.

But Nathan had said I could have my dance lessons, and Lori was taking me. That was all I needed for this day. I felt that once the "stupid x-rays" were done, things would be good.

"I need to chat with Mrs. Hinds," Lori said. "Get ready and we'll leave shortly."

"All right." I stepped out in the hall to watch Lori walk away. There was something different in how she moved, a stiffness, and it made me sad.

I didn't have to do anything to get ready other than change into the sweats. Then I put Little Blue in his bag and started to head down the hall to the back stairs. Then, on second thought, I returned to my room and took Little Blue out of his bag and put him on the bed.

"I'm going to leave you, Little Blue. Lori's in a bad frame of mind, and I don't want my attending to you to upset her."

Little Blue snorted, and I knew he didn't want me to leave him, but I felt it was best, and I headed for the stairs. But as I went down, I paused when I heard Mrs. Hinds say, "Be careful, Missus."

"Why, Mrs. Hinds," Lori asked, her voice anxious. "Why? There's something strange going on."

"Yes. Plenty strange things going on. X-rays for a healthy girl. And ... yes, plenty strange."

"So, you agree with me? About the fact that there's no need for invasive x-rays with a perfectly healthy girl who is far more agile than any ordinary mortal?"

"I more than agree with you, Missus. You hit the nail on the head, I believe, when you say, 'far more agile than any ordinary mortal.'"

"What do you mean?"

"Have you ever heard of Eos, Lori?"

"Well, yes, as it happens, I've heard this term twice in the last few days. From, in fact, that household troublemaker, and my *former* doctor, Edna. And I heard

Madame Colette whisper it when Dawn did her flying act. And now from you, Mrs. Hinds. What ....”

I heard Jude step in the back door. “Sorry to bother you. Taffy asked me to come fetch something from his room. Really sorry to interrupt your private conversation.”

I heard the discomfort in his voice, and could just picture how guilty Mrs. Hinds and Lori looked when he came, unexpectedly, in their midst.

“No, no, not interrupting a thing, Jude,” Lori said warmly. “I’m so glad you’ve not left us, with all the drama in this house.”

“Oh, well, ahm, it’s, ahm, entertaining.” Then Jude walked down the hall to Taffy’s room.

“Where *is* that girl,” Lori said. “We need to get on the road.”

Now I was trapped! I didn’t want to go into the kitchen when Jude would return there in moments, but I couldn’t get back upstairs before Lori saw me on the stairs. If I didn’t go down into the kitchen right away, she’d see I’d been listening on the stairway.

I stood and continued on down the stairs just as Lori started to come up. “I was beginning to think you got lost!” she said.

“Me too,” I laughed.

Jude came back in the kitchen. "Oh, hi, Dawn. Good to see you."

"Hi," I answered awkwardly. I had no ability to lie and so could not say it was good to see him too, because, well, it wasn't.

He looked at me as if trying to figure out if I really didn't like him. "Hmm, ah, I'd better get this pocket knife out to Taffy," he finally said, "before he cuts a finger off with the machete he's working with."

"*Machete!*" Mrs. Hinds wailed.

"Just kidding. But, he's got the wrong tool for the job." The back door slapped shut as Jude stepped outside, and Lori and Mrs. Hinds turned to look at me.

Lori shook her head. "Really, Dawn, you must at least be polite."

"But I cannot lie."

"You couldn't say, it's nice to see you too?'"

"No. It's not nice. I'm uncomfortable seeing him. But I think saying that *might* be worse than saying nothing. Although I'm not sure now, with the way you and Mrs. Hinds are looking at me like I did something really wrong."

"Poor boy, he must think he's a troll, that way you act," Lori said.

"He's not a troll. He's very nice looking, and he's human. I met a troll once. Very ugly. Ugly as you can imagine, and then some."

"I'll take your word for it," Lori said, distracted. "Let's get going. Mrs. Hinds, we'll continue our interrupted conversation later."

"Yes, Missus. I'll be here."

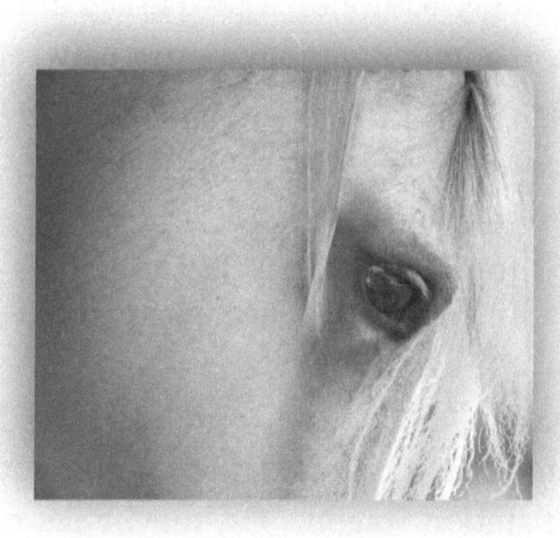

Chapter XXIII

Lori:
X-rays

Finally they were in the car and on the road. The continuing overcast skies matched Lori's dark and tail-spinning mood. She'd spent two days in the futile hope that her husband cared enough about her to at least come and talk with her. But he did not.

Her soul searching and troubled contemplations took her away from even superficial niceties with Dawn, which, when she thought of it, made her even more upset.

"Are you angry with me?" Dawn asked after they traveled for fifteen minutes without a word between them.

Lori glanced over at her. "No, dear. You're the very last person I'd be angry with. I'm mostly angry with myself."

"Really? But why, Lori, why are you angry with yourself? I can't imagine any reason why you'd be mad at yourself."

"It's ... complicated. Very complicated." She pulled into the center lane, gunned the engine and passed a family-filled station wagon. "Or, maybe it's not so complicated. I'm mad because, because I married Nathan. I'm mad at myself for not seeing that we are not a match. What was I thinking? And that's what I've been thinking the last two days, holed up in that little room, not even talking to you. Which is shameful. You don't deserve that sort of treatment."

"I did miss you," Dawn said. "But I didn't want to bother you. I thought, 'Lori needs time to herself. She's thinking about some things and she needs to be left alone.'"

"That's pretty accurate. But, still, I apologize for neglecting you."

"I don't mind, as long as it's not about me. Because if you were mad at me, I would want you to talk with me. I wouldn't want you to hide away." Dawn paused, then continued quietly, "Humans have a very difficult time communicating, it seems to me."

"Yeah, you got that right," Lori agreed.

"But Lori ...."

"Yes?"

"I want to say something, but I'm afraid to. Maybe it will make you really mad at me."

"Oh, well, I'm pretty much mad at everyone, so you might as well jump on the list."

"I don't want to be on the list, but I do want to say that, ahm, it feels to me like Nathan loves you. And what if it's not that he doesn't love you, but that he feels sort of like I have been feeling. That you need to be alone, that he doesn't want to bother you. That he's respecting you. Not neglecting you."

Lori took her eyes off the road for a lengthy moment, studying Dawn. "How do you come up with this stuff? You're just a kid."

"Well, Lori, age is subjective. One creature's short year is another's entire lifetime."

"Wait a minute, I have to pull over and write these wisdoms of yours down." She chuckled softly. "All right, you've succeeded in getting me to shift my mood. And—I'll give what you've said serious consideration. I need to set the bad frame of mind aside for now, and enjoy our day. Well, right after we get this onerous chore out of the way with 'Dr. Baduna.'"

They'd entered the parking lot of a down-at-the-heels strip mall. "Seems like an unlikely place for a ... oh, there it is." Lori pointed to a sign over a doorway: "Radiology, Dr. Charles Baduna."

She parked in front of the office, in a row of empty parking spaces. "Busy office," she said with a quiet note of sarcasm. "All right, let's get this over with."

"Yes," Dawn whispered.

Lori watched as Dawn unwillingly dragged herself out of the car.

"It'll be all right," Lori reassured, not convinced herself. There was something, though it was entirely unremarkable in every way, there was something about the front of the office that made her uneasy.

"I don't like it. It feels not nice," Dawn said.

"I'm having the same thought." Lori took Dawn's hand. "I've got you, you're safe with me."

"I know, Lori." She hung on tightly to Lori's hand.

They stepped through the door, and there, not four feet away, was a very tall, somewhat stoop-shouldered man, with a long and narrow, bald head. He appeared to hover over them. Lori tried to take a step back, but, as she stood at the door, there was nowhere to step back to.

"We're here for our nine a.m. appointment with Dr. Baduna."

"Yes. You're Lori Tanner, and this is your young charge, Dawn. I'm Dr. Baduna." His soft tone of voice seemed strained, as if he meant to keep it modulated, but as if it might break its bonds at any moment.

He came up to them, extending his hand to Lori, while giving Dawn an intense study.

Lori unwillingly briefly shook his hand, which, though huge, was peculiarly too soft for such a large man, and clammy-cold.

"I've been looking forward to your arrival. Please forgive the lack of staff. I generally only do radiology work on Wednesdays. But, to suit your schedule, I made an exception."

Puzzled, Lori began to protest, not having requested any special scheduling, as it was his assistant who made the appointment, according to Dr. Baduna's schedule. "I didn't ...."

"That's all right, I understand perfectly. Let's get started, shall we?" he said in his odd, too-soft, edgy voice. "Mrs. Tanner, why not wait here in my waiting area? Lots of magazines to occupy yourself with, while Dawn and I take some pictures."

"No, thanks. I'll come right along with Dawn."

"No need."

"Nevertheless ...."

"As you please." Dr Baduna led them through a doorway and closed the door behind them. "To your right."

The hall was nearly dark, and cold. Lori shivered. Dawn leaned into Lori and whispered, "It's cold!"

"*Ummmm,*" Lori agreed, her radar on full alert.

They stepped into a small, dimly-lit, room. Dr. Baduna handed Dawn a hospital gown. "Disrobe and slip this on, and then we'll take some pictures, all righty?" His voice went from tense to creepy. "I'll be in the next room, setting up the x-rays. Call me when you're ready."

Much to Lori's shock, he ran his hands along Dawn's shoulder blades, and down her spine. Dawn jumped nearly out of her skin.

"What was that?" Lori demanded.

"Not to worry. I'm a doctor. My main concern is with her spine. I just did a perfunctory spinal check."

"You might say something first. And further, Dawn needn't change into a hospital gown. She's in clothing that does not interfere with x-rays."

"Still, it is my standard procedure that all patients have their radiology exams in a hospital gown."

"I see," Lori said, as if she acquiesced.

"Very good. Just give me a few minutes to get set up." He stepped from the tiny, dark, disconcerting room.

Lori put her finger to her lips and grabbed Dawn's hand. She opened the door and peered into the hall. Then with Dawn in tow, she scurried out of the room, down the hall, through the door, across the waiting room, and out the front door. They jumped into the car, and were tearing from the parking lot when Dr. Baduna poked his giant head out the front door.

As they both shrieked with nervous giggles, Lori pulled onto the main road. "What was I thinking? Blindly doing what someone told me to do, completely against my intuition. I must be crazy."

"You're not crazy, Lori. You trusted someone who does not deserve your trust. And you figured it out."

"Better late than never, I guess. I mean, if I had even a tiny reason to think you need x-rays, which a person ought not be subjected to without good reason, why would I go to someone I've never met? We have a perfectly fine radiologist at the hospital. Bones get broken on a ranch. I must be sleep walking."

"You've had a lot on your mind. I'm a pretty big distraction, I think."

Lori chuckled nervously. "That's true, dear Dawn. But an extremely pleasant distraction." Then she shuddered. "He ...."

"Dr. Baduna is bad," Dawn said. "*Euh!* When he touched me, it went right through me."

"Yes. Me too, it's as if I felt him touch you. Creepy."

"I wonder what Little Blue would have done if I had him with me."

"Oh! I didn't even notice. Why don't you have your little horse with you?"

"I didn't want to do anything that might upset you. I left him at home. He made a noise when I told him I was leaving him there. Maybe he knew we were going to do something scary."

"Well, you needn't ever leave him again, Dawn, because of me, or anyone else. He's yours and you may do as you please. Goodness, you make me feel guilty. Don't let me scare you. Don't let anyone scare you."

"Except, Dr. Baduna. And Beau."

"*Oh dear!*" Lori shook her head in dismay. "I'm not sure you're all that safe in my care." She sighed, then shook her head again. "We have to change this mood. Let's get you out of those awful sweats and into some new clothes."

"I like the sweats, they feel nice. And ... and ...."

"I know, you don't want to go back to *Cyber-Style*. We won't. We won't even go to the mall. We'll go to my favorite little shop, right here."

Lori pulled into the parking lot of an exclusive shop. The frame of the wide, Victorian, bay window was painted a dark forest green and made up of little panes of glass, each catching the rays of the sun breaking through the days of clouds and rain. The wooden shingles on the facade of the shop added to its charm. A sign, "*Victorian Ladies*," hung over the pale green door.

"Oh! It's sweet looking, Lori. I could live here."

Lori laughed. "We'll have to ask the shopkeeper if she would mind a little mouse by the name of Dawn living in her shop. Let's see what we can find that you like as much as dreary grey sweats."

Inside, Lori watched Dawn as she took in the beautiful clothing, accessories, jewelry, and knick-knacks. "It smells lovely, like a field I once was in," Dawn said.

"It's lavender." Lori held up a bar of soap. "Is this what you smell?"

"Oh! Yes! I would like to have that by me."

"You can have it *on* you. I'll get you this soap, and you can take a bath with it, and I'll get you this little lavender scented candle, you can burn it, and I'll get you this body splash," she spritzed Dawn with the sampler, and Dawn giggled.

"That's beautiful!"

But Lori noticed she looked as if she would cry. "What's wrong, Dawn?"

"It reminds me of my ... of someone. But I don't want to talk about it now."

"No. We won't. Should I put these things back? Is it too painful?"

"No. It's sad-happy. I want them. I'm here, now, in this moment, with you, and we're making new, happy, memories." Changing the subject, Dawn stroked the fabric Lori held draped over her arm. "I like this very much. Isn't it pretty?"

"This plaid? You like it? I'm getting this pleated plaid wool skirt for myself, but if you like plaid, we can find something for you. Wool keeps you nice and warm when the weather turns cold, in the fall."

"It's very nice, the way the colors all cross one another and make other colors."

While Lori found a couple skirts for Dawn to try on, Dawn looked around on her own. Lori heard the shopkeeper and the two other women who were shopping, exclaiming.

"Oh, my, that is the color for you!" the shopkeeper declared. "Not everyone can wear it, but you! You're a princess, you're *royalty* in it."

"Yes, yes, quite stunning," the two women agreed.

Lori felt the shopkeeper was pouring it on a bit thick. She went around to the three-way mirror, where stood the original and three replicas of Dawn.

"*Wow!*" she whispered, taking in the extraordinary beauty of Dawn in a peacock blue, silk shirt, a color so intense it seemed nearly dimensional. "She's right, it's as if that color was special ordered, just for you. It's a show stopper."

"Well," Dawn turned shyly to Lori, "I very much like the color, but I don't want to stop a show, or anything like that."

"It's just a saying, dear. It'll be interesting to see what Madame Colette thinks of it."

"Madame Colette!" the shopkeeper declared. "Are you studying with Madame Colette?"

"She's just begun, but she has a rare talent."

"That goes without saying." The shopkeeper nodded. "Madame Colette is very fussy about who she works with." She turned her radiant smile to Dawn. "One day I may see you on the stage. And it wouldn't surprise me if you'll be wearing this color! I can say I knew you when!"

"When what?" Dawn asked.

The shopkeeper and Lori tittered.

"When you were on your way to becoming a star! You have the look, the carriage, everything! And I was the first to put you in your signature color!" the shop-keeper said.

"We won't forget you," Lori laughed, thinking that what the friendly little woman had just said may be prophetic.

They gathered their purchases, and when they got in the car, Lori pulled out her phone and entered a note. "Send a ticket to the shopkeeper at *Victorian Ladies* when Dawn has her first solo performance."

*   *

*J*ust as they arrived at Madame Colette's, the sun finally came out. The streets sparkled with the cleansing rains. Lori looked forward to seeing, and breathing in, Madame Colette's wonderful garden.

She parked near the wrought iron gate, just as the ever-present little girls exited. Lori and Dawn waited for them and their young mothers to leave, then made their way through the wrought iron gate, through the dark door, into the colorful, aromatic garden, and across the garden to the winding wrought iron stairway. For the first time, Dawn insisted on following behind Lori.

"Why?" Lori asked.

Dawn gestured to herself. "What if she doesn't like me in this color?"

"Well, that'll be just too bad! If *you* like it, that's all that matters."

"No. What Madame Colette thinks also matters. What you think, also matters."

"Come on, then, let's see what she thinks." Lori opened the door to the big studio. Madame Colette stood in the middle of the room, appearing to be deep in thought.

"Ah! There you are! I had some strange alarms going off in the previous class. I was meditating on the two of you ... Where's Dawn?" she asked, with consternation.

"She's right behind me. But your alarms were not wrong ...."

"Ah!" Madame Colette exclaimed, "That color!"

"Oh, no," Dawn cowered.

"That ... *that color!* On you! How did you know to wear that color?"

"The ... the shopkeeper told me to try it on."

"I'll kiss her forehead if ever I meet her! Perfect! Beyond perfect." She led Dawn to the wall of mirrors. "Look darling. Look at your future. *Stunning!*"

"She was afraid you wouldn't like it," Lori said.

"Nonsense. I love it. Here you arrive in your color, today. Today! As I begin your true training. You see how everything works together as one's intentions become clear. And, so, shall we get to our work?"

"But, for just a moment, Madame Colette, if I may, I'd like to tell you what we've just been through—the reason you were worried," Lori said.

"Oh, yes. I want to know, yes. This incredible, silken peacock blue took my mind. Tell me what happened."

"To make a long story short, Edna, my former doctor, has been insisting that I take Dawn for x-rays, which I've been resisting, because, why? There's nothing wrong with her. But we went today to appease her, as she was making threatening noises about the police, and I feared Dawn would be taken away. So we went. I didn't feel right about the place ...."

"It had bad energy even from outside," Dawn interjected. "And inside, it was too cold. And he ... he was weird ...."

"Yes," Lori agreed, "Extremely weird. Creepy. He tried to pry Dawn away from me, but I stuck to her like a burr. He took us into a little room, and then, without preamble, he ... he touched Dawn. He ran his big, creepy hands up and down her back."

"He's bad. He touched me and even Lori felt his bad energy," Dawn shivered.

"Yes. So, when he stepped out of the room, I grabbed Dawn's hand and we scurried like little squirrels out of there."

"Well, that was it, then, yes," Madame Colette said. "That's what troubled me. Wise, Lori, to leave. It takes bravery to do as you did."

"If it had been just me, I would have probably simply gone through it. But when his creepy energy touched Dawn ... *no!* I would not allow it. I wish I knew why he and Edna have this abnormal interest in Dawn. She's a lovely, talented, sweet girl. What's up with this weird obsession?"

"You ask an important question, Lori. And I believe you'll have a good insight to the answer before long. But in the meantime, continue taking excellent care of Dawn, and be suspicious of *any*thing."

"Well, now you've scared me," Lori said, frowning, feeling confused.

"Don't be frightened. But you both do need to be vigilant!" Madame Colette glanced at the giant clock on the wall. "Well, now, my valiant and peacock blue young student, shall we do some actual dance training today?"

"I would love that," Dawn agreed.

*   *

While Lori waited she settled on the little settee in the corner and thumbed through a— *strange enough!*—Lori thought, horse magazine that happened to be sitting on the little round table by her. She came to a full page ad that pinned her to the spot. Big bold letters declared:

Cavalia!

With a picture of half a dozen of the most gorgeous pure white Arabian horses, with flowing manes and tails, she'd ever seen.

Gripped by the text, she couldn't believe what she read—a horse show *with dancers!* Horses performing dressage and western tricks and a breathtaking array of other performances, interlaced with the world's most talented gymnasts, horses and humans in a breathtaking array of costumes, touring in the biggest, most breath-taking, multi-spired, pennant-tipped tent ever made.

And, as if wonders would never cease, *Cavalia* was currently running in Seattle, for only a few more days. A plan began to hatch in Lori's mind as she got out her phone to peer at the tiny videos of the performance.

How incredible it would be to see this event *live*. She must see it, and surely Dawn would love it. And, as Nathan's whole life was horses, he would enjoy it too, she felt certain.

Wouldn't it be a wonderful way to bring the three of them together, to see this incomparable production, filled with everything they loved? Even with all the other events of the day, she'd been replaying what Dawn had said, that she believed Nathan loved her, and had only kept his distance from her the past two days out of respect for her need to sort things out.

Filled with anticipation, she called the *Cavalia!* number and reserved three seats for the Saturday evening performance. She felt a tiny bit guilty not to include Taffy and Mrs. Hinds, but the point was for the three of them to bond. For Nathan to get to know and love Dawn as she knew and loved Dawn. To bring herself and Nathan close again.

It must be just the three of them. Joy-filled, she couldn't wait to rekindle the love in her marriage that she'd spent long hours the last couple days believing was over.

She could do her part. She could reach out. Nathan would be there. He would respond. Surely Dawn was right. Surely Nathan loved her. Surely he would adore sitting next to her, at a show such as he'd never seen in his life, with his arm around the woman he loved—the woman who was still, for only a couple more weeks, as they approached their first anniversary, his bride.

After paying for the reserved tickets, she felt herself grinning nearly uncontrollably. She couldn't help it, but she'd have to get it under control, or Dawn would insist she give up her surprise.

Lori stepped out on the balcony, looked down at the garden as it glowed in the sparkling sunlight. *Beautiful!*

She followed the deep purple iris around in their pattern, then the pale, pale pink iris, then the daisies, then the gladiolas. And, suddenly, she saw it! The invisible pattern.

The garden housed a huge, silent "Om." The sound of creation. The sound from which flowers, and dance, and horses, and *everything* came into being. The sacred mantra.

She meditated with gratitude on the flowery, perfumed *Om* until Dawn and Madame Colette came out to join her.

She smiled as they came to stand by her. "*Ommmm,*" she intoned.

"Yes, Lori. *Om.* Very good!" Madame Colette patted Lori on the shoulder. "Well, I must be on to my next class." She stepped back inside.

Lori, in a glow of happiness and peace, put her arm around Dawn. "How was your lesson?"

"She *really* started me on my work. She said, 'we start from today,' and then, I worked so hard. But I must work my discipline, every day."

"Excellent! You can have any of the spare rooms you need upstairs, and we'll get some mirrors. I'm happy to hear that you have serious work to do."

"Ummm, well, yes, but at *this* moment, I feel overwhelmed, and ... rather stupid and awkward."

"Nonsense! You may be overwhelmed, but you're not one bit stupid nor awkward. Just think how much you have to look forward to!"

They moved from the balcony to the wrought iron stairs. Dawn started down the stairs, but looked back up at Lori with curiosity. "Do you know something I don't?"

"It's possible," Lori answered, grinning.

Chapter XXIV

Lori:
Cavalia!

On the drive home, Lori argued with herself whether to tell Nathan about *Cavalia* privately, or with everyone present.

She finally opted to spring it at the dinner table, because, well, she and Nathan weren't talking right now, and it would be very awkward to get him alone, get them both communicating, explain the show to him and break the news that it was in Seattle. He hated long drives, whereas Lori loved a road trip on occasion, looking out the window at the countryside, changing the environment, appreciating everything and nothing as it flowed by like a movie.

Her reverie was interrupted by her phone ringing. Glancing at the incoming call, she saw it was Edna. No surprise. She scrolled through her incoming calls while getting onto the highway.

"Edna has called me eight times in the last couple hours! I'm glad I left my phone in the car. That's just abusive."

"I didn't think she was strange when I first met her," Dawn said. "But I now think she's very strange. Or she's suddenly become strange."

"Always strange or newly strange, she must stop this abuse. I'm not going to call her now, I'm too irritated. And I don't want to call her when we get home, either, because I don't want her to ruin my mood. I'll just have to put a block on her calls."

"So she'll call the loud jang-ly phone on the wall and bother Mrs. Hinds."

"Oh, *growl!* You're absolutely right. Well, we'll be home shortly. I'm shutting off the phone for now. What a nuisance!"

"Yes. And a worry, too," Dawn said.

"I imagine she's harmless."

"And Dr. Baduna?"

"He does *not* feel harmless. He feels a bit crazy with some completely unfathomable agenda. *Creeeeeepy!*"

"*Creeeeeepy!*" Dawn imitated, and they both laughed.

*   *

They had a casual light supper around the kitchen table with Jude staying, at Mrs. Hinds' insistence. Taffy sat next to Dawn, across from Lori. Lori saw he understood how uncomfortable Dawn was when forced to sit by Jude, and she was perfectly happy to be left to sit by the companionable young man.

Skirting the whole subject of Dr. Baduna, Lori jabbered on about the shopkeeper having discovered Dawn's true signature color, making much more of a story than was there, and then she moved in for the climax. "And then, to top the whole day off, while I waited patiently for Dawn during her lesson, I thumbed through a magazine and happened to stumble upon the holy grail. **Cavalia!** Oh my goodness, the most amazing horse show complete with gymnasts and dancers. I looked at the video snippets on my phone. Amazing! *A-mazing!*"

"*Cavalia!*" Jude exclaimed. "Oh, yes, it's an astounding production!"

Lori turned to Jude. "Are you familiar with it?"

Blythe Ayne - 289

"Yes. My parents took me to see it years ago in Portland. It has never left my mind."

"Well, there you see, Nathan. An assessment from, almost, the horse's mouth!"

Jude chuckled, but, strangely, Mrs. Hinds and Taffy remained silent. Dawn looked confused.

"Those dog and pony shows are a dime a dozen," Nathan groused. "Wouldn't go to one if you paid me."

"Oh. No, Nathan," Lori protested. "This is something truly different. There are gymnasts and dancers, and amazingly trained horses ... and ... and ...."

Lori felt her face fall, she felt her mood shift, she felt herself fall through the floor of the house and sink to the center of the earth. Or maybe down and right out the other side, and float forever and ever in the space between stars, where all was darkness.

"It sounds lovely," Dawn said in a very small whisper. "It sounds quite lovely."

"Well, I bought three second row tickets, and, also paid for the privilege of getting to walk through the stables and chat with the horses and performers afterwards. Saturday night. I had in mind, Nathan that you and Dawn and I would go."

"Wouldn't go if you paid me," Nathan repeated firmly.

"Honestly, Nathan," Mrs. Hinds said, "If I could reach you, Nathan, I'd kick you in the shin as hard as I could right now."

"Let me do it for you," Taffy added.

"Well," Lori said, unable to disguise her hurt, "Dawn and I will be going. And, I believe we'll stay the weekend. You found me under a rock in Seattle, Nathan, and I suppose I can take my friend and crawl back under that rock for a night or two.

"But, wait." Lori turned to Jude. "Maybe you'd like to go with us."

"Oh, I wouldn't think of taking Nathan's ticket."

"He just said I couldn't pay him to go. You wouldn't expect me to pay you to go, would you?"

"Most certainly not," Jude protested.

"It's settled then," Lori proclaimed. "Saturday, I'll pick you up at your place, Jude. I want to leave early and maybe get a lunch at my favorite little hole in the wall, and say hi to a couple friends I've essentially abandoned to be brought here between the villages of 'No' and 'Where.'

"Lovely supper, Mrs. Hinds, I enjoyed it immensely. But it's been an unusually long day, and I'm wiped out. If you'll excuse me." Before anyone could say anything, she stood and went up to her little room, down the hall from Dawn's.

Then she quietly cried herself to sleep.

*   *

Saturday couldn't come fast enough for Lori. She itched to be in Seattle, to see the skyline, to go to a couple of her old haunts, maybe see some of her neglected friends. Well, she finally argued with herself, she'd have to reel in some of those numerous plans. Also, Jude had taken her aside to tell her he would not be able to stay overnight in Seattle as he had committed himself to dog sit the neighbor's three dogs on Sunday.

"As much as I really would like to go, I'm afraid I can't if you're staying over," he said, conspicuously unhappy.

"Naa," Lori reassured him, "we're not staying over. It's too complicated on such short notice, don't worry about it, Jude. We'll have a great day."

"I hope so, Lori, but, you know, there's this other ... issue."

"What's that?"

"That Dawn doesn't like me."

"That's not true. She's just too shy for words."

"She doesn't seem 'shy' with anyone else."

"No one else around here is her age. Look, I'll let you drive on the way to Seattle and I'll sit in the front with you. Then Dawn can entertain herself in the back, and I think she'll relax. The thing is, we don't really know anything about her. Maybe she's never been around boys her age. Just go with us and enjoy yourself. It's not your job to make anyone else happy."

"That's what my mother always says to me. I guess it shows."

"Yes, it does. Anyway, you make Nathan, and Taffy very, *very* happy. And thus your 'make others happy' assignment is fulfilled."

Jude laughed. "If you say so. I really am looking forward to seeing *Cavalia* again. You sit there trying to take it in and you become awash with pixie dust or something. I was just a little kid, but I recall going into, like, a trance. It seemed like I became one with the horses and dancers. I wanted to see it again right away. I begged my folks to let me, but they said no. This really is like an almost mystical, amazing, wish fulfillment."

"I'm delighted to hear it, Jude. You're so helpful to Taffy and Nathan, it makes me happy to give you this gift of *Cavalia*. All right now, back to work with you."

After that chat, while Dawn hid out in her room trying to avoid Jude, Lori guessed, she went up to the master bedroom and filled a backpack and a suitcase with as much as they could hold and took them to her little room down the hall.

Then, in the middle of the night, she slipped down to the garage and put them in the trunk of her car. Upon returning to her little room she wrote a rather long letter, which she placed on the dresser, knowing no one would discover it before Sunday.

*　*

Saturday arrived with a fanfare of brilliant sunshine, and a delicate breeze that danced the shadows of oak leaves across the yard and into all the rooms.

Lori stopped by Dawn's room. "Are you ready for a fantastic day?"

"Ahm, yes. Sort of."

"Are you taking Blue?"

"I thought I would."

"Good! Run down and have some breakfast, I want to get on the road."

"All right," Dawn said, less than joyful.

"Don't kill yourself with happiness."

"I'm not."

Lori sat down beside Dawn on her bed. "I'll have Jude drive, and I'll sit in the front with him. Then you'll have the back seat all to yourself and Little Blue. You won't have to think of a single thing to say. You know I've got plenty to chatter on about, and Jude will be occupied with driving. How does that sound?"

Dawn perked up. "It sounds much better than the pictures I've been making."

"Good! Let's get at it."

"All right ... Boss."

"Funny." Lori watched Dawn as she went down the hall.

Dawn turned at the landing to glance back at Lori. "Aren't you coming?"

"I'll be there in a minute. I forgot something." She turned as if to go back to her room, and when she saw Dawn go down the stairs, she went into Dawn's room with a small satchel and gathered up a few items from her closet, bathroom and dresser drawers, then stuffed the satchel in her over-sized shoulder bag and went downstairs.

Mrs. Hinds had packed a few snacks and beverages in a little cooler for the road. Lori took it out to the car with her shoulder bag, stuffing them in the trunk with everything else. Then she went back inside, grabbed a slice of toast and hovered over Dawn as she finished her toast.

"All right, all right, let's go!" Finally, they were in the car. They waved at Mrs. Hinds, who watched them from the kitchen window as they left. They soon arrived at Jude's home, who stood waiting for them on the front porch, carrying a knapsack of his own. "Shall I stick this in the trunk?" he asked when Lori pulled up.

"Just throw it in the back with Dawn, there's plenty of room. I need to fill up the tank, and then, I'll turn the wheel over to you."

"Okay." He opened the back door and put his knapsack on the seat beside Dawn. "Hey, Dawn."

"Hi,'" Dawn said quietly, looking down.

Jude jumped into the passenger seat, and soon Lori stopped to fill the tank. She had Jude take over the driving, and they were finally on the road. Before long, they were singing silly songs—at least Lori and Jude were, as, to their surprise, Dawn didn't know any of them.

Lori's heart leapt when Seattle finally came into view. Had she missed it? Apparently, she told herself, given her bodily reaction. "Okay, Jude, you'd better let me take over. It's not the easiest city to navigate."

"I know," Jude said. "I've tried."

He pulled into a rest area, and they switched seats. Before long Lori drove into her old neighborhood, looking for her favorite haunts. But everything appeared different. Even things that were the same, were, somehow, different.

A bit shocked, she couldn't see herself fitting back into her previous life.

"Oh dear," she muttered, driving past the hole in the wall she'd been saying she couldn't wait to go to. "It looks like my favorite place is no longer here." Almost a lie, as it *was* there, but it didn't *seem* the same.

She drove to a little park nearby and stopped. "Good thing Mrs. Hinds packed those goodies, we can make a lunch of it."

They sat under big, old, friendly trees, whispering overhead in an off-the-Elliot Bay-breeze. Lori smiled as Dawn dared to engage in a bit of aimless chit-chat with Jude about the trees, the park, the view of the bay, and the ships on the water.

I could stay here forever. Lori thought, with these two beautiful, kind-hearted young people. She let her mind float away on the thought, when, all of a sudden,

Dawn was calling to her, and she discovered she'd fallen fast asleep in the warmth of the day and the gentle conversation between Jude and Dawn.

"I fell asleep!"

"Like a log," Jude noted.

"Goodness! Well, I've slept poorly the last few nights. Let's get to our destination! Horses and dancers!" Lori jumped up.

"Tricks and music," Dawn chirped.

"The biggest tent in the world!" Jude intoned, sweeping his arm to display the imaginary tent.

"Let's get to the real one!" Lori directed.

*   *

Soon, they stood beneath the most amazing tent any of them had ever seen, except Jude had seen it before. It seemed beyond imagining.

"I feel too tiny," Dawn said, looking up and up.

"Me too," Lori said in a little mouse voice, making Dawn and Jude giggle.

They passed along a walkway with gigantic pictures of beautiful people and horses, performing amazing feats.

Dawn suddenly grabbed Lori's hand, tense.

"What's the matter, sweetie?"

"I don't know. I ... I'm ... there's a feeling ... I'm ... it's too much ...."

"It'll be all right."

Jude looked at Dawn with concern, but said nothing. Inside they were taken to their seats. Lori insisted Dawn sit between the two of them, with Jude on the aisle.

Chapter XXV

Dawn:
On with the Show

I tried to understand the weird feelings rushing though me, but they were happening too rapidly. I began to wonder if I wasn't about to go through another transmogrification, right here among thousands of people.

Probably, though, I reasoned, it was the proximity of so many horses. They had deep memory, and perhaps *they sensed me!*

Would I distract them from their performance? It could be dangerous to performers and horses alike if the horses were distracted.

Sandwiched now, in the second row from the stage, between Lori and Jude, there wasn't much I could do. I tried to focus on the happy frame of mind I felt when Lori talked about *Cavalia!*—about the dancers with horses. Could anything be more beautiful or wonderful to see?

I would sit quietly, and watch and learn and enjoy, I told myself. That's all. Nothing more. Nothing less.

Finally, darkness and silence fell upon the audience. Then, slowly, softly, lights came up on the stage. The light was just like dawn. Through translucent curtains waving slightly like a breeze, I saw trees and grasses. Then horses wandered out onto the stage, so like a meadow. The horses were unbridled, unsaddled, just like the cayuse herd, just like my own, true family.

I clutched my hands together, making a tight fist in my lap. It was so beautiful! It was so difficult! Oh, if only Lori knew the turmoil in me, she'd understand.

The curtain slid aside and the lights came up on the stunning, astounding, gorgeous, brilliant horses. Palominos, quarter horses, sleek Arabians, all perfect in form. Then the performers began to come out, moving among the horses. It looked random, but I could see that each horse and every person knew their place. Everyone had a part in the dance.

Slowly a few of the horses began to canter, their people ran alongside them. They ran faster and faster. Then, up onto the horses the beautiful men and women leapt, graceful as grasses bending in the wind, sleek as clouds slipping from the moon.

"Oh," I whispered. "*Oh!*"

Lori reached over to take my hand, and discovered my tight, held together fingers, filled with tension.

She leaned close to me, "Relax, sweetie. They know what they're doing. Don't worry about them."

"Yes," was all I could say, forcing my hands to part and relax, even if they did not feel relaxed.

The lights came up slowly, slowly, in shades of orange and pink and lavender, just like early morning among the hills of home.

Oh, these humans were truly clever to produce this, so real, inside this tent. What was before me was bigger than the entire tent from the outside. I had no idea how they created that illusion.

Then I really did relax, realizing that the horses were professional. They not only knew exactly what they were doing, but they loved their people, and their people truly loved them. All they wanted was to give their ultimate best, their hearts opening, and opening yet further, as the audience went wild, clapping and cheering. The whole tent filled with happiness, welling up to the very peaks of the tent, flowing outside to all the world. I felt this crescendo of emotion like nothing I'd ever felt in my life.

The running, unbridled, unsaddled horses ran away off into the distance—*somehow!* becoming smaller as if at a great distance.

Then dancers came floating and running onto the stage, and leapt up onto colorful yet unreal horses that moved up and down, and around and around in a circle. The people did impossible things with their bodies such that, I wondered if they were Eos. They hung impossibly long in the air and twirled hundreds of times.

I sat transfixed. Could I, one day, do this? Could I make happiness for thousands of people, every day? There was *nothing* I'd rather do, than create this suspension from the sadness and woes of life, in this mystical space.

I relaxed yet more. As my tension left, my joy rose, and I felt my calling—to, perhaps, one day, be Eos in *Cavalia!*

Just as I felt better and more relaxed, out ran a small paint horse. He didn't look quite as perfect as the other horses. He didn't quite do as the other horses did. He didn't quite follow his person's movements.

Everything crashed in an instant. The little paint—*so like Blue.*

"Blue," I muttered. "Blue." I found myself gasping. *I couldn't breathe!* I thrashed and cried. *I couldn't breathe!*

Lori and Jude exchanged a worried look, and each of them took one of my hands. "Relax, Dawn, relax, dear," Lori whispered.

"*Niii* …. I tried to be quiet, but it wouldn't stop. "*Nii-ii!* Can't… breathe … *can't breathe*… Out … outside … Out, Lori, out …."

"Yes, yes, of course, Dawn, dear, of course. Jude stay here."

They stood and helped me stand. With her arm around me, Lori rushed me outdoors. The fresh evening air calmed me, and I began to breathe normally. "*Couldn't breathe!*"

"A panic attack, Dawn. A panic attack. You were hyperventilating. I'm sorry, I should have brought you outside sooner."

"Not your fault, Lori. You couldn't know. I just … couldn't breathe!"

"Let's sit here at this little table."

We sat and Lori patted my hand. "Can you tell me what set this off—this panic attack?"

"I *can* tell you. I mean, I know. But I don't think you'll believe me. I don't know if I ought to."

"Well, I think you must try. I need to know what would bring on such a serious reaction. Is it something you saw? Are we too close to the stage? Are you afraid of the horses? Are they too close to you? We can sit farther away."

"No, Lori, I love being close to the horses. Oh, I'm *so sorry*, you're missing the show, and poor Jude, he can't pay attention to it, with me having some weird fit out here."

"But we must know what your trigger is," Lori insisted.

"Then I will tell you. My trigger was that little paint, the one who didn't quite do what the others did, the one who didn't look quite like the others. He's like Blue, a little, scruffy cayuse paint. Blue. *Blue.*"

"You mean, your little stuffed horse?"

"No, I mean Blue, my brother, my full brother, Blue, a paint cayuse. We have the same mother and father. Except I'm Eos. Only females may be Eos. You met Blue, that first night in the paddock."

"I. Have. No. Idea. What. You. Are. Saying." Lori looked stunned and lost at me.

"I am Eos. I am Dawn. I am the dawn horse. I am of deep memory, I am of the tribe that, for eons—long before the dawn of human history—keeps life on Earth in balance through deep memory.

"Eos, when in horse form, has deep memory. Eos, when in human form, has work to do among humans to keep them in balance, because they do not have deep memory. Without deep memory, destruction is the result.

"Little Blue, my stuffed horse, became inhabited with the soul energy of my twin brother, the living Blue. When that little paint came onto the stage in the show just now—I couldn't handle it. *Too much!* Lori, it was too much. He reminded me of Blue, and I've gone through so much, it's impossible to tell you."

Lori shook her head. "Are you saying that ... did you say that ... are you trying to make me believe ... you are *sometimes a horse?!?!?*"

"Not sometimes. I was a horse, now I'm human. I'm Eos. I cannot become horse again except on solstice, or, perhaps, if urgently necessary, on equinox. I was the palomino that Nathan captured. You came out and saw me, and petted me. Then, that night, I transformed. And with these," I fluttered my hands, "I released Blue and my near brothers."

"Dawn, I can't take this in. You know, I really have to say, you seem sane, but this is crazy."

"I know, Lori. *I do know that.* Which is why I've not told you. But Madame Colette said the moment would arrive, and I would not be able to avoid it. And she was right. Right here, right now, with several thousand people."

"Madame Colette? You've told her about this ... this belief of yours?"

"I didn't have to tell her about it. She knew, when she saw me move."

"Yes," Lori said. "I heard her say it, and it was the second time that very day. But I had no idea what it was."

"There are no accidents, Lori. I was drawn to you, because you will care for me. You, almost immediately, got me to Madame Colette, another Eos. There's much I don't know, which is not usual. Most Eos have a teacher, but mine ... I lost mine very young.

"But, Lori, I feel so, *so* much better now. I needed to tell you. It was making me ill, keeping that secret from you. Now you know I'm Eos."

"I don't know what I know," Lori said. "But, if you feel you're over your panic attack, I would like to go back in, mostly, at this moment, for Jude's sake."

"Of course." I took Lori by the hand, and we returned to our seats. Although everyone around us gave us uncomfortable sidelong glances, Jude practically jumped up and down for joy to see us.

"Are you all right?" he whispered to me.

"Yes. I ... I'm fine. Watch the beautiful creatures, Jude. I'm *so sorry* to have interrupted your experience."

"Don't worry about that, Dawn, just as long as you're all right," Jude whispered in my ear.

After the show, and after repeated curtain calls, Lori and Jude and I made our way to the VIP tent. We were taken, with a number of other members of the audience who paid for the privilege, to meet a few of the performers, both equine and human.

Performers and audience were in awe when the little paint horse practically dragged his keeper over to me. When he reached me, he buried his head in my shoulder. His keeper tried to constrain him, but there was no dissuading the little horse.

"I'm sorry, miss," he said with a lovely rich French accent, "my horse may be small, but he is very strong willed."

"It's all right!" I hugged the little paint and whispered something in his ear. He made a soft response and nodded.

"*Ohhhh!*" everyone chorused, including the performers.

"What did you say to him?" one of the performers asked.

"I asked him to send a small but important message to another paint I know, and, of course, he
agreed."

Chapter XXVI

Lori:
Madame Colette

fter *Cavalia!* Lori drove, as Jude insisted that Dawn sit in front with her. Lori and Jude were very solicitous of her, though she protested that she was fine, and they were not to worry about her.

Before long, both Dawn and Jude were sound asleep. Lori couldn't blame them. It had been a long, intense, day. But a good day despite Dawn's strange fit. And she'd also gotten over her painful awkwardness around Jude. It looked like they might even become friends.

Of course, with Lori's current, and so far unrevealed plan, they would not have as much opportunity to grow that friendship. But that was not Lori's biggest concern of the moment.

Her biggest concern was where she and Dawn would stay tonight after she dropped Jude off, as the one thing she was certain of, she was not spending the night in Nathan's house where she no longer felt comfortable. Or welcome. Or happy.

Nathan had never shown this unattractive inflexibility when they first met in Seattle at a horse tack show, where Lori in a sparkling evening gown was a model showing off diamond studded bridles—the last thing in the world Nathan would buy, while Lori, herself, at the time, hardly knew a bit from a stirrup.

But she'd caught Nathan's eye, and Nathan had caught her eye. Oh, to get out of the rat-race of modeling, she'd thought at the time. Well, she wouldn't get back in it now, unhappy as she was to discover that Seattle did not strike the cord with her that it used to. After today, she realized, she did not want to live there again.

Yes, it was a fabulous place to visit. She loved it as she loved no other city. She just didn't love *cities* enough to live in one anymore.

These contemplations, she told herself, needed to be sorted through at another time. She had a much more urgent concern at the moment. Where, besides the car in a rest area, would she and Dawn spend the night?

She could, of course, check into a hotel. But she feared spending money when she wasn't sure what she actually had access to. As mean and distant as Nathan had been of late, she could imagine him trying to cut her off. She knew enough about the law to know he wouldn't win that round in the state of Washington, but he could make it difficult for her in the immediate future.

The shock of this thought settled on her. Where had their love gone? She remembered it, when it was new, two years ago. When they talked of their amazement, finding love in a world of alienation and greed. But, in the last year of marriage, little by little, they'd grown apart. Lori was sure it was mostly on Nathan's side, who seemed half the time to not even be aware of her presence, let alone suggest that they *do* something together. Or even have an interesting conversation.

And now, with the sudden appearance of Dawn in their midst, it caused everything that was not good, rumbling and stirring about in the basement of their faulted relationship, to come flying up to the surface. Tension, poor communication, criticism, frustration, exasperation, clashing of wills—and all those problems' cousins and siblings, swirling around their relationship, finally became unavoidable.

In addition, Lori reasoned, Dawn really needed her, and Nathan … really didn't. Lori weighed the challenges of one against the losses of the other. Again, Dawn won. Dawn was no challenge at all. Well, until tonight. But setting Dawn's peculiar story aside for the moment—which she *really* could not deal with right now—Dawn was no challenge. While not having Dawn in her life felt like a huge loss.

Meanwhile, Nathan was a daily challenge, causing her to feel tense and unloved. But pragmatically, the loss of physical comfort and luxury that would be the result of a divorce would be an additional—and huge—challenge.

Another loss would be Taffy, and to a slightly lesser degree, Mrs. Hinds. Yes, those two people she now considered friends, though they probably did not reciprocate the thought, would be a painful loss.

Lori arrived at Jude's home before coming to a solution about her own night's lodging.

Sleepily, he climbed out of the car. "Goodnight, Lori. Thank you so much for a really super-wonderful day. I'll never forget it. I mean that in a good way."

"I'm glad to hear it. Off to bed with you now. You've been sleeping for an hour, and it's past your bedtime."

Jude laughed. "I can't believe I fell asleep with two such fascinating people to talk with."

"Thank you, sweetie, although Dawn fell asleep before you did."

"True." He tipped an imaginary hat and hurried into his home. It looked so cozy and inviting.

Lori, far beyond exhausted, was sorely tempted to simply go back to the ranch and up to her little room, where it was safe. Not so much cozy and not so much inviting, with all the tension between herself and Nathan, but surely safe and warm.

Dawn stirred, half-awake. "Good night Jude," she said.

"He's in his home now, little horse-girl. Go back to sleep."

"Is he?" She reached out for Little Blue, in his shoulder bag on the seat beside her. "All right. Having a *wonderful* dream of running with my herd."

"That's nice, Dawn. Why don't you go back to it?"

"I think I ...."

Lori drove around for a while, but as she, too, began to drift into sleep, she knew she must park somewhere. The only place that came to mind was the block owned by Madame Colette. Not a very savory part of town, but Lori had become used to it, and what had before caused her to be hyper-vigilant didn't even bother her now. There was protection from Madame Colette's energy, and the giant soundless flower *Om* behind the wrought iron gate held for her an unseen, but peacefully felt, presence.

Although, on another hand, it was late Saturday night and the bars were still open—she ought to think twice about sleeping in her car in a neighborhood replete with rowdy night spots.

However, she soon parked in front of the wrought iron gate and pulled the comforter she'd put in the back seat over herself and Dawn. She covered Dawn's bright blonde hair that caught the weak streetlight like a spotlight.

Then she tried to relax.

But she could not. Too much to think about. She didn't even want to run through her mind this "Eos" thing. Not right now. She didn't know enough to make progress with her thoughts. She'd just run in circles, and she needed to fix her attention on her own life. On her failed marriage. On her failed self. She had nothing to fall back on. Not like Dawn, with her unnatural ability to move. The only "talent" she had was physical beauty, and that had a shelf life that the timer ticked away on.

She had no family. In that regard, she and Dawn shared plenty. In that regard, they needed each other.

But even there, Dawn had already, thanks to Lori, established a close tie with someone. A relationship that, candidly, did not include Lori.

Would it really, she asked herself, be so awful to continue living with Nathan? She had luxury, three squares a day, interesting chit-chat with the help. And she could get involved in some civic volunteering. Like bored housewives did. Nathan had not set his foot down firmly that Dawn must leave, and so, it was a good safe-haven for her, as well.

But, in a word, no.

No. She would not live a loveless marriage. What was the point? She had seen too many people in their loveless relationships, living loveless lives, becoming crotchety, angry that the love had fled when, perhaps, *they* ought to have fled.

She didn't believe in walking away from a marriage for small slights. But staying in the sham of a marriage where she was not civilly addressed was not good for anyone.

With these disturbing and unresolved thoughts, Lori had almost managed to fall asleep when Dawn jumped up, wide awake. She threw the comforter off her.

"Where are we? We should be home by now." She spied the wrought iron gate. "*Ahhh-iiii-eee! What* are you doing here? You don't have to talk with Madame Colette *right now* about Eos."

"No, I don't, Dawn. That's not why I'm here. I'm here because I simply couldn't imagine another place to park for a few hours, as I must sleep. More to the point, I'm not going back to Nathan. I have left him. The trunk is full of our belongings, and, as of the moment we left the driveway of the Tanner Ranch this morning, we've been wandering around homeless."

"No, Lori, no! This isn't right. You need to go home. You and Nathan will fix it. Love gets wounded, but it needn't break."

"I know this is hard on you, Dawn."

"Hard on me? I'm not even thinking about me. I'm thinking about you. About ... about your best friend, Taffy."

"Taffy's not ...."

"Yes, he is, Lori, and you know it. And you're becoming friends with Mrs. Hinds, and your oak trees, and even your friendship with Jude. Oh, no, he'll be so hurt. If you leave tonight, like this, he'll always have that in his memory. You'll ruin this beautiful day forever in his memory."

"No it won't," Lori protested. "He'll understand. He was there when Nathan dealt the final blow. Jude made the day great for you and me by being a real man and a real friend, when Nathan just behaved insensitively and like a spoiled child. I'm so tired of it. Of him, Dawn. I really am. I deserve to be treated better. And I want to role model self-respect for you, too. I want you to know it's not okay to tolerate being neglected, criticized ...."

"Nathan doesn't criticize you!"

"He does, when you don't hear him. And he does, by not accepting you. By fighting with me about you. By being silly and jealous, and again, childish about you. It's extremely unattractive, Dawn. A love relationship is complicated, but one of the first things that made me take notice of Nathan, and made him stand out in a sea of men, literally at that horse accessories show the day I first saw him, was his sure sense of self. Or that's how it seemed, but it's a false facade.

"Anyway, I'm very sorry, but that's why we're in the car, not in beds."

"All right then, here we are. But why are you sitting in the car? Why didn't you go in and talk with Madame Colette?"

"Because it's almost one a.m. I had thought to go to a motel, as much as I hate them, but I really don't know how much money I have, and I must be frugal until I see how I can support us."

"Oh, dear," Dawn cried. "Couldn't you have waited to do this until I'm able to make some money?"

"Goodness, Dawn, that thought never crossed my mind."

"I think we ought to go in and talk with Madame Colette."

"It's too late, Dawn."

"But she said I could come to her, any time, day or night, if I ever needed to."

"Really? Well, that's very sweet of her. But I doubt she meant right away in less than a week, coming in the middle of the night, and oh yes, by the way, dragging someone else along with you, too."

Lori succeeded in making Dawn chuckle. "No, she didn't put it that way, exactly. But, still, she *did* say it. And here we are."

"We'll just have to wait a few hours until it's at least passing decent to knock on someone's door."

"She told me she often does her own dance work in the night, because, well, never mind why right now. Just that she does. Let's drive around to the other side of the block and look up at the main studios. If the lights are on, we'll go up, all right?"

"If the gate will open."

"Let's go see if the lights are on."

"All right." Lori started the engine and drove around the block and looked up.

A soft light, like candlelight, glowed from the windows of the smaller studio room, a dancing shadow flowed on the wall in the fiery glow.

"Oh!" Dawn sighed, awe struck. "Look! Look! What grace!" She turned to Lori, eyes sparkling, "See! I told you!"

"But, as you note in awe, I hate to disturb her moving meditation."

"She'll be fine," Dawn whispered.

"You seem very sure of your knowledge of her."

"Of course, Lori. We're Eos."

*　　*

Dawn insisted. Lori drove back around the block and parked where they had been, and got out. The gate opened under Lori's hand, and also, the door beyond.

What she hadn't been prepared for was the nearly overwhelming redolence of the night blooming jasmine and other night blooming flowers in the garden. So heady, she felt a bit tipsy.

They climbed the winding wrought iron stairs, and half-way up the haunting music that floated out to them, such as nothing Lori had ever heard, stopped. Madame Colette came to the balcony. "Who goes?"

"It's us, Madame Colette, Dawn, and Lori."

"Dawn and Lori, at one a.m. on a Saturday night after seeing *Cavalia*, I believe, if my intuition and my perception of your little penciled note on my magazine are in tune with reality."

"Yes, dear Madame Colette," Lori barely whispered, so chagrined at their abnormal behavior. "You've squarely hit the nail on the head with every point. I apologize profusely for our intrusion."

"Do you intend to continue standing there chatting away, or are you coming up?"

"We're coming up," Dawn affirmed, continuing up, and stepping into the small studio. Lori, after hesitation, finally joined her.

"There now, you did it!" Madame Colette said. "Let us sit and chat." She moved to a chaise lounge and sat, spreading her brilliant purple, lavender, blue, and green gown out around her, gesturing for Lori and Dawn to join her.

Lori sat at the far end of the chaise lounge, while Dawn plopped happily on the floor before her teacher.

"Going on the premise that the two of you have been solidly on my mind all evening," Madame Colette began, "and I, though the thought surprised me, rather much anticipated your arrival, I think it best to dive right in."

"Well, I, ahm, that is, you see, *hmmmm*, can't seem to broach ...." Lori stuttered and stumbled.

"Lori believes she has left Nathan," Dawn stated. "He's been deeply asleep in their relationship, and she feels unloved and disrespected. She invited him to *Cavalia*, and he said he wouldn't go if she paid him. She was severely hurt. I felt her pain from across the table. She turned to Jude, the boy Nathan retained to help with the ranch work and asked him if he'd like to go with us.

"It happens that he had gone before, and he very much wanted to go again.

"I believe Nathan truly loves Lori. But he is, for sure, making a mess of it."

Madame Colette had been nodding, nodding, nodding through Dawn's explanation. "I *seeeeee* ...." she mused. "Most interesting. Well, first, Lori, I'm sorry for your heart, that it is disillusioned and in pain. But, *ah!*

such are the vagaries of the human heart! I, for one, have not found a man to equate with an equine heart.

"But that's not the point at this moment. I'm certain Nathan is a very good man. However, I can also imagine he may not be complicated enough for you. You're very bright. You're complicated. You need nuance. You love romance. And you'll give ten times what you get.

"But there's the problem! Because you give ten times more than you get, *so much* of what you give goes unnoticed. Not because it wouldn't be appreciated, but simply because it's more than an uncomplicated man can perceive.

"I think he may just not see it. But, ah me, does the thought bear contemplation at this moment? I think not. I think the moment calls for pragmatic handling in physical terms because I'm looking at two beautiful women so tired they're about ready to walk on their hands and not know it. Especially Dawn, who is quite capable of doing so."

"I am?!?"

"Indeed. But that's a thought for another time. Right now, let's put the two of you to bed. You've been sitting out on the street needlessly when you could have been all snuggled in a bed. Think about that!"

Madame Colette jumped up, picked up a gigantic flashlight, blew out the candles, and led them back down the winding wrought iron stairs. They walked through the garden to the side wall of the block of buildings. Madame Colette brought out a key—*from somewhere!*—and stuck it in the little keyhole of a little door, with pale lavender curtains in the window. The three of them stepped inside. The room had captured the aroma of the night blooming jasmine. Lori felt she might fall down from dizziness.

"The night blooming jasmine," Madame Colette said, noting Lori's stagger. "Quite heady. Drunk on aroma. It's a true thing. The molecules you breathe giving you a buzz. Trust me, you will sleep as angels have never slept.

"Now, what am I saying? I imagine angels never sleep in the first place. All right, you'll sleep in the arms of angels. That's better." Madame Colette flipped a switch, and a muted lavender light glowed in the tiny, darling room. "Kitchen and little breakfast table."

She led Dawn and Lori further into the tiny apartment. "Here, a minuscule sitting room. Here, a bedroom for a mouse. In you go, mouse." Madame Colette gently directed Dawn into the tiny room as she turned on the light, unveiling a room of all shades of blue from baby blue to the exact peacock blue of Dawn's silk blouse that she wore.

Lori couldn't believe Madame Colette called Dawn a mouse, just like she had, herself, the day she got this very blouse—everything a web she found most strange.

And yet, intriguing and—*believable!*

"A little bathroom between the two bed chambers, and in this little room, dear Lori, I hope you will find your angel sleep." Madame Colette turned on a light to reveal a room of yellows soft as a duckling's down to bright as a cheerful sunflower.

"Oh, *too sweet!*" Lori exclaimed. The room, yes, but mostly she loved—and couldn't wait to be in—the yellowy little bed, piled high with pillows, pillows, pillows.

"Nighty-night, my dears. There are night clothes in the little closets, if you desire to change." Madame Colette exited through the lavender-curtained door, closing it behind her.

Lori looked longingly at the bed, wanting nothing more than to go immediately to sleep. But a nagging realization made her sit on the edge of the bed and pull out her phone. It was not only wrong to simply disappear without a word, other than the little note upstairs in the bedroom she'd appropriated, which may not be discovered for some time, it was also counterproductive—Nathan or Mrs. Hinds would call the police when she and Dawn didn't come home, after first alerting and alarming Jude's family.

She texted a message to Mrs. Hinds. "Not coming home tonight. Please read note upstairs in the room I've been staying in." Terse and unfriendly, but the best she could do at the moment.

She sat holding the phone, trying to send a message to Nathan, but, instead, looked at the blank screen until she fell asleep over it. Later, she set the phone on the bedside table, kicked off her shoes and crawled under the lovely comforter, fully clothed.

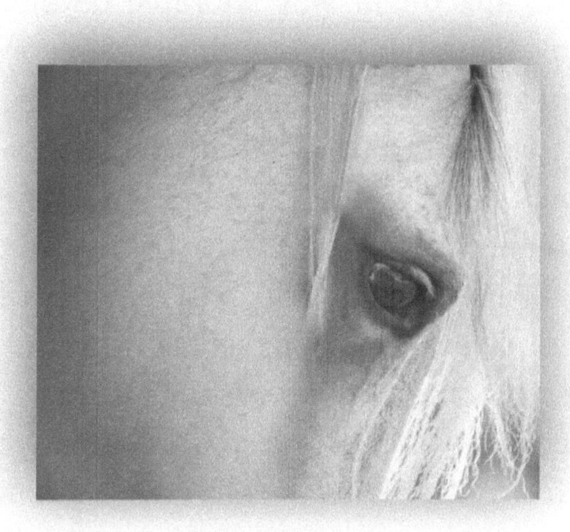

Chapter XXVII

Lori:
A Job Well Done

When Lori woke up in the pixie dust room late the next morning, it took her a few moments to recall where she was. And why.

Then she contemplated the seemingly impossible odds that Madame Colette had a place for her and her young charge to live while major life changes were ironed out.

The little apartment was adorable beyond describing. Nothing about her surroundings offered even a clue they were in a part of town run down at the heels.

The sun poured through the little cottage-like windows. The day would warm up, she felt, into a proper summer day.

She flung her feet over the edge of the bed and spied her phone sitting precariously over the edge of the bedside table, and recalled falling asleep with the phone in hand, trying to write a few words to Nathan.

She picked up the phone and saw that there were messages from Mrs. Hinds, Taffy and Nathan, but she refused to read them.

She began, "Nathan, I'm not reading these messages from your household right now. I need time and space to think. The nights I spent in the little bedroom at the opposite end of the hall, I urgently wanted you to come and talk with me. I wanted you to pay attention to me.

"But now, I need you to please leave me alone. Dawn and I are safe. You can mention to Mrs. Hinds that we are where dance thrives." She hit send without closure.

She stood and put her phone in her shoulder bag, and the shoulder bag in the closet. There, just as Madame Colette had said, were night clothes. But not any old night clothes. There hung several pristine white, beautiful, flowing, lacy Victorian night gowns. Lori stroked the delicate laces, the satin ribbons, the filmy, gossamer silk and light-weight cotton.

Thinking about Madame Colette's bright colors and flowing caftans, Lori wondered at these nightgowns, so much like her own Victorian inclinations, but very different from Madame Colette's style.

Lori made her way into the kitchen. On the diminutive table she happily saw a bowl of fruit, full and brimming over. She didn't remember seeing it there the previous night.

She was *ravenous!*

A peace settled over her as she surveyed the calm and colorful surroundings. Thoughts of *Cavalia* flowed through her memory—the exquisite horses, the gorgeous performers, the flawless production from beginning to end, including the event afterwards, when the little paint horse came up and hugged Dawn.

How, she found herself wondering, could Nathan, an inveterate horseman, not be first in line to buy tickets? If only from professional curiosity, wouldn't he wonder what breed of horses they preferred for such a production, wouldn't he be curious how well-trained they were, what styles they engaged? Wouldn't he be interested in what their gear was like?

She hoped he dismissed *Cavalia* because he *thought* he knew what it was, not because he *actually* knew what it was.

At least it resonated with Jude, and it had been a delight to share the experience with him.

Interesting ... they'd not had a single word of discussion about Eos last night. But now it hung like a thought balloon over her head.

Lori cut up two apples, peeled and sectioned two oranges, peeled and sliced two bananas, added a handful of grapes, and tossed them together. She put half the fruit salad in a bowl for Dawn, and sat at the table enjoying her own.

Now then. She must think seriously. What must she do to make a life for herself and Dawn? She'd be happy to live right here where Madame Colette placed her, if she could afford the rent. But she couldn't afford anything. So the first problem remained the biggest problem.

Madame Colette waved to her through the tiny window.

Lori stood and welcomed her in. "I don't know when I've slept like that! I expected the street noises to bother me, but I didn't hear a thing."

"Excellent. Good insulation in this building."

"But now, dear Madame Colette, for my burning question."

"I'm sure I'll have a watering answer."

"*Ha!*" Lori laughed. "I hope that's true. My burning question is, well I just realize, I have several questions. First of all, is this place available for rent? I adore it, and I know Dawn does too. Second of all, if it is available how much is the rent, and third of all, what day is rent due? And then, the all-time most important question, do you have any ideas about what I might do to earn money to pay the rent?"

Madame Colette took a small bunch of grapes and pulled them off, one by one, answering Lori's question.

"One little grape, yes, the apartment is available to only very special people. Two little grapes, the rent is not money, it's barter. Three little grapes, due date is utterly flexible, according to what we both agree works for us.

"Four little grapes, there's about a gazillion-and-one things I need done around here, and if you don't mind doing things I hate, and that I've never been able to get away from feeling like they're a waste of time, like depositing money in the bank, and paying utility bills, and running around getting things and getting rid of things. And just ... *THINGS*, I would happily accept you doing *things* as rent.

"You'd be getting the raw end of the deal if you do some of this *stuff*. You don't know how I hate the bank, the post office, paying bills, all of that time-sink...."

"But, that sounds perfect, Madame Colette. I love to do that sort of thing. Mrs. Hinds has the household all shipshape, and I don't get to do anything. I love to organize things. I love to find the patterns in things."

"Lots of patterns to be found in my messy business, Lori." Madame Colette laughed.

Dawn came into the kitchen, joining them at the table. "It sounds like you've come to an agreement."

"I believe we have," Lori smiled at Dawn. "I can take care of both of us and do good work at the same time. It's a *miracle!*"

Madame Colette handed Dawn the bowl of cut up fruit and a spoon. "Here, dear, have some fruit."

Dawn took the spoon, but sat, unmoving.

"What's the matter?" Madame Colette asked.

"I ... feel ... so ... bad."

"Why? Are you sick?" Madame Colette and Lori asked at the same time.

"Not that kind of bad. I feel terrible that it's my fault that Lori and Nathan are apart. If I'd never come into their lives ...."

"Nonsense," Madame Colette interrupted. "You're not the *fault*, you're the *catalyst*. Your presence brought to the surface festering problems. You're not to blame."

"Goodness, you've said it neatly, Madame Colette," Lori said, surprised. "The tension between Nathan and myself has been growing. I ... I didn't realize it until a catalyst came along, something that he and I feel differently about.

"All the noise and muddle and distractions got swept off the game board. There he and I were, facing one another with our deep-seated differences. Thank you Dawn for being that catalyst. But I apologize that you've had to witness our ... our dysfunction."

"It's all part of our work, Dawn," Madame Colette said, getting up and reaching into cupboards and fussing with things in drawers, suddenly producing a pot of tea in their midst. "You'll discover that wherever you go, Dawn, you will compel people to look into their hand mirrors. You'll make people see themselves.

"Most people don't like that, because it means they have work to do. Most people don't like to take on their work. But that's not your concern. Your concern is the eternal calling of Eos. To work to preserve this beautiful Earth. And do that we must, to help humanity find its way.

"Thus, you must learn not to take personally that which is the work of the people you meet."

After pouring tea, Madame Colette sat down between them. "Now then, you two, tell me all about *Cavalia* while we enjoy our tea. After which, I'll share with you some of the mysteries of Eos, as there is much that even Dawn does not yet know.

"And *then*, dear Lori, we'll dig into my projects that need attention. I'll let you begin to do that which you claim to love, *organize*."

*   *

Lori blossomed in the authority given to her by Madame Colette. And, for her part, Madame Colette crowed in delight to not have to interrupt her work putting on street clothes, which she claimed to loathe, to run around from bank to post office, to office supply store, and every other "mind-numbingly boring place in kingdom come."

However, at the same time Lori discovered, much to her surprise, that she found herself thinking about Nathan far more than she imagined she ever would, after deciding the relationship was over. She kept thinking about how much she missed making him laugh.

True, Nathan was taciturn by nature. But, that had been one of the traits she'd initially found attractive. Now a quiet argument rose in her thoughts that it wasn't fair to like a trait in a person, and then turn around and decide *not* to like it, and blame the person who possessed the trait that she'd initially found attractive. That was a problem with *herself*, not with Nathan.

And more to the point, it had been the challenge of cracking his "taciturn-ness" that was fun. She'd succeeded in making him giggle uncontrollably like a *school girl* exactly twice.

Those were delightful, intimate moments. Those were the moments that built the *House of Love*.

Maybe she'd give her inflexible stance some more thought. Maybe a bit of distance and ... and something to *do* that gave her life meaning ... could heal broken hearts.

Chapter XXVIII

Dawn: Kidnapped!

It was a beautiful summer day, and I loved my life!

I loved what Madame Colette taught me about dance, about the human body, about my own body, and its ability to move, and all the secrets she taught me about defying gravity, ancient, *ancient*, arcane knowledge.

Although I occasionally succeeded in spontaneously defying gravity for moments, I now began to know how it worked.

But there was more—so much more!—to this life in Madame Colette's Dance Studio, I thought as I sat at the little window in the little apartment, facing the summer blooming flowers in the garden.

At the moment, Madame Colette was teaching, and Lori was off doing a hundred-and-one errands, making Madame Colette deliriously joyful. And Lori seemed fairly joy-filled as well.

Lori had asked me if I wanted to go with her on her run about the little town, like she did every time. Initially I always said yes, but recently, I realized that Lori and I both need moments to ourselves, and I began to say I would stay home to practice my dance.

But today, I wanted only to relax and enjoy the summer day. There was something in the air that reminded me of the summer long ago, when Blue and I were born. Twins who looked as different as possible—from Blue's little wild horse body, black and white paint coat but almost shocking, bluer-than-blue-sky eyes, and my long-legged, pale blonde coat, sweeping mane and tail, even as a new foal, and golden eyes.

It was a day like this that I recalled the two of us romping in a field of wild daisies that stretched as far as we could see. Oh! Daisies were delicious! Our mother and several of the other horses attended to us, everyone filled with joy with the new beautiful babies and the summer warmth that reached into our very bones. Even our mother and the other horses kicked up their heels, and whinnied.

Wild horses, dancing through wild daisies.

All was right with nature.

Smiling down at Little Blue in my hands, I remembered that perfect day. It was good to have a perfect day to recall, forever and always.

This day beckoned to me, so I put Little Blue in his shoulder bag, and stepped out into the garden. I thought for a fleeting moment I'd leave a note for Lori, but I knew I'd be back before she returned, so no need.

I wandered through the garden—and there! I encountered a stand of cheerful, white-faced daisies! I smiled at the thought that I had no inclination to eat them now. I went through the door and then through the wrought iron gate, and out to the sidewalk.

I'd never gone for a walk alone since Lori and I had moved into Madame Colette's apartment, and I felt it was long past due. I had always been the one to explore, dragging the other timid young horses along.

As I turned the corner, proud of myself for taking things in my own hands, I hesitated, listening to the music issuing from the studio above. Then, to my shock, it looked like ... Beau ... on the sidewalk in front of me, trying to look in one of the windows, just above his reach, on the street side of our apartment.

Was it Beau? What was he doing here? A voice in me told me to turn and run back inside and up the winding stairs to Madame Colette. But another voice, indignant and furious at the unmitigated gall of Beau to try and peer into the windows of my home made me slip up to him, while he stood on his toes trying to see inside. Yes, as much as I'd hoped my eyes were deceiving me, and this awful peeping Tom was *not* Beau, it proved, in fact, to be him.

"*What are you doing?*" I nearly shouted in his ear.

He jumped back several feet, engaging in a series of gyrations to keep from falling.

"*You!*" He laughed a strange, undecipherable laugh. "You. I'm looking for you."

"What kind of sick are you, anyway? Just take your crummy, broken mind off me."

"Yeah. Whatever." He reached out and grabbed me. "It's her," he shouted.

A meaty, gigantic hulk of a man—or whatever it was—lumbered out of a van parked beside us on the street.

I struggled mightily and started to scream, but the giant put his hand over my mouth, and quick as lightning, threw me in the back of the van, while Beau climbed into the driver's seat and maneuvered back and forth out of the parking space, banging into the cars in front and behind the van. Only when he managed to tear out into the road did the hulking thug release me.

"What are you doing? What are you doing, Beau, this is, *this is illegal!*"

"Shut up. I don't care. Shut up." He swerved the van back and forth on the road, and, as there was nothing to hold onto in the back, the thug and I went rolling from wall to wall of the van, smacking into the walls and each other.

I finally crawled into the farthest corner of the van, holding my shoulder bag close to my chest. Holding Little Blue close. "Tell Blue I've been kidnapped. Tell Blue I've been kidnapped," I whispered to him.

"*Got her!*" Beau chortled to someone. I decided he was talking with someone on his phone.

There were no windows in the back of the van. I became silent, focusing on the turns and making a mind map of the route we were taking. My initial fright had interfered with tracking the first few turns, but now, as I followed the route, it seemed, strangely enough, that Beau was headed toward the ranch.

But then, no, now he turned and headed north. Soon, we'd be in the forest. Why? *Why?*

Yes, there was the scent of the forest. Then, I saw the shadow of the trees overtake the interior of the van. I could see the passing forms of pine trees.

I felt the van leave the main road and slip around on dirt with Beau's terrible driving. Suddenly he slammed on the brakes with all his might, sending me and the gigantic thug forward into the back of the seats.

Beau laughed uproariously as if he'd just heard the best joke ever as we struggled to upright ourselves.

"Don't do that," the thug said.

"*Tee-hee!* Break any bones? Get her out of there. Dr. Baduna wants her in the cabin now, and fast. There's no one around here, but he doesn't want to risk her being seen."

Beau threw the sliding door on the side of the van open. "*Move! Move!*"

The thug grabbed me, while I clutched my shoulder bag. He carried me as if I weighed nothing into the cabin, his hand over my mouth.

"In the back, he's in the back," Beau said.

I was carried like a log of wood to the back of the small cabin and plopped down without ceremony on a metal table.

The room had only a very pale light coming through two windows, covered in some opaque material that allowed no view of the outside.

"Nice of you to drop by," A sinister, yet unpleasantly familiar voice said from the dark corner of the room. "Idiot boy, what's in that bag she's carrying?"

Beau dragged the bag off my shoulder and peered inside, while I did everything in my power not to cry out. I knew if I showed that I cared about the little "toy" inside, they would keep it from me.

Beau guffawed. "It's a stuffed horse."

He pulled it out and wagged it about in the air.

"Enough. Put it back, give it to her. We don't need to concern ourselves with toys."

Beau jammed and crammed Little Blue back into the shoulder bag abusively and threw it at me. "Jeez, Dawn, a stuffed animal? How old are you?"

"Shut up!" Dr. Baduna ordered. "Girls always like stuffed animals. Be quiet, I'm trying to think."

"But, I got her! *I got her!* Isn't that good?"

"Yes. You finally got her. I might ask why it took you days and days to succeed in doing so. But I won't."

"Wasn't easy," Beau whined. "I had to find out where she was. I had to figure out a lot of things. I had to go kiss my dad's behind, and act like I wanted to be back there to find out where she was. I think I did great!"

"Well, that makes one of us. Now go away some-where so I can have a decent talk with her."

"Where should I go?" Beau whined some more. "We're in a forest, for cripes sake. There's not even any internet. I can't even play a video game."

"*I don't care!*" Dr. Baduna roared, jumping up to his full height. "*Just get the hell outta here!*"

Beau jumped, fear in his eyes, as he scurried out of the room. I heard the front door slam.

"Now then," Dr. Baduna said, making a grimace I imagined he thought passed for a smile, "Just the two of us!" He pulled the chair from the shadows in front of me, and sat.

"I'm not angry with you," he said softly, "that you left me with x-rays all ready to be shot, watching Lori and you laugh as you sped away. I'm not mad at you, you couldn't help what she did. But—I am still sort of mad. I don't think anyone has ever treated me that way."

I *wanted* to say, "*Really*? How is that possible?" But my instinct told me to say nothing.

"Well, never mind. What's important is, you're here now, and I'm about to make both of us famous. I'll prove Eos exists, and that you are one."

There it was! Why he and Edna were so creepy. I hugged Little Blue close, sending my thoughts to my brother, hoping against hope that he heard me, felt me, sensed me, and that he could get a bearing on where I was, even though I only had a vague idea myself.

"First we'll take those x-rays you ran away from before. Unfortunately, the equipment here is not as modern as what I have in my radiology office, so it's not as safe. But, oh well, you made your choice."

"Well," I ventured, trying to sound as calm as the summer day outside, "you have me now, and there's no Lori, why not take me to your office where the equipment is better? It probably produces better images, too."

Dr. Baduna hesitated for a few seconds, then snorted. "Nice try! Nope, I'm not trusting anything. Stand up, turn around," he demanded.

I played a variety of scenarios in my mind about jumping and running. But I knew I would not escape. Better to be agreeable than to push this insane man's insanity.

"*I said* ...." he growled, his weird grin turning into simply his teeth showing.

I stood and turned.

Dr. Baduna ran his huge, soft, cold, hand down my spine, then around my shoulder blades.

"Damn," he whispered. "The anomaly that was there even those few days ago is gone. *Damn!* You'd better hope something shows on the x-ray."

It was true that I wondered how, with merely an x-ray or two, he planned on proving the existence of Eos.

As if I'd asked my question aloud he continued, "First the x-rays, then the blood test, then the bone marrow, and so on and so forth. I believe every step of the way I'll discover anomalies that I can write in my paper that will put forth to medical science, and science in general, the existence of the transmogrifying species, Eos.

"I don't suppose you'd care to make both of our jobs easier by simply telling me you're Eos, so that I have your affirmation as a significant part of my work."

"What's 'ess'?" I asked with my best imitation of complete oblivion.

"*Eos! Eos!* You know what I'm saying. Don't try to toy with me. All right, now then, sit back up here on this table." But before waiting for me to do it on my own, he hefted me onto the table. "Sorry to have to do this part, but I can't have you getting away." He tethered my right hand to the metal table with a rope that only let me stand or sit.

"Now, to set things up." He went into the small closet in the room, where I heard sounds I cared not to know anything about. But feared I soon would.

Chapter XXIX

Lori:
An Old-Fashioned Posse

ori returned to the apartment in the late afternoon, feeling nearly as fantastic as she'd ever felt. She'd unknotted a financial muddle of Madame Colette's that confirmed she really earned her keep. She couldn't wait to tell her about the success, but, of course, it would have to wait until after the last class.

She made a plan to take Dawn, and Madame Colette if she wanted to join them, to the small park nearby for a casual picnic, on this most summery of summer days.

She began to put together a picnic in the sweet little kitchen, then paused to ask Dawn if there was anything in particular she'd like to have included in the picnic basket.

She sensed that Dawn was not in the apartment, although there was something rather strange about the feeling, as though Dawn had very recently been there.

Lori ran up the winding stairs to the studio room Dawn worked in, but, much to her surprise, Dawn was not there.

Anxiety began to overtake her, while reasoning that there was nothing to be anxious about. She stepped in the doorway of Madame Colette's class, hating to bother her.

"Dawn?" She mouthed to Madame Colette.

She shook her head and shrugged, coming over to Lori.

"Dawn is not in the apartment, she's not in her studio room, she left no note."

"That's not good!" Madame Colette exclaimed. "No, not good at all." She looked at the clock on the wall. "All right students, early out tonight, off you go. Tell your parents the next class will be fifteen minutes longer."

The young students looked at her in surprise. She *never* let class out early.

"Stay with them, Lori, as they gather themselves, while I get changed and make a phone call." Madame Colette scurried from the studio and into the next room, informing the parents that the class was over, and that she would run the class fifteen minutes later next session.

"My mom won't be here until the end of class," a little girl said.

"Do you have a good friend in class?" Lori asked.

"Yes." She pointed to the only boy in the class.

"Let's see if his mother can take you home." She took the little girl by the hand and stepped in among the flurry of parents and children in the next room. She saw the little boy go to one of the pretty young mothers. "Hi there, do you think you can take this little girl home? Oh, wait, her mother is probably on the way ... hmmm."

"I'll call her, I have her number," the boy's mother said. "It's a bit out of my way, but I'll take her home no problem. Is everything all right?"

"Not to worry. Thank you for being so helpful!"

The room emptied and Lori called Mrs. Hinds—although they had texted one another a few times, this would be the first time she talked to Mrs. Hinds since she left.

"Tanner Ranch," Mrs. Hinds said.

"It's Lori."

"Oh, Lori, Oh! It's so good to hear you voice, I just can't tell you. How are you? I'm so glad you called."

Lori was taken aback by Mrs. Hind's warmth. It was uncharacteristic, but she could not give it thought at the moment.

"I'm all right. But the reason I'm calling is, well, it appears Dawn is missing. And I thought to check, just in case she went there. I mean, I don't know what's going on, but I just had this instinct to call you."

"Oh, no," Mrs. Hinds whispered.

Lori could tell she was putting something together in her mind. "Oh no, what?"

"Dear me, I just don't know. I hope this doesn't have anything to do with it, but Edna called me, again with her story about the police wanting to know about Dawn, which is just a big crock. She insisted on talking to Dawn, and I said she wasn't here right now.

"I didn't know how to handle it. Next day, Beau was here, trying to wheedle his way back into the house, saying it's so awful at his Aunt Louise's because she makes him shower every day. Thank goodness.

"Anyway, he was in the barn, verbally abusing Jude and Taffy from what they say, and then he came sneaking into the house. Nathan and I didn't know it, and right at that moment I said to Nathan, 'well, he sure doesn't need to know that they're with Madame Colette.'

"When we saw Beau, we exchanged a look like, '*oh, no!*' and I hoped like crazy he didn't hear me. But I'm terrified to think maybe he did."

"But, Mrs. Hinds, what relationship does Beau have with Edna?"

"Well, a weird one. When she had her cap set for Nathan, she tried to cotton up to Beau. Of course, as you know, he's 'uncottonable.' But if Dr. Baduna ...."

"Oh, Mrs. Hinds, this is really terrible news. Of course, Edna might do Dr. Baduna's bidding. If they're trying to ...." She couldn't finish her sentence. "Here's Madame Colette, she needs to talk with me. Call me if anything ...."

"I will, Lori, I will. Awful, just awful ...." So upset, Mrs. Hinds clicked off without even a good-bye.

Lori hardly recognized Madame Colette, wearing jeans and a plaid shirt. "I called my friend, Officer Mandrake," she said. "He said he's headed for the Tanner Ranch."

"Your *friend!*" Lori exclaimed, amazed. "A big, burly, guy, kinda scary? He was one of the two officers who came to the ranch when Dawn first ... ah ... arrived."

"I know."

"You do?"

"After I met Dawn, I was the one who kept him informed about Dawn's life, so the police left you alone."

"And all the times Edna said they were calling and bothering her?"

"Not true."

"No. Of course not. I didn't believe her either. It was Baduna, trying to get his creepy hands on Dawn, nagging Edna. Mrs. Hinds just told me that Beau was at the ranch, and he snuck into the kitchen the precise moment she said to Nathan that Beau sure didn't need to know Dawn and I are with you."

"That's terrible."

"If he kidnapped her, maybe he took her to Baduna's radiology office."

"Right," Madame Colette said. "Let's go," They hurried down the winding stairs, through the door, and out the wrought iron gate.

Lori drove madly to the awful office she hoped never to be near again. They were both disappointed to see the place closed up tight.

"It was a bit much to hope for," Lori said, hanging her head. "I know!" She started up the engine and headed for Edna's office. "I'll face Edna to her *face!*"

In Edna's reception area, Lori and Madame Colette barged past the receptionist. Lori hurried up to the only closed door and banged on it. "Need to talk to you right now, Edna."

"I'm with a patient," Edna replied, indignant.

"Come out or we're coming in. No ceremony. I'm not making an idle threat."

"Is that Lori Tanner?"

"It is."

"Will you kindly wait?"

"*I. Will. Not!*"

"Do I have to call the police?"

"Oh, please do! Though you needn't, as Officer Mandrake has already been called."

Edna stepped out of the room, closing the door behind her. She bid them follow her down the hall, and the three of them entered another room. Edna closed the door. "*What* is going on?"

"You would do well to be truthful," Lori warned. "We believe Dawn may have been kidnapped, by Baduna. I suggest you shed any light on this that you can, to reduce your inevitable sentence. And, by the way, you're fired. You're no longer my doctor, nor the doctor of anyone I know. That is, if you're still in practice when this is over."

Edna looked as if she might begin to cry. Lori wondered if that was because she actually cared about a young girl, or if she was only concerned about the possible end of her career.

"I'll tell you everything I know, Lori! First of all, Dr. Baduna has not returned any of my calls since he hooked up with Beau. That's been a few days. They seem to be made of the same cloth, if you ask me. Anyway, years ago he took me to a weird cabin he has in the woods. He was so proud of it, because he had it all outfitted for medical 'research' he called it.

"He's always had this obsession with Eos. So determined to prove they exist. I believe they exist, but I'm not obsessed with it."

"Let's go! Where's this 'weird cabin?'" Lori tugged at Edna's sleeve, leading her back down the hall to the front door. Madame Colette followed close behind.

"Oh dear! Cynthia," Edna called to the receptionist as Lori pulled her through the door, "cancel all my appointments. Tell Mr. Godash he can get dressed and go home. Oh, dear!"

In the parking lot, Lori escorted Edna into the back seat of her car while Madame Colette got in the other side. She started the engine, but she didn't know where she was headed. *Where is this cabin? I'm serious now.* She gave Edna a look in the rear- view mirror that affirmed her words.

"I don't know exactly. It's sort of out there not far from the ranch, as I recall. I remember thinking he was so creepy about this whole Eos thing, and his 'secret lab' was awfully close to civilization."

Lori turned to Madame Colette. "What should I do?"

"We need to gather a search team," she answered.

"We do. That's right. Oh, Anubis!"

"Are you swearing creatively, or are you calling upon an ancient Egyptian god?" Madame Colette asked.

"Neither. Well, maybe I *am* doing the latter, without fully realizing it. Anubis is the neighbor's dog. He was inordinately attached to Dawn, on sight. Then she told me she'd befriended him during the time she'd disappeared. But if the cabin is in the government forest near the ranch as Edna suggests, maybe Anubis can help.”

While driving at breakneck speed, Lori dialed Mrs. Hinds again. “We’re on our way. Edna thinks Dawn may be in the forest beyond Mr. Wise’s property.”

“We’ll saddle up, then,” Mrs. Hinds said. “Officer Mandrake called and is on his way, and Nathan said he’d comb the countryside, inch by inch to find Dawn.”

Lori blinked in surprise. “Nathan said that? Not Taffy?”

“Taffy agrees, of course. I agree, of course. But, yes, Nathan said it.”

At the same time, Madame Colette called Officer Mandrake and got an update on his progress.

As they tore into the driveway at the ranch, the first thing Lori saw was Nathan on Vladimir. He looked phenomenal. “*Oh, my!*” she whispered. Be still my heart, she thought.

Taffy sat astride Steed, and even greater than all former shocks, there sat Mrs. Hinds, a striking figure on Goldie, in western riding jeans and cowboy shirt.

“Oh! Mrs. Hinds, fine form!” Lori called, jumping out of the car. They had saddled up Twinkle for her. “I’ve never seen you on horseback!”

“No one messes with my girls!” Mrs. Hinds exclaimed, meaning business.

"Taffy, I think Madame Colette might be good on Steed."

"Sure, Lori, anything you say." He jumped down from Steed, and went to the barn to saddle up one of the other horses for himself.

"Officer Mandrake will be here shortly," Madame Colette called after Taffy, "if you could saddle a mount for him, as well."

Jude came flying into the driveway, and jumped out of his bug. "Came as fast as I could, Mrs. H," he said to Mrs. Hinds.

Mrs. H? Lori thought. My, they've become close.

"Get the dune buggy from the garage," Nathan said. "Keys are on the wall. Edna can ride with you. But help Taffy saddle up a couple mounts, first."

"Will do!" Jude answered.

Officer Mandrake came into the driveway in his civilian car, and he, too, popped out of his car in riding gear and cowboy boots. "Great, a real, old-time posse!"

Lori heard a dog barking excitedly, and soon enough, Timothy on Arion came running full tilt into the yard, hardly able to stop his mount. "Whoa, Arion, don't run anyone down."

Anubis leapt and barked and tore off toward the hills and then came back, clearly begging everyone to follow him. He looked up at Lori. Why won't you follow me? he seemed to be saying.

"We're coming," she said, looking down at him. She turned to Timothy. "I thought we'd come to your place and go from there."

"Better to go across the hills. I realized I'd save the party time if I came here."

"He's right," Nathan agreed. "Good thinking, Timothy."

Nathan's glance encountered Lori's look, and a wordless exchange passed between them that four books of poetry could not convey.

Taffy came up on Venus, leading Orion for Officer Mandrake, while Jude, in the dune buggy, pulled up to Edna, and she climbed in.

"Fasten your safety belt," Jude and Nathan said together.

Fear running across her features, Edna *fastened her safety belt*.

Everyone now mounted, the party took off across the hills. The giant, patient oaks looked down upon them, rooted seers through the generations, watching, with equanimity, the human drama unfold.

When the group reached the hill overlooking Timothy Wise's farmstead, they paused.

"Okay," Lori said, "Edna, you have the best idea where this lab is, lead the way."

She waved to the forest beyond the Wise property. "You can see the county road entering the forest. We need to get down to that, and then I think I'll know where to go once we're there."

Anubis charged down the hill, trying to get the pokey posse to follow him. He tore ahead as Jude threw the dune buggy into gear, and they went flying down the hill with Edna yelling "*woooooo-hooooo-hoooooo!*" all the way down.

The late afternoon's shadows lengthened and danced among the horses' legs, whose long shadows played across the land in syncopated rhythm. The golden sunlight splashed and frolicked on the flaxen hides of the palominos, and sank into the tans and browns of the other high-bred horses, but they all, of one mind, tore with raging beauty across the countryside, bent on one, numinous objective—

To save Eos.

When they arrived at the bottom of the long hill, they raced past the Wise farmstead, chickens in the yard squawking at the unusual sight, with their master in the midst of it.

The group slowed as they came to the dark road entering the forest.

They clopped along while Edna tried to get her bearings. "It's been a long time. I know we left the main road and went onto a dirt road. It seems like we went to the right."

When they arrived at a dirt road, they took it, peering through the thick of the giant, silent, trees for a cabin, until they came to a fork in the road.

"Oh no," Edna sighed, distressed. "I think, go right."

Anubis began howling, running down the left fork of the road and dashing back.

"To the left," Lori called, asking everything of Twinkle she had to give. Anubis was right, of course. As the sun sank, time became progressively more precious. She felt herself close to Dawn—she could feel her fear. "I'm coming, Dawn. I'm coming," she whispered.

As Twinkle nimbly flew among the trees, Lori heard the thunder of hooves coming from the near distance. Hundreds of hooves pounded the earth, just as they had for eons upon eons, the ancient, the primal sound of the thundering hooves of the herd. Lori couldn't see them yet, but she knew it was the cayuse, tearing through the forest with the same objective as her own.

Taffy and Nathan came roaring up on either side of her, Anubis howling in the lead.

And there!

There through the forest, the lengthening shadows making giants of the cayuse, they now ran parallel to Lori, Nathan, and Taffy. One hundred, two hundred, three hundred, four hundred, and more, wild horses, headed to the same destination.

"There, Nathan, in the lead," Taffy pointed, shouting, "there's that little black and white paint we captured that night, with those cayuse."

"Ah, naa, Taffy, all paints are the same."

"No," Taffy argued, "Not that one. That one is different. That one has a fire. *He's got a fire!*"

As the huge herd on one side and the small band on the other flew through the forest, converging upon the same location, they drew closer and closer together.

Indeed, Lori thought, he has a fire. He's saving his sister. He's saving Dawn.

Then the cabin became visible. Small, unassuming, with a couple of tiny, fogged, windows.

Lori was still at some distance when she saw the little black and white paint tear up to the cabin. Raising up he smashed with all his might into the wall, tearing at it. Several other cayuse, rushing up, did the same. The window tore open and Anubis leapt inside. In moments, they saw Dawn spring through the destroyed window frame, and jump onto the fierce little paint horse. They tore away with the cayuse, leaving the cabin in near shambles.

Dr. Baduna ran out, with Beau and the thug, all yelling for their lives, running to the van.

Officer Mandrake charged up to them and stood his mount in front of the van, while Mrs. Hinds and Madame Colette blocked the rear.

"Halt in the name of the law," Officer Mandrake cried.

"Who do you think you are?" Dr. Baduna yelled.

"I'm Officer Mandrake, a Kittitas County, Washington, sheriff, and you're under arrest. You have the right to remain silent. Anything you say can and will be used against you in a court of law. You have the right to speak to an attorney, and to have an attorney present during any questioning."

Lori broke away from the group, flying after the cayuse.

Twinkle, understanding the goal, gave more than her all, dancing among the trees, the shadows, confusing to Lori, but Twinkle appeared to see with a different vision as she pursued the cayuse.

Soon, they were parallel with the back of the herd. Gradually Twinkle gained on Blue and Dawn. As they raced toward the sunset, Lori saw Dawn begin to slip from Blue, and terror took her, fearing Dawn was about to fall.

But no! What she saw! *What she saw!*

The phenomenally beautiful form of Dawn as Eos, as the perfectly-formed little palomino, ran beside her brother, neck and neck, glancing at one another, a smile passing between them from their eyes. Twinkle pulled up alongside them, the three of them, their necks stretched out, their tails streaming.

Then Lori felt herself slipping from Twinkle's back. She ran between Dawn and Twinkle. She looked to her right, and there! There was Twinkle, beside her!

Lori ran full tilt, keeping up with Blue and Dawn and Twinkle, flying into the glorious sunset, the streaming gold and pink and lavender bathing them, and they, too, became a part of the bursting colors of sunset.

She'd never experienced such a total boundless freedom. *Freedom!* She felt she was flying. She knew Twinkle's and Dawn's and Blue's feelings. Their energy, their hearts, their *very being*, knit together as one.

Dawn looked at her with knowing and love.

Oh, Eos, Oh, Horse! Grace and glory, love and peace, joy and understanding....

Chapter XXX

Celebration

As evening, that sly thief, stole the brilliant colors of the sunset, the herd slowed its thundering, joyful, shared-mind, shared-heart, hurtle across the open land. Among dusk's shadows Lori found herself riding at a calm canter on Twinkle, beside Dawn riding Blue.

As if waking from a wonderful dream, Lori noticed that the rest of the herd had slipped away, continuing on to where they would spend their night, sleeping under the ever-rotating, warm, summer night stars.

The two horses and riders crested a hill. Looking down, Lori saw the ranch spread out below—the staid, serious house with its white columns, the graceful, imperturbable oaks lining the driveway, the long, white horse barn, the several horses milling about in the paddock, their attention drawn, Lori could see, to the mounted riders in the yard.

Lori deduced that the rest of her party had taken a leisurely stroll on gravel roads, back to the ranch, and had just arrived. They were no doubt wondering where Dawn and Lori were, not about to dismount until they decided what next to do.

Lori and Dawn shared the thought that the wonderful, valiant horses were exhausted, having been put to a task that was not usual in any way. They needed to have saddles and bridles taken off, needed a loving curry, a long drink of water, and to enjoy their favorite dinner.

Wordlessly, they ambled down the hill in the night toward the welcoming lights that came on as they approached.

*   *

As Lori and Dawn rode up, Nathan, Taffy, Madame Colette, Mrs. Hinds, Timothy, and Officer Mandrake all rode up to them, with Jude rushing up on foot, Anubis bounding alongside him, barking and tail wagging, thrilled with everything around him, reflecting the mood of the entire party.

"My girl, my Dawn!" Mrs. Hinds exclaimed, a tear streaking down her face. Lori saw it, even if the light was dim, and no one could ever tell her otherwise. "Are you all right? Did that monster—what a horrible hulk of man—did he hurt you?"

"No, dear Mrs. Hinds," Dawn said compassionately, seeing Mrs. Hinds' distress. "He didn't hurt me. I'm all right. I'm ...." she reached down and hugged Blue, bareback and without bridle, as much one with him as she could be. "I'm more than all right." She looked at each person and horse in turn.

"Thank you, everyone, for rescuing me. Blue would not have been able to outrun their van. If not for Anubis, who gnawed through the rope I was being restrained by, I would not have been able to escape." She held up her wrist, where remained a tightly knotted rope with a dangling, roughly-torn end. She looked down at Anubis, who nearly leapt from his fur, trying to reach up to her. "Thank you, my beautiful, canine friend.

"But now, I believe, our horses have exceeded reasonable expectations, and must be attended to."

"Yes," Lori agreed, "Let's head to the barn and put up the horses. And then, *let's celebrate!*"

"*Yay!*" Taffy exclaimed, "But first ...." He rode over beside Dawn, got out his pocket knife and cut the rope off her wrist, while everyone cheered.

"If someone would attend to Goldie so I can pull out the celebration box ...." Mrs. Hinds said.

"Of course, dear," Lori took Goldie's reins. "But please, don't put yourself out, Mrs. Hinds."

"I won't." Which, everyone knew was Mrs. Hinds-speak for, "*party will be had!*"

But the party began in the barn as, after dismounting, everyone hugged everyone, and hugged the horses, and most, *most* especially, hugged Blue, who lapped it up like a puppy, his blue eyes shining. Though not for a moment did he move from Dawn's side.

After the horses were pampered, curried, watered, fed, and bedded with fresh straw, the human members of the party, and Anubis, headed for the house, while Dawn stayed behind for a few minutes, forehead to forehead with Blue. Lori stood aside during their exchange. Dawn then came up to Lori, and she—*finally!*—was able to give her the gigantic, private hug, she'd been waiting to share.

"Dear Dawn, I was so frightened for you!"

"I was frightened too, Lori. But you and ...." she looked back at Blue, who watched them intently, "Blue ...." She could say nothing more.

Lori nodded, putting her arm around Dawn as they walked to the house.

"*Yay!*" everyone cheered when they came through the door. "*Yay, Dawn! Yay Lori!*"

Somehow, in those few minutes, Mrs. Hinds had managed to change back into an unremarkable, yet spanking clean and pressed shapeless housedress, had pulled together platters of munchies and veggies and cookies, and pitchers of juices and a couple of carafes of hot beverages, with stacks of plates and glasses and cups and silverware and napkins, as if the party had been planned for weeks, and prepped for days.

"Mrs. Hinds," Lori exclaimed, "you are truly amazing."

"Oh, well ...." she replied shyly when all eyes turned to her.

"You, Mrs. Hinds," Dawn exclaimed, "you were on horseback! I didn't know you rode!"

"I rode in my childhood. I did trick riding and dressage, and, well everything, more or less." Then she added a very quiet comment. "I was Washington State Miss Rodeo one year."

"Whoa!" Taffy said. "Wait ... *wait!* Eliza Hinds. Eliza! Eliza Williams. You're *Eliza Williams! OMG*, Mrs. Hinds, *Mrs. Hinds!* I was utterly in love with you that year. Which doesn't mean anything, 'cause every man and boy in the state was in love with you!"

He shook his head in stunned amazement. "Why did I never put that together?"

"Because eventually my year was over and there was another Miss Rodeo. I married one of those adoring boys, and fell out of the public limelight. Sorry Taffy, you didn't make a play...."

Everyone laughed and Taffy grinned, "My error. I was too shy to even talk to you, though you came to the ranch I was working that summer a couple times ...."

"Well, anyway, I married Mr. Hinds, and had a couple children, and grew round, and you see the result before you today."

"One of the most beautiful people on earth," Lori said, giving Mrs. Hinds a hug.

"*Yes, indeed!*" Nathan exclaimed, raising his glass of punch. "To Mrs. Hinds!"

"*To Mrs. Hinds!*" everyone intoned, raising their glass, or if they didn't have one yet, raising a phantom glass.

"Well!" Mrs. Hinds said, all business, "Enough about me! This is a celebration for our girls, for Dawn, rescued and in our midst, and for Lori, who brought a posse together in record-breaking time that any sheriff would be proud of."

"So true!" Officer Mandrake said. "With Baduna and his thug hauled off to jail, and with that sad case, Beau, no offense, Nathan...."

"None taken," Nathan said.

"That sad case, Beau, spending a well-earned night in juvenile hall, we applaud Lori's brilliance and bravery."

Again, glasses raised to a roaring cheer. *"To Lori! To Dawn!"*

"To Blue," Dawn said softly.

"To Blue! *To Blue!* **To Blue!**" everyone roared louder and louder, so that certainly Blue, and all the horses, heard it in their cozy stalls.

"Let it be known," Nathan declared, raising his voice above the cheers, "that the cayuse will, from this moment forward, forever and always, be safe and welcome on any land owned by Tanner Ranch.

"The wild horses will never be chased, never harassed, never harmed. They will always be welcome to come and feed, they will always be welcome to come and drink."

"Yes, yes," everyone affirmed. "To the cayuse!"

"Very good, Nathan," Taffy said, reaching up and patting him on the shoulder, "Very, very good!"

Madame Colette made her way through the crowd and handed Dawn a rolled-up bundle of fabric. "I dismounted at the cabin and rescued this."

On sight, Dawn and Lori knew what it was—Little Blue, safely inside his rolled-up shoulder bag. *"Oh! Teacher,"*

Dawn sighed, hugging Little Blue close, "Thank you! *Thank you!*"

No one could say for certain-sure, but those who stood closest to Dawn could have sworn that a soft neigh issued from the bundle in her hands.

*   *

*T*affy put on some quiet music while everyone chatted, curled up inside the glow of love and companionship, recounting the events.

Officer Mandrake sat near Madame Colette on the sofa, engaged in a soulful conversation. Jude, with Anubis between them, finally had the opportunity to stand by Dawn.

"I was so worried, Dawn, when I heard you were missing. I didn't know what to do!"

Dawn looked down at Anubis and patted him, as he gazed up at her adoringly. "Well, thank you, Jude," she answered awkwardly. "Because you followed Anubis ... I don't know what might have happened had the party gone the other way when you came to the fork in the road, like Lori told me almost happened. Blue and the herd would have been there, but without Anubis so quickly chewing through that rope ...."

Jude knelt down and hugged Anubis. "Hero dog!"

When he stood, Dawn screwed up her courage and hugged Jude, whispering in his ear, *"hero boy!"*

Eos ~ 366

He grinned like his mouth would run right off his face and jump up and down in the middle of the room. But he was unable to utter a single word.

In the far corner of the room where the wee settee faced the night-shining window more than the festive room—or, perhaps, Nathan moved it just a bit in that direction—Lori agreed to sit by Nathan.

They sat with their backs to their friends, while Nathan took Lori's hands in his, and, without pre-amble, began, "my darling bride, I've been a mad man without you. And I was some kind of mad man before you left here, the way I neglected you. I truly don't know what was the matter with me. Ignoring you, then acting like a spoiled child when Dawn came into our lives.

"There's no mistake in how you knew to name her, as she has brought the Dawn to everyone in this room." He looked down at their beautiful hands, held together. "But no one more than myself. I've had a true awaken-ing about the depth and breadth of my love for you.

"It may not even have crossed your mind," Nathan continued, "but our anniversary is in three days."

"Oh, yes, Nathan, it has more than crossed my mind ...." Lori kept to herself for the moment that she had planned to come to him on their anniversary and suggest they start anew.

"You are a profound and brilliant teacher-of-love, and I've been a terrible, sleeping-in-class student," Nathan said shyly. "Can you find it in your heart to forgive me?"

"I can and do, Nathan." Lori said, so softly she barely heard herself.

"And so, I dare ask," Nathan inhaled nervously, and Lori wondered what he could possibly be about to ask that would make him so nervous. The only other time he appeared this nervous was when he asked her ....

"Will you marry me?" he blurted. "Will you marry me *again*? Will you marry this broken down man? This man, selfish and self-centered? This man for whom life has no meaning, whatsoever, without you? This man who has learned more in the past year than his entire life before, because of you, intrepid, valiant, moral teacher—will you marry me in three days?"

"Yes," Lori said simply. "I will marry you. Again."

Nathan jumped up, facing the room. "We're getting married!"

Everyone looked a bit puzzled and, perhaps, a bit uncomfortable.

"In three days, on our first anniversary, we're getting married *again.*"

Lori stood and turned to face her beloved friends, while Nathan wrapped his arm sweetly around her.

"Hooray! Congratulations!" everyone shouted over one another.

Lori exchanged a look with Dawn, whose tears ran down her cheeks unashamedly. Then she saw the same look, the same tears, upon Mrs. Hinds and Taffy's smiling faces.

And she knew, *she knew*—she had arrived home at last.

The End

Thank You

Thank you for reading ***EOS – The Long, Dark Road of Horse & Human.*** As a thank you for taking the journey with Dawn and Lori, here's a story you might enjoy. Although it's about horses, it's unrelated to ***Eos***. In fact, it's possible that it's largely autobiographical. I hope you enjoy it.

You can download ***Banner*** by inputting this link:

https://bookhip.com/RJZWWXK

I live in the midst (and often the mist) of ten acres of forest with domestic and wild creatures as family and companions, where I create an ever-growing inventory of books and short stories.

After I received my Doctorate from the University of California at Irvine in the School of Social Sciences, I moved to the Pacific Northwest to write and to have a modest private psychotherapy practice in a small town not much bigger than a village.

Finally, I decided it was time to put my full focus on my writing, where, through the world-shrinking internet, I could "meet" greater numbers of people. *Where I could meet you!*

All the creatures in my forest and I are glad you "stopped by." I'd love to hear from you if you'd like to write to me. Here's my email address:

Blythe@BlytheAyne.com

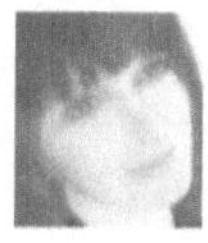

And here's my website:

www.BlytheAyne.com

And my **Boutique of Books**:

https://shop.BlytheAyne.com

'Til We Meet Again,

Blythe

Books & Audiobooks by Blythe Ayne
Fiction:
Joy Forest Cozy Mystery Series:
A Loveliness of Ladybugs
A Haras of Horses
A Clowder of Cats
A Gaggle of Geese
A Round of Robins – The Novella
A Round of Robins – The Novel

The Darling Undesirables Series:
The Heart of Leo - short story prequel
The Darling Undesirables
Moons Rising
The Inventor's Clone
Heart's Quest

Novel:
Eos– The Long, Dark Road of Horse and Human

YA Series – The City Under Seattle
With Thea Thomas:
The People in the Mirror
Millie in the Mirror
The Angel in the Mirror

Middle Grade Novel:
Matthew's Forest

Novellas & Short Story Collections:
5 *Minute Stories*
13 Lovely Frights for Lonely Nights
When Fields Hum & Glow

Children's Illustrated Books:
The Rat Who Didn't Like Rats
The Rat Who Didn't Like Christmas

Nonfiction
Excellent Life Series:
Love Is The Answer
45 Ways To Excellent Life
Life Flows on the River of Love
Horn of Plenty – The Cornucopia of Your Life
Finding Your Path, Engaging Your Purpose

How to Save Your Life Series:
Save Your Life with Basic Baking Soda
Save Your Life with Awesome Apple Cider Vinegar
Save Your Life with the Dynamic Duo – D3 and K2
Save Your Life With The Power Of pH Balance
Save Your Life With The Phenomenal Lemon
Save Your Life with Stupendous Spices
Save Your Life with the Elixir of Water